SIGHT SEE UNSEEN

SIGHT SEE UNSEEN

Matt Parravano

DOSTE Publishing, LLC.

Cover design by Pamela Tarbutton and Matthew Parravano

DOSTE Publishing, LLC.
Austin, TX
First Edition: December 2020

Scripture passages are taken from the Holy Bible (King James Version)

Library of Congress Cataloging-in-Publication Data

Names: Parravano, Matthew, author
Title: Sight See Unseen / Matt Parravano
Description: First Edition. | Austin : DOSTE Publishing, 2020
Identifiers: LCCN 2020921382 | ISBN 978-1-7359944-1-3 (hardcover) |
ISBN 978-1-7359944-3-7 (paperback) |
ISBN 978-1-7359944-0-6 (ebook) | ISBN 978-1-7359944-2-0 (audio file)
Drama, Thriller, Suspense, Fiction

For Gramma & Grampa

CONTENTS

	Page
Chapter 1	1
Chapter 2	29
Chapter 3	40
Chapter 4	48
Chapter 5	63
Chapter 6	72
Chapter 7	82
Chapter 8	89
Chapter 9	107
Chapter 10	120
Chapter 11	126
Chapter 12	139
Chapter 13	148
Chapter 14	164
Chapter 15	171
Chapter 16	178
Chapter 17	200
Chapter 18	209
Chapter 19	219
Chapter 20	227
Chapter 21	228
Chapter 22	233
Chapter 23	235
Chapter 24	240
Chapter 25	242

"I've got one eye open and the other on you."

—Matty P.

please continue

CH. 1

'WHATTA YOU WANT!

Whatta Ya want!
What do *you* want?
What do you ... *want*?'

He said it to himself backwards and forwards. In many different ways and in so many decibels on the way to where paradise exists. "Hey kid! Whattya want!" He couldn't help himself. Tried to even make a song of it. "What pray tell would you want ... today?" He didn't even know what *pray tell* meant. Just heard it on an old black and white flicker movie and it sounded good to him.

That was the greeting he received from old man Johnson every time he tried to hand him his morning paper. He wasn't even his paperboy. Just saw it dangling in the old timer's rhododendrons and figured he have a hard time getting it out of them. Heck, he wasn't even old enough to peddle papers yet, but he didn't know that. Never said a word to Johnson. Just rang the bell. Handed it to him and went on his way.

It was another cold, brisk January morning in New England. Massachusetts to be more precise. The sun had just peeked over the horizon and the wind would howl through the woods and whisper between the trees. There were a few lone surviving leaves left on a few scattered branches but for the most part old man winter had taken them. Throughout the neighborhoods you could get that distinctive aroma of burning leaves. A bit musty, but all of it said winter. Ice had formed throughout the streets and on roof tops. That black ice can be a killer when it's on the roads and you can't see it while you're driving or if you walk over some then you find out the hard way as you're smack down face first on the concrete. The public transportation division does their best to salt the main roads and your car gets the same kind of white lines on the side of the doors as your baseball cap does from the sweat of wearing it too long and never washing it. The crazy birds are all south by now, so the woods have a peaceful calm to them.

The kid was walking in and out of the trees on and off the wooded path. One of those games children play with themselves. Kind of like stepping specifically so not to step on the grooved lines of the concrete. Perhaps it's a derivative of hopscotch.

He had his hockey stick in one hand, skates laced and tied over his shoulder and a couple of pucks in his pockets. As he neared closer to the pond his heart would beat faster and faster. The anticipation to get on the ice was starting to consume him. He was the first one there this morning. Had the whole ice all to himself (so far). Today was especially sweet. The ice was smooth and clear. No bumps in it or snow patches to hinder the puck or break a stride. There must have been a little rain the night before to clear things up on the water and then freeze again at just the right time.

Lacing up his skates as he usually did every other Saturday was a bit of a ceremonious ritual. Always the left skate first then the right. He was as methodical as any other athlete much to his senior. Mind you, he's in single digits at present, but still, I guess it's instinctual. When you get comfortable with a procedure or if you have a good game doing something other than the ordinary it usually stays with you. Just ask El Mejor why the piece of velcro was always stitched into the right side of his hockey pants.

Another aspect made this weekend a little different as well. Remember when I mentioned what he did every *other* Saturday? This was an off weekend where he didn't see his father. The kid's parents got divorced when he was a baby, and he was being raised by his grandparents (on his mother's side). They were hard workers and as honest as the day is long. His Grandfather Sven was almost retired. He is a tall, towering man with a deep, gentle, bellowing voice. A wave of curly hair in front was always parted with pristine accuracy and his attire was in complete complement to the day's activities. If it was a workday or evening event a highly starched collar, bow tie and perfectly creased pants were required. If it was mowing the lawn or chopping up wood for the fireplace only a flannel shirt and well-worn trousers would suffice.

He was kind in gesture and manner and his word was his bond. If he told you he would do something for you, you could take it to the bank. No questions. He was liked by all as well. All the neighbors and extended family held Sven in the highest regard. Great sense of humor too. One day he had taken his nephew Warren to lunch downtown. When they were finished, they stepped outside onto the street and his nephew noticed the town drunk stumbling into the sides of the buildings and meandering aimlessly at 1 o'clock in the afternoon. Warren only being eleven at the time said,

"Hey Unc, why is that guy walking like that? What's wrong with him?"

Without missing a beat he replied, "Oh him, his shoes are too tight."

Sven was extremely physically strong. It was a natural strength. Not the body builder kind for showing off. He had a motorcycle back in the day. An old Indian Scout I think it was with the suicide clutch. His brothers would try and ride it when he wasn't home. The way they all described that bike was when Sven rode it, it did what *he* wanted it to do. When they rode it, it did what *it* wanted to do.

He was drafted into the military in 193- and had served as an Army Corp. Engineer in WWII. As I understand it, he didn't speak of the war very much when he first returned. The hard parts were when they had to dig trenches to stay in as the bullets were flying over their heads. While they were in Germany a fellow platoon member of his (Gene) took notice of how well liked he was as well as having a gift for being good with numbers. When they got home from the war Gene asked him to come work for him in his bottling plant. Been with him ever since.

When Sven left for basic training, he had to leave behind his wife Diletta and their two baby girls. Diletta is a short petite little thing. She had grown up on a dairy farm and was the youngest of nine. While Sven was courting Diletta he would drive up to her father's farm in his old Ford Model-T that was on its last legs. Always dressed handsomely and with flowers or candy. Diletta's father once said that he had more respect for Sven than a few of his own boys. Sven wouldn't hesitate to roll up his sleeves and milk a cow or two then repair a fence. His family was extremely poor, while hers was a little more established. During the depression Diletta always had eggs from the chickens, milk, and a pig or two to be slaughtered to feed the family.

Diletta has short brown hair and impeccable manners. She loved her daddy too. As a kid she always had to sit by his side (especially at dinner time). When she was old enough to learn to drive the milk truck for deliveries it was, "I want Papa to teach me."

Sven was managing an IGA grocery store when they first met. He would take her to the Sons of Italy Hall for dances on Saturday night. Her curfew was 11 o'clock and she was never brought home late. I think they went together for four years before they got married and honeymooned in Florida. She loved to wear her flower dress on the Saturday night occasions with simple and modest shoes. Then she would ask her mother if she could borrow a necklace or earrings since she didn't have any of her own. These gala events were always waited upon with great anticipation by the both of them. A chance to forget the trials and tribulations associated with the laborious tasks involved with running a dairy farm as well as the tremendous responsibilities that go with managing a functional grocery store.

On one distinctive Saturday night the two were having a delightful evening dancing and conversing with friends. Diletta would usually order an old fashioned and Sven liked his scotch on the rocks (he always said that scotch is the hardest drink to get used to but once you do it's the most satisfying (he's right). All of a sudden, out of nowhere comes Leo De Luca. He and his family owned a garage in town. The De Lucas were known for being as cheap as they come.

“Watcha drinkin’?" Leo said to Diletta.

“A bourbon old fashioned." She replied.

“I've never had one before. Can I have a sip? Just to try it.”

"Sure Leo.”

After she gently pushed the glass towards him. With one big gulp he downs almost the entire thing.

"Wow, these are good!" He said as he left despairing remnants in the glass then walked away.

Sven turned to her,

“Don’t worry, I’ll get you another.”

When Sven went to war, she had to go to work in a factory on the line doing piece work. Her job was to put bearings into metal casings. Diletta had an excellent business acumen. She repeatedly told the kid so many stories where she was going to buy stock in a fast-food company at fifty cents a share or how since she and Sven had been renting a house in the summer on Cape Cod (since 194-) that it would be better if they just bought one. After all, by the time 196- rolled around they had been renting for twenty something years and inviting the whole family to join every year. Brand new homes were going up in Dennis and

West Dennis for $10,000 fully furnished. Kinda like lake front property back then. Nobody wanted it. But those ideas just got pushed aside.

Oh, I digress. Hockey. That was the kid's thing. Loved it. His Father got him started at a real early age. You see in Rhode Island (that's where his father lived). Hockey is like football is in Texas. Don't believe me? Ever heard of The Academy in Woonsocket? No? Shame on you. They've produced over 20 NHL players. That may not sound like much, but when you think of the stats where 1 in 50,000 play division 1 and 1 in 500,000 play professional (worldwide), and put that into a state you can drive across in an hour. It puts things in a little different perspective. It means something.

When he was just starting his dad would have to get him dressed and ready for skating.

"First things first, you have to put on your dingleberry protector." He would say to him. But when his father was rolling up his hockey socks and sliding him into his protective pants the kid would always ask,

"When will the yellow, black and white show on my socks?"

You see there is only 1 team in these parts for puck. That's right, the Big Bad Boston Bruins. From the early days of Milt Schmidt, Dit Clapper & Eddie Shore to the man, the myth, and the legend. The greatest player ever to strap on a pair of skates. Who ruled the ice with an iron hand, number 4 Mr. Bobby Orr! The Bruins are not only a part of the fabric. They are the spool, the sewing machine, the tailor, the ... well, you get my jive.

But man, every two-weeks,

"Dad, when are my socks gonna show? Dad, when are my socks gonna show?"

His hockey pants went down to his ankles, so it never looked like he was wearing any socks. Yeah, the kid isn't exactly overbearing in stature. He's about 3' whatever. Very thin bone structure and as strong as a baby rabbit. Straight brown hair that tends to have a mind of its own with developing cowlicks. He can be awkward at times not knowing what to say or then saying too much (the latter of course getting him into trouble then beat up). He tends to let a lot bother him and it gives him anxiety. Nervous exuberance some might say, but none the less it doesn't show the pearly whites any.

One of his many achilles heels he's carried is that he has always cared a tremendous amount about what people think of him (especially those closest). To an unhealthy level. To the contrary, he's not of the slightest concern what the popular kids think of him. It's just an extreme awareness of what his family says about him.

No one has confirmed if he's actually ambidextrous. I guess you would have to say yes, he is since he shoots the puck lefty, bats lefty, throws righty, writes righty. His father got him a guitar for his birthday one year when he was young. A wonderful little generic acoustic job that had the highest action imaginable. The only thing wrong was that it was a left-handed guitar (and as certain the kid started to play it righty). His father stood there for a moment then said,

"Heh? Why did I think you were left-handed?" (no one ever thought to just re-string the thing righty, so it sat in the basement for years and years).

He's not strong on his skates. Gets bumped around quite a bit on the ice. But what he may lack in physical magnitude he certainly makes up for in crazy. And by crazy, I mean he talks to his equipment. OCD in its infancy.

As the morning continued a few of the others arrived at the pond. His best friend Brandon would always be there. They've known each other since kindergarten. At that age the kid was as awkward as it gets. Never really spoke outside the house, so only spoke when spoken to. Brandon was willing to reach out to him and ask him questions. No one ever did that before.

"What do you think about those finger paints we did? I couldn't get mine to come out right."

That was what broke the ice. The kid waited for a minute and then looked around to see if there was someone else he could be talking to. Brandon waited patiently with a smile on his face and a look of ‘no rush, take your time’. He has displayed a tremendous amount of patience with him throughout the years.

When the kid finally realized he was talking to him, he didn’t know what to say. A couple seconds later he finally came out with,

“I wasn't sure what was going on there. It kinda was a surprise.”

The two spoke to each other for another couple minutes then the bell rang. “See ya!" “Okay, see ya!" Each said.

The next day Brandon said hello to him again (first). The boy was a bit more comfortable this time. Not so jumpy. As they were talking back and forth Brandon asked him if he wanted to come over after school and ride bikes or something. This once again threw our hero for a loop. He didn’t know what to say to this either. He had never been invited over anyone's house before. He didn't even know if he was allowed. Everything in his house he had to ask.

“I’m not sure if I can. I gotta ask my gramma."

"Don't you mean your ma?" Brandon asked.

"No, I live with my gramma and grampa."

"Oh, okay." (Brandon didn’t think it was weird or anything). "Just let me know if you can and which day. We can ride bikes any day or play street hockey in my driveway if you want.”

The kid's eyes light up. “You like hockey too?”

“Oh ya! My dad takes me to Franklin for the public skate. Westborough too, sometimes. The mite league is startin' up soon. You play?”

The kid could hardly breathe. He was too excited for words. He never talked about hockey with anyone his own age before. Practically hyperventilating he shouted,

“Oh ya! The B’s are the best! When I’m with my dad he takes me to Cranston rink for public skate every two weeks. One of these days he says my socks are gonna show! I shoot pucks in my basement ‘till then, then I ..."

"Where's Cranston rink? I never heard of it." Brandon was thinking he might pass out if he didn't cut him off really quick and give him a breather.

"It's in Rhode Island. My dad picks me up every two weeks and I stay with him there for the weekend then he brings me back on Sunday night. It's the rules I guess."

Brandon never heard of such a thing, but he would never insult his new admirer. "Okay, just let me know if you wanna come over sometime this week. I'll see ya."

"See ya."

Then Brandon headed to the cafeteria for lunch. The kid went running up and down the hallway like a Tasmanian beast. To have a chance to shoot pucks with a friend. He had never been here before. The cubbies were flying by as a complete blur. Got to the end of the hall, about faced then started going again at full speed past the classrooms. Then out of nowhere,

"Where's the fire?" (he got stopped dead in his tracks)

"Mr. Moore. Hi."

"Where's the fire son? You're running up and down these halls like a silverback guerilla. I figured there must be some emergency I don't know about. What is it?"

Trying to catch his breath and talk at the same time he blurted out,

"It's a chance to shoot pucks and ride bikes and I think I have a friend now and he plays hockey too and he lives with his dad and ma and he never made fun of me and I think ..."

"Okay, okay son just relax. Breathe in, breathe out. It's about lunch time why don't you head to the cafeteria. Who knows what your blood sugar level is at right now."

"Okay Mr. Moore. I'll see ya."

"Alright, just keep it under a hundred miles an hour."

The rest of the day took forever to get through. He had trouble sitting in his seat. Couldn't concentrate on any of the lessons the rest of the afternoon. When that final bell of the day rang, he ran out of the school and all the way home (forgetting he rode his bike there). Got home, came flying through the screen door, left his books outside by the breezeway and ran up to gramma who was cleaning the dandelions she had picked earlier that day.

"Can I go shoot pucks at Brandon's house and ride bikes and play street hockey? I have a friend now and he likes hockey too and riding bikes and I think he likes the Bruins too, can I go?"

"Speakin' of bikes, where's yours?" Gramma asked, "I didn't hear you slam it against the side of the house when you came home."

That's when it hit him,

"Oh, I musta left it at school. I didn't ride it home."

"We already have one hayseed in the family in your aunt. You ain't gonna be another. Run back to school, get your bike, then come home and tell me about your boyfriend. I'll be right here."

Twice in one day he got stopped in his tracks. This time he was walking not running back to get his bike. Didn't have that much energy to double-time it all the way again. He saw his lonely two wheels sitting there on the rack all by itself. Unlocked it and rode home. Told gramma all about his new friend and that he was invited over. When he got the details of where he would be and for how long he was allowed to go. That was when and how he met his first best friend.

Ah crap! Here comes some pain. The McGreeley brothers. Or commonly known as the McGreedys. They're puck hogs. Don't know how to pass or set up a play. If that weren't enough, they're the biggest and strongest on the ice. The kid gets frustrated with them often. Usually loses his temper at one or both and they end up checking him into a snowbank or tree. When they finally got enough players for a game there were never any netminders. No one in the neighborhood has enough money for goalie pads or any real goalie equipment of any kind. Teams are divvied up. Brandon, Stanley, John (another good friend) and the kid are up against the McGreeleys, Kevin Livingston and Billy Delvechio (The Italian Ice cream ... puff). Brute strength vs. speed and agility. Gonna be a long day. And nobody ever remembers to bring anything to eat or drink. How can you play puck all day on just what you had for breakfast?

The sun was going down and it was getting dark. The final tally was 5 games to 1. And the kid only got knocked around 3 times today.

Back home gramma had supper started.

"I'm starving! What's for dinner?" The kid yelled out as he came busting through the door.

Over the years many people have asked why he talks to his grandparents the same way they talk to their parents. He always replied that they *were* his parents, and it wasn't like he visited them twice a year on holidays where you get the *coochie coochie coo* talk. When he explained it that way they got it.

"How'd ya do today boy?" Grampa asked him.

"We won." He informed his senior with an intense desire for the food. "Hey Pop, are The Dukes on tonight?"

He always called him Pop. It was their own way to each other, and that was their favorite show to watch together. The Dukes of Hazzard. Gramp got the biggest kick out of Rosco P. Coltrane and Boss Hogg and the kid loved the General Lee especially with the jumps and chase scenes. I have to note as well that he got thoroughly embarrassed when the opening credits would come on and the scene where Daisy Duke is standing there in her tiny bikini. The kid would always say something to him to sort of break his own embarrassment at that moment. Something like,

"When's the next Bruins home game? Think we can get tickets?"

Gramp would say,

"What for? We can see it right here just fine and not have to fight any traffic or the crowds." That was another way of saying, *can't afford it.*

Just then a commercial for a remedy came on the tv.

The kid asked him,

"Pop, what's gonommonorrhea ...?"

"It's when your joint drips."

Joint ... joint, he thought to himself and looked at his elbow,

"What joint?" He asked so curiously.

"Your joint." Gramp said as he pointed to his crotch.

That night the kid went to bed right after the Dukes was over. Had a hard time keeping his eyes open while it was on after playing pond hockey all day. Gramma walked into the den a few minutes earlier (before the show was over) and as he was dozing off she exclaimed,

"What, are ya sleepin?"

"No." He replied, "I'm just resting my eyelids."

She vehemently retorted,

"Well, go to bed then! And rest your eyelids upstairs. We got Sunday mass tomorrow morning."

This day was done. The kid slept like a baby that night (which makes sense since just a few years ago he was). His bed is in the same room as the elders (who each had their own bedding as well). There was a guest room but that had to be kept pristine for the infrequent overnight company they *might possibly* get annually. I guess it makes sense somewhere somehow.

7am came mighty quick that Sunday. Catholic mass wait for no man. Except a priest if he is running late. Gotta wear your Sunday best which for him meant pressed corduroys, hush puppies, a collar shirt and his Bruins jacket.

"How come Grampa ain't gotta go to church?" He asked.

"Don't worry about it." She told him.

Now religion is muy importante in this house. So important that Sister Vincent from Blessed Sacrament Church would frequently come over and may or may not stay overnight (maybe that's who the guestroom was always saved for?). On more than one occasion one of the priests would be invited to a Friday night dinner. One evening Father Fitzgerald arrived for supper. The usual conversation occurred, *how's things, what's new,* etc...etc... etc... As the evening progressed Father Fitz happened to mention that they were short on altar boys. The kid overheard this and said,

"You need altar boys Father Fitz? I can be an altar boy."

"You wanna be an altar boy? Sure thing, I can make that happen."

The dinner went on as usual with Father Fitzgerald smoking his Marlboro reds and enjoying the table wine. Jokes were told and everyone was laughing. As the night ended the priest was led out by gramma. As he left the door to the breezeway she proclaimed,

"See you Sunday!"

"Okay Diletta, see you then! And I'll get things rolling for his initiation."

He got in his 4 door Mercury sedan and drove off. She waved goodbye, closed the door, turned around to him and said,

"You are *not* going to be an altar boy."

The kid just stood there perplexed. Not understanding a thing. She was protecting him (and I think you know from what).

She walked back to the kitchen and he went downstairs to the basement to shoot pucks. Never a word was spoken about it again.

Another Sunday, Gramma and he went to church together as usual. After the service was (once again) the same routine. Meet all the other old birds at The Mug n' Muffin where they would drink coffee and chew the fat about who knows what. He always had to sit through it and have an orange juice with a bagel, english muffin or something. The perpetual talk of,

"Her food is so bland."

"That's because she doesn't use any salt!"

"Are you gonna be the one to tell her?"

"Oh, no."

It was the longest hour and a half of his life.

As soon as they got home, he would immediately put his play clothes on and head to the pond to skate. Everyone was already there by now, so it was a matter of who was going to let him play on their team. Just another Sunday.

The next morning the kid arose and got ready for school. As luck would have it, his house was 9/10 of a mile from the school. He once asked grampa,

"Hey Pop, why won't the bus ever pick me up for school?"

"Why?" Grampa replied, "Remember that day we were riding along, and I stopped directly in front of your school. When we got home the odometer on the car only read 9 out of 10. Not a full mile. That's why. But the good news is you still have your trusty steed!" (that's what Grampa called his homemade bicycle that his father built for him from parts at the junkyard, Benny's store and the local five and dime). Yeah, to a young year old his bike is heavy duty.

This day he got to school, and he must have arrived a little early because on the front steps to the entrance was Sally Ellington sitting there with her best friend Jennifer seemingly waiting for him. He didn't know what to think of it. They were never sitting there before. He said good morning to both of them and they replied back with the same. Sally asked what he was going to do at recess.

He said, "The usual. Play kill the kid."

This was a primitive exhibition of football. Whoever had the ball would get tackled by the crowd, then throw the ball straight up in the air. The next one to catch it would run as much as he could in any direction until getting tackled. The process was then repeated several, several times. Not highly sophisticated, but as far as recess games go it was right up there.

Sally said, "Okay, see you then."

Somehow, someway the news travels. And in the first or second grade if the news is that someone likes someone else, that news is going to be made known to everyone at recess. It appears that little Miss Ellington has somewhat of a crush on the kid (unbeknownst to him). Lunch time had just finished, and everyone was in line to go outside. When they all got to the playground area of the school yard the game of kill the kid had just begun, but something was a little different. There were 2 girls playing this time. Sally and Jennifer were in the mix.

"Aw man! Now we can't play tackle if girls are playing." Someone yelled out.

"Don't you worry." Jennifer came back with, "You stupid boys can't run anyway, and will never catch us!" (she was a spitfire)

So, the game commenced. It almost appeared that everyone knew and was in on it (even Brandon). Come to find out that the object of today's game was to get the ball to Sally (or the kid), then tackle the both of them together and mush each one as close as they could to get them to kiss. It almost worked. Someone threw Sally the ball. She caught it. A couple guys got a hold of the kid and got him right next to her. Then the whole crowd tackled them to the ground and shouted,

"Kiss! Kiss! Kiss!"

Really, the kid didn't know what to do. After all, his life was hockey. But that wasn't going to suffice this crowd. He gave her a peck on the cheek, and everyone cheered then continued the game. It was his first kiss, and it was mandatory. None the less, he thought about it all day and was flying on air.

That night after dinner he went down to the basement. The basement was his sanctuary. It's where he could fire pucks against the cement wall, throw a ball or simply escape the trials and tribulations of being different. This night he had a new agenda. He was going to write Sally a poem and give it to her the next day at school. Now I can't recall the entirety of this masterpiece, but there is one line from it that is ensconced in my mind for all of time. He wrote to her, *your hair is as brown as the dirt on the ground.* It almost made headlines.

There was another event that happened in the basement. What was it? Oh yeah. So, he was down there again shooting pucks and stick handling around table legs and decoys he created in his mind and on the floor. This one day he was getting hot and sweaty, and he got thirsty. Grampa kept an old General Electric refrigerator in the basement to store things. So, he opens the door to the fridge, and he sees a green and silver can on the shelf. Ginger Ale is a particular choice of his. He cracked that can open and chugged it down. At first, he thought, *Canada Dry sure tastes funny today?* But what the heck, he was thirsty. After he finished the can, he couldn't find his hockey stick. Where'd it go? He looked for it and bumped into Grampa's desk. Found it shortly thereafter, but now where was the puck? He bumped into a few things on the way to finding the puck as well. Gramma yelled down to him from the top of the stairs,

"Come on up here, I need a hand with this!"

He stumbled his way up the stairs.

"What's wrong with you?" She said, "You look starry-eyed."

"I don't know?" He said, "I had a can of ginger ale downstairs and now everything seems different."

She went down to the basement herself to see what's what. On the ground next to the fridge was an empty can of Gennesee Cream Ale. The kid was crocked. She went back upstairs.

"Boy, you didn't drink no ginger ale! You drank real ale. Don't you know the difference between the two?"

I do now (he thought).

"Well, the can is green. And I saw a G on it and the word Ale on the can. It musta gotta be ginger ale." He said.

"Watchu mean must be? It ain't!" She came back with.

Then grampa came back from the grocery store and as soon as he walked in, he noticed.

"What's wrong with him?" He asked.

"He got into a can of your ale downstairs. Thought it was ginger ale." Gramma told him.

Sven couldn't stop laughing.

"Well, he'll sleep good tonight." He said.

The weekend was coming up. This was the one where his father was granted custody and would pick him up on Friday evening to have him until Sunday night. Actually, the boy would start to get anxious on Wednesday for these weekends. As soon as he saw his father's van pull into the driveway (and noticed him walking up the steps to the porch) the kid would spaz, bang through the door and jump into his arms (it was how they greeted each other every time).

"How's my boy?" His father would say to him.

"I'm good." He replied. "Did you see the Bruins game the other night Dad?

"I sure did. How many points did number four have that night?"

"He had three." The kid announced, "Two goals and one assist."

"That's right." His father confirmed, "Have you been practicing? Skating is very important and don't forget about your backhand. It's good to have a strong backhand for the loose pucks around the net."

"Yeah, I've been practicing every day."

"Very good." His father affirmed.

His father's name is Alfredo, but everyone called him Fredo and over the years the nickname of Freddy had its life as well. There was certainly no love lost between Sven and Alfredo. Whenever Fredo came into the house he wouldn't go 2 feet past the entrance. There was an end seat on the inside right near the door and he *might* sit down and talk to Diletta for a few seconds. Grampa would be around the corner at the kitchen table playing solitaire. I don't think they ever had a conversation together in front of the kid.

One day it dawned on the boy to ask grampa the question,

"Hey Pop, how come you never meet Dad when he comes to pick me up on the weekends?"

He got his answer swift and abruptly.

"The only reason I let him set foot in this house is because of you." He told him.

That was the only time they ever talked about it.

Diletta reminded Alfredo that he has school early Monday so to have him back at a decent hour Sunday night would be appropriate. He nodded and soon the two were on the road to Providence for another weekend together.

These weekends were what the kid lived for. To be with his father. They would go to the Cranston Ice Rink and check out the high school hockey games that were going on.

They would get Dell's Lemonade. His father worked for the government. I think he made maps. The man was large in stature and had a temper. He always wore a beard that was neatly trimmed and blended smoothly with his short straight brown hair. Light blue eyes accented his large ethnic nose that gave character. At approximately 240 pounds and 6'2" he held an equilibrium of blended muscle and fat. Strength was a given and fear of any kind didn't seem prevalent. By this I mean he liked to fight. A certain level of anticipation to a brawl at any given place and time. Often (and especially at the bars), he and his band the Easy Riders would play at on the weekends. He played guitar in a semi-country, blues, rock, pop quartet. It wouldn't take much throughout the course of a night to have an argument at the pool table or the counter. He'd be on stage sometimes during the first set then throw his guitar down, jump off the stage and get in the mix. The drummer and bass player would look at each other and roll their eyes as if to say, *here we go again*. When he got back to playing the lead singer would be like,

"Hey man, we got 2 sets left to go, pace yourself."

But he was as hard-headed as they come. If he told you that the chair you were sitting on was from England, but it had *Made in China* stamped directly on it he would talk for 50 minutes about the wood or the glue or the tools that were used to fabricate the stupid thing were originally from England so that means it's *from England*. Eventually most people would nod their head and remove themselves from his area, but he never gets the hint. Then he would stand there. Eyes wide open. A continuous expression on his face of, *okay, now what?*

He liked motorcycles as well. Had two Harley hogs over the years. Another odd trait he demonstrated is how whenever he was working on them (or his cars) and he was adding engine oil he would sit there and let the quart can drip, and drip, and drip, and drip, and ... *drip,* until it would literally stop dripping. This would often take upwards of 25 minutes. As if the reading on the dipstick (once entering the crankcase) could be humanly detectable by the naked eye from when the first pour that occurred to the final drip 1,200 seconds later. He also walked ever so slightly peculiar with his toes pointed out a few degrees from center. You wouldn't notice it at initial encounter or even after a few interactions, but eventually something would trigger something, and you'd say to yourself, *that's a little different.*

But he loved his son very much and wanted to have custody of his boy. One weekend he figured why go through the formalities and red tape of the court system. He'd just keep him. Didn't bring him back that Sunday night. 7 o'clock turned to 8 o'clock. 8 o'clock turned to 9 o'clock. The house was eerily quiet. Grampa was playing solitaire at the kitchen table as usual. Gramma was upstairs but started to make her way down the staircase. You could hear the cracking of each step she made as she walked to the kitchen where her husband was sitting. He looked at her over his glasses and noticed she had her rosary beads in her hand. He continued to play the card game.

"Do you think they are okay?" She asked him.

"I'm sure they are." He replied, "They probably have car trouble and are nowhere near any payphones. You know that old jalopy van of his is a death trap. They probably won't pull into the driveway until 11 o'clock and then ..."

"Then what?" She said boldly.

"Then good luck getting him up for school tomorrow."

9 o'clock turned to 10pm, 10 pm went to 11 then 11 hit midnight. Not a sound. Not the slightest clamor. One or two lonely crickets outside but that was it. Even the birds were asleep by now. *What do we do?* She asked herself. This had never happened before. Sure, the two families were not fond of each other, and his father had historically tried to get away with as much as he could so he could spend more time with his son, but kidnapping? She honestly believed he wouldn't do such a thing.

Gramma stayed up all night without a minute of sleep. One set of rosary beads around her neck and the other wrapped around her wrist and hand as she stared out the window. That morning grampa got up even earlier than he normally does. He was downstairs by 5am and saw what a nervous wreck she was. After putting a pot of coffee on, he turned to his wife. She saw the look in his eye that it was time for action.

"Who should we call first?" She asked him.

"Call Janine. Maybe she's heard something, knows something."

Gramma picked up the old yellow receiver and started to turn the rotary dial to call her daughter. Janine didn't answer until the 7th ring.

"Hello?" She said.

"Hey it's me. Is he with you? His father didn't bring him home last night so I'm hoping he's with you."

"What!" Janine jumped out of bed. "What do you mean he didn't bring him home last night! No, he's not here with me."

"I was afraid of that." Gramma said softly, "Should Daddy and I call to Fredo's mother?"

"No, no. I'll do it. I'm his mother I'll call. I know he likes to take his time bringing him back, but this is ridiculous."

Janine put her robe on as an instinctual measure of security and proceeded to call her ex-in laws. She punched the numbers with one hand and bit her nails on the other. *Ring, Ring, Ring, Ring, Ring*. No answer. She called again. *Ring, Ring, Ring, Ring*. A half a sleep voice answered on the other end,

"Hello."

"Where's my son! What's going on! Who do you think you are!" She kept going.

"What the hell time is it?" He said.

"It's time my son should be getting ready for school here in Massachusetts *not* Rhode Island! What's wrong with you!"

As he laid there on his mattress on the floor (the kid had the couch to sleep on) Alfredo stated,

"I had a three-party executive meeting with me, myself and I and we are of the majority opinion that we want our son to live together with us and, the board agreed. The motion was passed and now put into effect. Executed if you will."

"This is not a joke Fredo, my mother and father are frantic right now. Its illegal what you are doing."

"Legal Schmegal, Potatoe Potato." It's all he could come up with.

"I'm serious, you can't just keep our child. You know that in the eyes of the court his grandparents (my parents) have legal custody of him."

"Yeah, I thought about that part of it too. The board was not in favor of going through 'Due Process' or 'Proper Channels' or even those overly repetitious 'Required Forms' (as he stated each of the terms with as much intellect as he could muster and made air quotes with his free hand). The executives are in complete agreement that we will raise him ourselves and provide for him the only way a natural father can."

"Don't do this Freddy. You won't win. If you really want custody of him then do it legally. You're only making yourself look more incompetent as it is. This is *not* the way!"

"I have to go now. It appears that with great pleasure it is time for me to make breakfast for my boy. My number one son looks hungry. Honeynut cheerios perhaps son?"

"Is he up? Put him on the phone!"

"Hey little man, your mom wants to talk with you."

He passed the kid the phone.

"Hi Ma."

"Are you okay? Are you alright? How do you feel? What are you doing? Do you need anything? Are you okay? How do you feel?"

"Yeah, sure. I'm fine. The phone woke me up. Dad said I could stay longer than just the weekend this time. I'm about to have breakfast. We got Honey Nut Cheerios, Count Chocula, Boo Berry, Frosted Flakes, Franken Berry and a couple others I can't remember right now."

"Okay. You have fun with your dad. I'll see you soon. I love you."

"Love you too Ma."

"Thank you honey, please put your father back on the line."

"Satisfied? You interrupted our beautiful, delicious, fine, wonderful, tasty breakfast."

"He's missing school you *moron*! What do you think happens once the school realizes he hasn't been in attendance? He hasn't been taken out of enrollment! What questions do you think they will have for us? Guess what happens then!"

"My corn flakes are getting soggy. I will be hanging up now. Have a pleasant morning and/or afternoon."

-click-

All that she heard next was the dial tone. As Janine put the receiver back to the holder she murmured,

"*Dumbass*."

When she picked up the phone to call her mother and father back and update them a sense of calm had come over her. Even though the kid was technically being illegally kidnapped, she knew he was safe. His father loved him very much and would never hurt him.

Ring! Ring! "Hello?"

"He's okay Ma."

"Thank you, Jesus." Gramma expressed softly,

"What happened? What's going on?"

"Well, it appears that Alfredo wants primary custody of our son and he decided to bypass any legislative procedure. He thinks he can just keep him and that will be it. No questions asked."

"What? What's wrong with him? Why would he think he can do such a thing?"

"That's just it. He's not thinking Ma. This is a completely emotional response and action. I think he misses his son during the week and wants to be with him all the time. The thought process of what's transpired and how to logically progress with re-adjusting the outcome has completely surpassed his pathology."

"Heh? Say that again but a whole lot slower."

"He misses his son and it hurts him. He's thinking with his heart and not acknowledging that daddy and you are the legal guardians."

"Oh, I see. Well, what should we do now? He obviously won't be going to his school today. I doubt the principal will call here if he misses a few days, but what about after that? What do you think we should do?"

Janine paused for a moment then replied,

"I know it, I mentioned something to that effect to Fredo on the phone just now. Let's see if he comes to his senses in the next few days. Maybe he will realize what he's done and bring him back. Let me think about it."

"Okay." Gramma confirmed, "Did you talk with him?"

"Oh yeah, he's fine. They were just starting breakfast. He was making him cereal."

"That's my job." Gramma let out.

"I know Ma, I know."

Almost a week had passed by and no update had occurred. Grampa turned to Gramma and said,

"It's not the same without him is it."

"No, I know it." She replied, "It's too quiet. I never before noticed that humming sound the Frigidaire makes. I was sitting here at the kitchen table just yesterday and all of a sudden it hit me like a gust of wind. That electrical ice box likes to hum a little tune throughout the day. It gave a cough here and there, then almost a little hiccup. Like it was catching its breath and then, right to a hum."

"Be careful it doesn't fart in your direction." He said with a calming grin.

"Remember our old ice box?" She asked him, "That thing dripped and dripped and dripped into that little ceramic pan we had for it. Loud drips too! Not the faucet kind. But it's funny, I can't think of a specific point in time I noticed the drips of the ice box, but I'll always remember when I realized the hum of the Frigidaire."

Then the phone took off. *Brrriing! Brrriing! Brrriing!* Gramma jumped out of her seat to get it,

"Hello?"

“Hi Ma, it’s me. Did he bring him back yet?”

“No, he hasn’t brung him back yet. Would I be talking about ice box drips if he did?”

“Heh? What?”

“Never mind.”

“Okay, I’ll call over there again to see what they are doing. I imagine Fredo must have taken off from work for the week. I’ll call you back.”

“Alright.” Gramma then hung up.

Janine started to pace back and forth. She wasn’t quite sure how she was going to approach the situation this time. Last time there was a bit more adrenaline flowing. This time it’s a case of catching more flies with honey than with vinegar. She took a sip of her lukewarm tea and started to dial. Ring! Ring!

"Hello?"

"Oh, hello Yvette. It's Janine. How are you?”

Alfredo’s mother has a distinctive soft tone to her voice that Janine recognized immediately.

“I'm fine." She replied in a slightly condescending tone.

Yvette never had much use for Janine. For whatever reason she didn't feel she was good enough for her son as a wife.

"Is my son there? I'd like to speak with him.”

"He's in the bathroom right now." She informed Janine unsentimentally.

"Oh, okay. How about Fredo? Is he available?”

"He's at work right now.”

"So, he leaves our son with you all day while he goes to work?"

"Of course, he can't just stop working. How is he going to pay for things?"

"So let me see if I have this correct, all this time he has had our son in his custody, he's been going to work while you have been taking care of him?"

"Yes girl.”

"Has he come out of the bathroom yet?"

“Has he come out of the bathroom yet? No, not yet."

"Is he constipated? Sometimes he gets constipated if he hasn't had enough fiber in his diet. Did you know that?" Janine said a bit sternly.

Yvette responded,

"Would you like me to have him call you when he gets out?"

"Yes, please do."

"Alright bye." -click- (she hung up)

Janine's blood was boiling before she put down the receiver. She was thinking to herself ... (He wanted his son so badly, but he's leaving him with her all day. No school. No friends. What are they left to do all day?)

As the kid came out of the bathroom, he was still fixing his trousers.

"Oh, let me help you Nonny." (*it's an old-school Italian term of endearment. The grandmother calls her grandson Nonny, and the grandson calls his grandmother Nonny. I think it may be similar in other ethnic origins as well)*

"What are we going to do today?" He asked her. "Can we go to the park? Can we go ride bikes? Can we go to the hockey rink?"

He was rattling off everything he did with his father.

"Oh no Nonny." She said, "We have to go grocery shopping, then I have to get my driver's license renewed at the motor vehicle department, then we have to stop by St. Augustine's to light a candle. We have a lot to do today."

"Okay Nonny, I'll get my coat and hat for the ride."

She put him in the car, and they went off to run all the errands of the day. He went along and into all the buildings of each stop with her. Didn't say much, just observed the different places he had never been to before on his usual court appointed visits.

5:30pm came up pretty quickly when she noticed it,

"We have to get home soon! Your father will be home from work at six and I have to make supper."

They drove home as fast as she could drive. She had the soup on quick and started some pizza bread with hot dogs. He turned on the tv and simply watched what was on the current station (didn't bother to change to anything).

A few minutes after 6pm his father came through the door. He wasn't wearing the big smile the kid was used to seeing when he picked him up every other weekend.

"Hi Dad, how'd it go today?"

There was a slight pause before his response,

"Ah, just another day in the meat grinder."

The kid didn't know what that meant but he got the feeling that he shouldn't even ask.

"What's for supper tonight Ma?" (Fredo immediately diverted his attention away).

"We've got some pizza bread. I think I have enough for a salad and something I can whip up real quick."

Freddy looked around the room of the kitchen as the kid looked back at the television and then to him again.

"Well, let's see if we have enough for an iced coffee." He stated with little emotion.

As the three of them sat at the dinner table the conversation between the only two adults usually got very heated. Yvette would begin by saying, "You need to ...!"

This is where you could literally fill in the blank with any possible situation, act, occurrence or realization that a mother believes her son should have. Sort of like a B-17 machine gunner unleashing the artillery. Freddy would listen at first, but then respond loudly back in Italian. The volumes of both would go up about every 20-30 seconds and then ... *silence.* Imagine two people hollering at each other as their form of communication for 6-7 minutes and then nothing. The kid would just sit back and watch the fireworks. A few more minutes passed as the three of them ate their dinner.

"Hey Dad, can we hit the batting cages at Rocky Point tomorrow?"

"No little man, I've got to work."

"How about public skate at the rink the next day?"

"Well, I have to go to work every day of the week up until Friday. I only have Saturdays and Sundays off."

Yvette looked at him across the table as if to say, *well, now you've got him, what are you going to do with him.*

The next few days were more of the same. Fredo went to work, and the kid was left with his nonny throughout the day. He was always very respectful of her, but she could tell he was getting restless and antsy. The kid couldn't sit still. He was always jumping out of his seat or running up to her asking every little question that came to mind,

"What are we doing today? What's that bird? Who just called on the telephone? What's this music? Can we pick cherries in the park?"

Yvette wasn't prepared.

As she shook her head in frustration there was also a tremendous amount of sadness. She loved her grandson with all her heart. The hard truth hit her that day that this situation was not going to work out. It wasn't what was best for him (and she knew it). Just then the phone rang,

"Yvette, please let me speak to my son right now!"

A quiet, "Yes dear" is all she said back. She gave the phone to the boy.

Janine expressed with great concern,

"Honey are you okay? How are you? Do you need anything? Did you go to the bathroom alright?"

"Hi Ma, yeah I'm okay. What's new? How's Gramma and Grampa?"

"We all miss you so very much honey. Gramma and Grampa ask me about you every day."

There was a little hurting feeling in his throat, but he didn't know what it was. He didn't want to cry in front of nonny, so he held it in but then his voice cracked,

"Tell Gramma & Grampa I'm fine."

"Okay honey I will. If you need anything at all just call me. Nonny has my number."

"Okay Ma, I will."

"I'll see you soon."

"K Ma, bye."

He gave the phone back to Yvette.

"Yvette, this is ..."

"I know Janine. I'll have a talk with Fredo tonight."

"Thank you."

They both hung up at the same time.

When Fredo came home from work that night they had a heart to heart about the situation. She said to him,

"We both love him very much, but I think a big part of his life is there with them. If we think about what's best for him, I think we have to consider that living there (with them) during the week and you getting him on weekends might be it."

Alfredo sat back in his chair, didn't say a word then let out a heavy sigh. An hour later the two were driving back to Massachusetts. While they were in the van the kid turned to his father,

"This long weekend was a little different than all the others."

"Yeah, I know beanzo. It was just a little change of pace for us. A little spice to mix things up a little. Everything is *a okay* though."

About a half past nine the old beat-up van pulled into the driveway. Sven was playing cards at the kitchen table and continued to play although always paying distinct attention in the background. Fredo and his son said goodbye in the van. It was the first time he didn't walk him up to the door. As the kid ran up the steps to see gramma waiting for him, he smiled at her, and she opened the screen door. He walked in and waved goodbye to his father. Gramma looked at Fredo as he sat behind the steering wheel. He could feel her look. What is more, he knew she was right.

CH. 2

Diletta and Sven had two children. Delores and Janine.

Janine (as you know) being his mother and Delores his Aunt. Janine is teeny tiny. Always has been. As a child she was a bit sickly and developed a bad case of asthma. Allergies took a predominant role in her youth, and she had to get shots injected on a regular basis. At 95lbs. with short brown hair and brown eyes she can have a tendency to blend in with the crowd. Often getting overlooked or blocked when the large family photos or business pictures are taken. She's not the least bit bothered by her inconspicuousness. She rather prefers it. JC Penney off the rack is just fine. She's an intellect. Attire is a mere necessity. I suppose it is a bit different though for women of similar IQ. as opposed to men of the same. What I mean by this is how Einstein had 7 outfits each being the exact same so he wouldn't have to waste thought on what he would wear. She's certainly not at his level of disregard for her ensembles, but by no means will Joan Collins be in contact to get beauty tips.

Her glasses tend to overextend in the classical sense and sweaters can often be wrinkly and sometimes torn. Shoes are always penny loafers and usually on the verge of needing to be re-soled. As a child you can imagine the torment she had to endure from the various socialites in elementary and through high school. When she was elected class valedictorian all the years of mockery, negligence by peers, and being completely off the radar for any Saturday night dates seemed to be justified in one single afternoon. An absolute gorgeous Saturday in June with a distinct breeze that cooled everyone in their gowns. This graduation ceremony was a bit more prestigious than any year prior. The superintendent of the entire school district was the MC. He had connections with a few of the muckety mucks down at city hall, so he was able to convince the mayor to show up and present the award for the institutions' highest level of academic achievement. As Janine sat there in sustained elation this guy gave what ended up being a 45-minute recount of all the years budget goals, accomplishments, and plans for the future. You name it, he just went on and on and on. After so much redundancy he finally got to the matter at hand. By this time the jocks, greasers, most of the band and another third of the student body had already checked out and were dozing off in their seats. Mr. Mayor brings it home by saying,

"But today we are here in glorious celebration of this year's graduating class and its illustrious valedictorian Miss Janine Jalinski. Miss Jalinski has proven herself to be a veritable titan in the fields of mathematics, physics, science, and engineering. Her intellectual prowess has earned her a full academic scholarship to the Massachusetts Institute of Technology where it is my understanding that she intends to pursue a career in the computer sciences. So, without further ado, I give you Walpole High class of 19— valedictorian, Janine Jalinski!"

By this time even the birds flying above were anxious. With her heart racing a mile a minute, knees wobbling and palms sweating profusely she slowly made her way to the podium. As the crowd's applause slowly came to a halt, she placed her well-rehearsed speech carefully on the podium. At the exact moment she adjusted her glasses and brought the microphone close in, it happened. One of the above hollow boned carnivores flying just low enough to be heard (as well as seen), pooped like a seagull directly on her right shoulder. The faculty and staff held themselves, but the first few rows of student body regressed back to adolescents with whistles, jeers and the most common robust applause usually reserved for the cafeteria when someone drops their tray. If the lottery had been legalized, she could have run to the closest convenience store and simply wait for her numbers to roll out. As it was, she held her composure. Mr. Chara, the P.E. teacher, handed her his handkerchief and she was able to wipe most of it away. Take two.

"Fellow students, distinguished guests, faculty and staff, Superintendent Oates and Mayor Janney. It is an esteemed privilege to be here with you today." As she delivered her 35-page acknowledgement of every aspect of her academic career thus far, Sven and Diletta sat in the audience with so much pride and joy for their little girl that they were both in tears (Sven a bit more choked up than an actual wipe of the eyes). They both had to go to work at such a young age so to have two children graduating high school at the same time and one of them carrying the flag for the entire class, made them the happiest mama and papa in the world. They were just happy Delores graduated.

Janine's speech concluded with an optimistic view of society, the world, and all the plants and animals that live in it. All that kind of stuff. Then the whole crowd clapped again. She collected her notes and went back to her seat on the stage. The ceremony ended with the marching band playing Pomp and Circumstance. People gathered in the parking lot a while to socialize. Mr. Richards, her advanced calculus teacher, came over to say goodbye. He was elder in years and looked at his students more like his kids.

"Wonderful speech young lady." He said to her.

"Thank you, Mr. Richards."

"What are your plans for the summer?"

"Oh, it's so exciting (she could hardly contain herself as she replied while having a hard time catching her breath). I have a summer internship at Padias in their computer development department. They have established a new division and are applying resources to create ..."

She went on for another eight minutes of details that Richards politely nodded to and expressed a sincere enough level of interest to show genuine appreciation for. When she concluded he said,

"Well, my dear, you have certainly earned it. Congratulations on such a stellar academic performance here. I know you will be a valuable asset and complete success in all your future endeavors."

She thanked him politely then Mr. Richards walked away into the crowd. Many other faculty members expressed their appreciation to her that day. By the end of it all everyone's mouth hurt from smiling so much.

The two sisters are as different as night and day. Delores has a mean streak in her and it has never gone away. There was one story I heard when they were in grade school. Delores knew that Janine didn't get along with this girl Gloria in their class. I really don't even know if Gloria knew that Delores and Janine were sisters. Anyway, one day Delores asked Gloria if she would like to come over to their house after school (unbeknownst to Janine). The girl said yes and when the last bell rang that day, they both headed over to Delores' house. Janine was always doing extra homework after school, so she got home a little later than her sister. When Delores saw Janine come through the door, she immediately told Gloria to hide behind the sofa so they could scare her. Gloria obliged (not even knowing who her sister was). Janine sat down and Delores started to ask her how her day was and other forms of the usual. Then she asked her,

"Hey, what do you think of Gloria Laguna?"

"Don't get me started about that witch!" Janine proclaimed, "She's as bad as they come!"

And before Janine even finished her sentence. Gloria popped out from behind the couch. Didn't say a word to either and walked out. Delores just stood there with her estranged smile for what she accomplished. The funny thing too, Delores didn't even like Gloria.

Janine always excelled in school. From the very beginning she was the brightest one in her class. Especially with numbers. Calculus 1 & 2 were not even a challenge. She understood imaginary numbers better than her imaginary friends. That's another interesting point. What she excels at intellectually, she lacks socially. Janine didn't have any friends growing up. Socially disparate to say the least. And as we all know kids can be brutally truthful about their feelings at times. So, sufficed to say, she took her fair share of ribbing as a child.

Janine always persevered. Finding solutions was the excitement. She received full academic scholarship awards from all the Ivy League schools as well as a vast number of Technical Universities. In the end she chose to stay right in her backyard and go to MIT.

Delores, not so much. Delores believes in the lifestyle, *when the going gets tough, quit. It ain't worth doing*. She really didn't even try in school. Just had fun and was the social butterfly. She got a job at Plimpton Press after graduation where she met her future husband. They ended up having two kids (a boy and a girl) and living in the burbs. Basically, her life has been a Norman Rockwell painting with the husband, kids, dog, cat, house, and white picket fence. She's the poster child for Gen-Xrs who believe you can be lazy and still live in a $500,000 home.

As Janine was getting closer and closer to her freshman year at MIT she really wanted to live at home and commute. She was petrified to live in a dorm. The thought of having a stranger as a roommate, community bathrooms and having to go to the cafeteria everyday sent unwavering panic to her central nervous system. Diletta and Sven believed it would be good for her to experience this aspect of college life. That it would assist in making her a more 'well rounded' individual. So that September morning in 196-

they took her to her first day of school kicking and screaming just like it was kindergarten all over again.

They got her settled in her room where she basically just cried the whole time. Diletta made up her bed and Sven walked around the dorm room introducing himself to everyone and cracking jokes (I told you everyone liked Grampa). When it came time for them to leave Janine's eyes were as red and puffy as they could be. She had boogers hanging from her nose with no desire for a Kleenex. Diletta wiped her face and assured her they were only an hour away. The funny thing here, I was once told there is no correlation between intelligence and emotions. They are mutually exclusive. I think that's correct. As smart as Janine is, the rational side never hit that her mother and father were only an hour drive away. And that was with traffic! There are many scenarios where intellect and emotion do not appear to have a connection.

Janine didn't have a thing to eat that first night on campus. She just sat in her room, alone. Her roommate didn't arrive until the next day. I would have liked to have been a fly on the wall. Can you imagine that introduction? New girl walks in, "Hi! I'm ..." Janine runs out of the room without saying a word and no idea where she's going. Then has to come back and start all over again. I would have paid money to see that.

Once she got to her classes, she was fine. The stress of discussions on a social level escaped her. She could lose herself in her studies. That's where she was comfortable. That's where her inhibitions lowered. Creating algorithms to solve problems was her forte. In a sea of 4.0 GPAs, she impressed her professors so much that they wanted to publish some of her work. When they realized how socially inept she was, they decided against it since the attention she would receive would have been too overwhelming for her.

It wasn't until her senior year at MIT that she went on the first date of her life. They met in the chess club and were paired up to play each other. His name was Ramon. During their first few matches he would try to make small talk with her in between moves. At first, she thought it was meant to divert her attention away from the game. She beat him every time. But then she realized he was sincere. Ramon and Janine went on a few dates. He soon realized there was nothing there. No connection. She didn't let him in, although she had no idea that she was so distant. When Ramon stopped calling Janine asked herself, *What's wrong with me? Why aren't I ...?*

After graduation she spent the summer on Cape Cod with her family. This season they rented in Falmouth and would head to the Shorecrest on weekends. While waiting for her ice cream cone this young man slowly and secretly slid up next to her. When she reached over the counter, he very discreetly bumped her elbow. She watched the vanilla chocolate swirl fall to the pavement in suspended animation. When it finally landed and began melting before her eyes he said, "I'm so sorry. I didn't see you there. Please allow me to get you a new one."

That's who she married seven months later. Alfredo Calletti. An Italian from Rhode Island. He was supposed to go to Providence College but dropped out after a semester.

He picked her up in his father's shiny bright Cadillac. Guineas from Rhode Island and New York all drove Caddys in those days. I think they went to a Hungarian restaurant that night, not sure. All I know is that after that first date Fredo wanted a second date and a third and a fourth and a ...

It appears he enjoyed meeting his intellectual superior. They had a beautiful wedding ceremony and reception in Old Saybrook. Then spent their honeymoon in Greece. I saw a few pictures from that trip. There isn't one photograph where they are standing side by side. It's bizarre. You know how you would think newlyweds on their honeymoon would be gazing into each other's eyes mesmerized with all that gooshy love or something. Not here. Not these two. She's either walking ahead of him or in the picture all by herself. Peculiar.

It wasn't until a few years later that the kid was born. There it is. We got there. We finally made it. I can imagine you were wondering where when how who what where when we were going to bridge this gap. But the marriage didn't last very long. He couldn't hide his stripes for an extended period of time. Actually, it was a truly short while after the wedding when Freddy came home, slammed his fist on the table and said to her,

"Now you're going to see what a bastard I really am!"

He lived up to it too. There was a time when the baby was crying. Alfredo and Janine were in bed, he turned to her and said,

"Hey, the kid's crying."

I guess she didn't get out of the bed fast enough for him 'cuz he pushed her with his foot. She fell out and landed on the floor. She was in excruciating pain because the kid broke her tailbone coming out of the birth canal. It hadn't fully healed yet.

They were married for less than a year then got a divorce. I think grampa even saw it coming. He told me of a time when they were dating. Fredo was over their house when he saw Sven's golf clubs in the garage. He said to him,

"Hey, let me wash those for you."

Sven replied,

"I don't need them washed Freddy they're fine."

"No, no, no." Fredo insisted, "I'll wash them for you, bring 'em back, and they'll look brand new."

"Fredo, I don't need them washed." Sven had to repeat.

One more time it was there again, "I'll have them shiny and bright."

"Go ahead Fredo. Take the clubs."

Sven knew he would never see them again.

But the moment that it came to fruition was the day Janine and Fredo were married. Both Diletta and Sven knew how important it was to Janine. They paid for everything. The entire wedding, reception and three days of festivities at their house since family members came from all over the East coast. I think it totaled about $4,000. Not a small sum for an honest, working-class family in those days. After the ceremony and reception, right before the bride and groom were leaving to catch the plane to go on their honeymoon Sven turned to his daughter and said,

"You can always come home." He knew.

After the divorce, Janine won custody of the kid and they lived in a one-bedroom apartment in Boston, until ...

Janine was working with top level security clearance and Monday through Friday would have to pass through 4 separate check points. She was working for Ratheon in their government division of bio-chemical reactors. Since the kid was a baby, she hired a nanny that would take care of him during the week prior to getting home at night. Also, often dropping him off at her parent's house for three to four days at a time as well. Diletta and Sven never refused her.

Shortly after being granted custody Janine was woken up in the middle of the night by her crying baby. She didn't know what to do. She just stood there over his crib and stared at him. The crying got louder and louder. She started to wonder if her neighbors could hear. Tapping her foot and biting her nails her first thought was to make a phone call.

Ring! Ring! Ring!

"Hello?"

"Ma, you hear that in the background. He's been like that for half an hour. What do you think it is?"

"Janine, are you kidding me? When was the last time you fed him?"

"The nanny fed him at dinner time before I got home from work."

"Go into your ice box and see how many bottles of milk there are and give him one. You may have to warm it up a bit. At his age they take a bottle every two or three hours, sometimes more if they're hungry."

She went into the kitchen and noticed five small bottles with *formula* written on the side. She didn't know what temperature it needed to be, so she just pushed it against her body and hoped for the best. While picking him up she didn't know to support his head but soon realized she needed to stabilize his position. Then, leaning back in her chair, one arm with him and the other placing the bottle gently to his mouth the crying subsided. Diletta stayed on the phone a brief while longer in silence and then hung up.

She knew it was under control now. As Janine was feeding him, she could faintly hear the dial tone of the receiver she forgot to hang up. She just closed her eyes.

A few weeks later another similar scenario occurred but with a much different outcome. The kid was crying and crying non-stop. Janine got a bottle of formula. He wouldn't take it. She tried rocking him to sleep as gently as she knew how. He wouldn't stop crying. She checked his cloth diaper. Nothing wet in the front. Nothing in the back. He kept crying. After an hour she called her mother again.

"Ma, I'm at my wits end. I don't know what to give him. He doesn't want a bottle. He doesn't need a changing. I don't even think he wants to be held. What else is there in life at this age?"

"Okay, Janine feel his forehead and tell me if it's warm."

Janine returned to the wailing crib then back on the phone.

"Yeah, I guess he's a little warm, but I would be too if I was screaming crying for an hour and a half."

"Has it been that long? Get dressed. Get him bundled and meet us at the ER."

Janine was a bit surprised to hear her mother say, "ER", but it didn't register that it could be anything serious. When she arrived with him Sven and Diletta were already there in the waiting room. Diletta put her hand on his forehead,

"Nurse! Please help us. My grandson appears to be running a temperature."

The nurse took the baby from Janine and wheeled him into the ICU pediatric division of Boston Children's Hospital. The three took a seat in the waiting room and sat there together not saying a word for over an hour.

There after the nurse came through the doors of the reception area,

"Who is the boys' mother?"

"I am." Janine informed her.

"It appears he has scarlet fever. We're running a few tests to confirm. We'll report back to you when we can."

And in an automated fashion the nurse turned around and went back to her rounds.

"I want to ask something of you both." Janine looked down at the floor as she spoke to her parents. "I want to ask if you would be willing to accept legal guardianship of my son."

The words came out with little emotion and more in a manner of sensibility.

"Oh honey, what are you talking about? This isn't your fault." Diletta continued to console her daughter, "You didn't cause any of this to happen. It's just a part of life. We'll get through this and many other things."

"I've been asking myself questions and trying to come up with the most logical solutions. I feel extremely inadequate with my maternal instincts. I fear that I do not react correctly and (or) efficiently when it comes to the daily emotional, physical, or psychological needs he has. I feel that I am lacking in certain primary areas. I believe I am inadequate and at this juncture of his life he would certainly be in better care with the two of you."

There was a long section of silence as nobody knew what to say. Diletta looked over at Sven for a second then back at Janine.

"So, honey what are you saying? Do you want to go down to the courthouse and have papers drawn up that have me and daddy as his parents?"

"Yes." She said while having her eyes fixated on the tile floor.

About a half hour later the nurse came back with her update,

"He should be fine. We have given him some Pedialyte and hydrated him intravenously. You will be able to take him home in a couple hours."

They all left the hospital together shortly thereafter. A few months later the kid was legally under the guardianship of his grandparents. The subject of why was never discussed again.

CH. 3

Ratheon is where she met Ted. Ted Sullivan. Originally from Vermont. He's a bit smaller in physical makeup than most of his male counterparts. When he graduated high school, he weighed 125lbs. All through elementary and middle school he was the smallest one in his class. Always picked last (or sometimes not at all) on the playground. There were numerous days throughout the school year where the teachers would see him alone on the fence or just sitting on the ground while the other kids (including the girls) would be playing baseball or dodge ball. Every now and then someone would chime in at roll call for picking teams and add a ... *Who's lucky enough to get Ted today?* An interesting characteristic to note is that even at this young stage in his life he never showed any emotion with it. If it bothered him, nobody knew. If it angered him, nobody could tell. If it frustrated him, no one (not even the staff) could even guess. Whatever he felt he held it all in and simply waited for the bell to ring to go to class. Once back at their neatly uniform desks, most of the kids were sweating profusely and would have to wait in line at the water bubbler. Ted would just sit there. A subtle little grin, or more often than not, no expression at all. Just his pencil in hand eagerly awaiting the continuation of the day's lesson. As an A & B student of his own, his report card was his paycheck. And that's exactly how he looked at it. Even in grade school. When he came home each semester, and if he had all A's staring back at him, he knew his parents would reward him. In effect, he got preferential treatment over his brother and sister who achieved the same for some reason. Have you ever known parents to play favorites with their kids? Have you ever known it to have a positive effect?

When junior high came around Ted learned to socialize a little more. He had a good friend named Alexander whom he would play backgammon with quite often. They were inseparable by 7th grade and only ate lunch with each other at school. Alexander lived about two miles away from Ted's home. One weekend Ted asked Alexander if he wanted to go to the museum with him on Sunday morning. They were having an exhibit on mythical creatures, and he didn't feel like going alone again. Alexander said he had to go to church with his family at the same time the exhibit was being displayed. Alex asked Ted,

"Don't you go to church too?"

"No." Ted replied, "We're agnostic."

Alexander looked extremely perplexed. "What's Ag ... Agnnnostix?" He asked.

"It's when you say there either is or isn't a God."

"Heh?" (Alex was still confused).

"It's when you say sure ... why not or sure maybe there is and maybe there isn't."

"Oh." It was all Alex could think of to say at this point.

A couple hours later Ted was riding his bike to the museum by himself. Along the dirt roads there were always turtles and frogs trying to cross and get to the water nearby.

Any other day he would assist and carry them to the water's edge. Not this time. He was late to the event.

Ted was unassuming at first glance. Very reserved. Quiet. Wasn't the smooth-talking type that woos women. It was an accident that he and Janine met. The cafeteria at Ratheon was jam packed for lunch one day. The only seat that was open was across from Janine. He asked if he could sit there, and she said yes. As he settled into his seat Ted adjusted his silverware and juice glass, he noticed she was reading a magazine on astrophysics. He mustered up the nerve to ask her what the article was about. She then replied,

"String theory. It is a relatively new theoretical framework in which the point-like particles of particle physics are replaced by one-dimensional objects. It describes how these strings propagate through space and interact with each other. On distance scales larger than the string scale, a string looks just like an ordinary particle, with its mass, charge, and other properties determined by the vibrational state of the string. In string theory, one of the many vibrational states of the string corresponds to the graviton, a quantum mechanical particle that carries gravitational force. Thus, being a new theory of quantum gravity."

"I see." Ted replied.

Not knowing a word of what she was talking about.

"Is that your area of expertise?" He asked her.

"No, I was brought in to assist in developing Ratheon's bioreactor division. We need to eliminate fouling in the heat exchangers."

He was no closer to understanding what it is she did.

"What do you do?" She asked him.

"I work in data processing." Ted informed her without nearly as much elaboration.

They continued their lunch in the sea of employees at the cafeteria. Janine was reserved in her expression and tone. No signals of happiness or sadness during their conversation. No emotion to speak of, but she wouldn't let the conversation just die out. Whenever there was that brief moment of silence, she would break that barrier with a

"Where did you grow up?" or "Do you have any brothers or sisters?" Every time Ted thought he was sinking she reeled him back up ever so subtly. A good half hour had passed when she looked at her watch.

"Excuse me, I've got to get back to the lab." She informed him as she was gathering her belongings and cleaning up her tray.

Ted replied to her with a smile,

"This was extremely enjoyable. It was such a pleasure to meet you. I hope we can get together for lunch again sometime ... my treat!"

She was caught off guard. Today's lunch started off like all those years in jr. high and high school. Alone at a table. She was used to it by now. She was comfortable with it. Suddenly in familiar surroundings enters an unfamiliar scenario. She politely responded,

"Yeah, okay. Have a good day."

And without a second glance Ted was left there with his crumbs of meatloaf, ¼ cup of apple juice, little sliver of chocolate cake and hope. But he was happy. Very, very happy.

When he got back to his area nobody else noticed (at first), that he had a grin on from ear to ear. He started to review some charts but couldn't keep his mind focused. Two seconds later Al Burke from marketing popped around the corner.

"Hey, Ted. What did we finalize on the ... what the heck are you so happy about?"

"Al, I met her."

"Met who?"

"Her. Don't ask me her last name. Don't ask me where she's from. She told me but I just can't remember right now. Don't ask me what she does, she's smarter than you, me and ten astronauts combined. I just know it's her."

"O ... kay ..." Al responded very slowly as he had never seen Ted this way in all the time they had worked together. "Does *her* have a first name?" He asked.

"Janine, Janine something."

Al thought to himself, *ah, Janine. Janine something that works somewhere and does whatever. Sure, that cleans it up.*

"Okay man, hey I'm glad you found your Helen of Troy. When you land back down here on earth can you give me a ring. I just need a couple of notes from the last meeting of the minds we had with the brass."

"Sure." Ted replied with a glow of happiness.

Al just rolled his eyes and went on his way. *Puppy love? At his age?* he thought to himself.

When Janine got back to her lab, she was unfazed. It was business as usual. She was setting up variable arrays. A mock re-enactment of transposing a vector by adding a dot prime to evaluate the various outcomes and analyze the data that each outline provided. A newsletter had trickled down throughout her division regarding funding for certain projects which may have to be delayed as sources of revenue appear to be diverted. It was a bit unique that information like this was put into print. It was usually only verbal and in certain circles.

As her experimental procedures continued, William Bourque, the Chief Executive Officer of the organization strolled into her domain. He walked in with his hands in his pockets. Nonchalantly looking around at the various instruments, gauges, and devices that he certainly had no idea how to operate. Janine didn't even notice he entered the room as she was completely encompassed in her activity. A few moments later,

"Good afternoon Janine. How are you?"

She could smell cigarette smoke on his person with the subtly of his infamous single malt scotch.

"Hi William, just one moment please."

This wasn't the most crucial point in her analysis, but she took her work so seriously that she couldn't stop ever so abruptly. She then tightened the valve to off and turned to him.

"Hey, sorry I didn't see you when you first came in. I'm good. What's up?"

William cleared his throat then,

"I'm calling an executive meeting on Friday and was hoping you would join us. There is only going to be about four of us there. Larry, Ed, Michael, and you if you can make it. Hoping to run some ideas by everyone and your input would be greatly appreciated."

"Yeah, I'm sure I can make it. What are the topics of discussion?" She inquired.

"Well, I'm actually waiting to spring that on everyone there and then. I want to try something new. I'm looking to get everyone's initial reaction, thoughts, feedback on the subject from the moment they hear it. Kind of an instinctual reaction. Not having weeks or even days to process the information. It'll be straight from their gut. Then of course we can re-group a week or two later after everyone digests all that we've covered."

"Wow, this *is* a new technique (for us any way). Yeah, I will be there. What time?" Her curiosity had been piqued by this new approach and she was all in.

"10am in the Montgomery Room. 39th floor." William confirmed, "See you then!"

A second later, William strolled out of the lab as smoothly as he walked in, and without a sound.

Janine dropped her token into the slot of the Boston Red Line transit for her ride home that night. She continued to think about the psychological dynamic of what William presented earlier that day. There was an underlying level of erudition to the thought pattern that is involved. Not giving the subjects time to prepare for a discussion because the subjects are not told what the topic of discussion is. Their responses will be virginal. Without any contamination from a previous stimulus.

She lay awake that night under the covers staring at her ceiling still pondering the meeting to be on Friday. The only other possible action that could be taken to get the most instinctual reaction by the subjects would be to call the meeting immediately. This would take each subject out of their environment or current task rather abruptly. Then bring said subjects to the area for discussion. Perhaps the logistics of this would cause a barrier. Where is everyone?

How soon can you round them up? How much time would they have without any notice of any kind? People react to the same stimulus in different fashions. Some people focus. Some people fold. (then her mind went even further) What if that was a root element for sibling rivalry? A parent has two or three children. The parent only knows one form of discipline, praise or instruction and administers their authority to each of their children in the exact same manner only to find the results and outcomes are different from child to child. Little Johnny comes home with a report card of all Cs and one D. The father lays into him seven ways 'till Sunday ... *What's wrong with you? Haven't ya got any brains? You could have stayed home and got the same grades!* Then his brother Billy comes home with almost the same kind of report card and it's all over again. The father gives him what for. Little Johnny was so distraught, embarrassed or ashamed that he never wanted a reaction like that from his parents again. So, he buckles down. Studies as hard as he can and got his grades up. All Bs and one A. Little Billy doesn't have the same reaction to his father's rants and raves. Perhaps he takes his dad's reprimands much more personally and processes it in a manner that he feels inadequate in some way. As time goes on little Billy loses interest in performing and doesn't care anymore. An underlying animosity between the two siblings gets created and then what? Cain v. Abel? This would be what we are trying to avoid. So, possible solutions? But first another question. How does a parent react to their child's behavior in a customized fashion to each child's specific needs without creating an aura of favoritism thus creating any hostility within the fabric of the ecosystem?

Janine made a mental file of the situation and turned out the light. By now she was well aware of her tangents and the many avenues they do progress. *Tomorrow's another day*, she had to say to herself.

The next day she skipped lunch entirely as she was completely consumed with her data gathering. Ted walked into the seating area after getting his lunch tray filled (with a big bright gleam), only to see all new faces at the table he shared just yesterday. *Maybe she is at a new area?* He thought. He walked with his tray up and down the rows, in between the tables of beaming faces and clinking silverware. An enjoyable sound he realized he took for granted for so many years.

Ted didn't see her anywhere. He kept walking through in an orderly fashion, but his grinning cheeks grew less and less with each pass by. When he had finally walked in and out and completely through the whole cafeteria twice, he called it quits. He went back to his area and ate lunch alone.

Al saw Ted somberly walking back from the cafeteria with all of his food and couldn't resist,

"Hey Romeo! What gives? Why aren't you with your one true love having lunch?"

"She wasn't there today." He replied modestly.

"Did you guys make plans for today?" Al asked.

"No, it was more or less left up in the air. I guess I was hoping to have a déjà vu type moment."

"Is French food the theme this week in the caf?"

Ted just looked at Al really quick. He knew his jokes were stale.

"Man, can I just look at your notes from the meeting fast time I..."

"Here, take 'em. Learn 'em, live 'em, love 'em."

"Gracias amigo." Then Al took off.

Ted finished his lunch by himself with his latest Racing Illuminated magazine.

CH. 4

Friday came and Janine arrived to work a half an hour earlier than her usual 6:30am. She set up her lab the same as she did every other day. Gave a dab of that odd smelling goldfish food to the lonely pet she kept near the window for aesthetics. After taking a few more sips of her coffee she looked at the clock. Almost 9:30am. She never used a daily planner and rarely had to open the rolodex. Dates, times, or events were locked into her short-term memory and then never left. She could recount the when and where of a meeting from eight years ago. What the weather was like that day. The price of gasoline.

Two of the invitees arrived in the Montgomery room exceedingly early that day. Ed Bluestein the Executive Vice President of Engineering and Michael Bonfiglio the Enterprise Architect. They had known each other for years and were quite close. Ed was a heavier set gentleman. Not obese, but certainly not thin. He had curly red hair and reddish/brown eyebrows that accented his freckles. He stood about 5'11" and sharp as a tack (but then again everyone here today is exceptionally gifted in the brains department. You don't get to have titles like they do if you don't know your butt from third base).

Michael was the Mr. Venetian Blind Smooth of the Execs. We're talking $1,100 tailored suits, $2,700 Rolex, brand new Jaguar every two years, a town house on Beacon Hill, condo in Aspen, house on Cape Cod, a boat here a motorcycle there. The list of toys goes on and on. And did the ladies love him! So much so that he went and had a vasectomy a few years ago. He believed in his motto, 'Life is too good to get caught in the family trap'. He wine'd 'em, dine'd 'em, and then realigned 'em as fast as he could. Some dames would get it, understand the picture, and just go with the flow. Some would be heartbroken, cry and need consolation. He was good at that. Always knew the right thing to say to let them down gently. Some would get angry. Start throwing things or breaking things. An antique vase from the Ming Dynasty got hurled across the veranda one time. None of it even bothered him. All his artifacts were insured so he would get paid 5 times what he bought them at. To replace one 500-year-old statue with another 450-year-old statue was no big whoop.

When Ed and Michael walked into the meeting room Michael made a bee-line for the liquor cabinet. The 39th floor kept nothing but 10x distilled vodka, 100% agave tequila, 30-year-old single malt scotch, Kentucky bourbon and certainly the finest beer and wine selection available.

"What's your flavor of the day amigo?"

Michael had already poured his own and was ready to get Ed going with him.

"Aw, it's way too early for me. You know that."

Ed never had a sip before 5pm.

"Eduardo! It's Friday! Live a little!"

"Can't. The wife and I have a dinner/introduction, introduction/dinner (whatever you want to call it), with some commercial real estate mogul she's trying to get as an account. She reminded me this morning that I have to be at the top of my game. So, in my mind, that simply means I can't start drinkin' until after I shake their hands."

"Man, thank you for reminding me why I'm still and always will be single."

"Hey, where are you guys on the Frinseheed-Barton deal?" Ed asked quickly to change the subject. He'd been in these domestic conversations before with Michael and wasn't up for another one this early in the day.

"We just had the dog and pony show last week. It was more of the usual look up here not over there." Michael made his all too familiar raised arm finger snap signal indicating that this was yet just another presentation filled with half-truths, words of double/triple meanings and subtle innuendos to purposely perplex his audience into believing what he was saying while still leaving himself the luxury of renouncing anything he may need to. Ed just looked at him with a straight face and replied,

"So, it's a done deal."

"Oh yeah. Michael said proudly.

Ed let a couple seconds pass and then,

"Ever bother you?"

"What, the game?" Michael replied, "It's chess, trying to see 5 moves ahead."

"Yeah, some people call it chess. Others call it dirty pool. I'm just trying to get an idea of where you are mentally in the whole ball of wax."

Ed was feeling more inquisitive today. He continued,

"Have you ever read the Torah?"

"Not cover to cover," Michael said.

"Me neither, but there are more than one indication alluding that we *are* what we pretend to be."

Michael just looked at him,

"Brother, I sold my soul years ago."

Ed just nodded with empathy then tried to assure him,

"It's not too late to get it back."

"Wanna hear a *bring it home* moment I've thought about if I were to ever have kids?"

Ed sat in his chair listening attentively.

Michael continued,

"Say I find, *the one*. Settle down and move to the burbs. The years go by, our children are in school, they play sports, music ... whatever. Then one day a note from the principal's office comes in the mail. It tells me that my son cheated on a test and will now have detention for a week. What would I (in all honesty) be able to say, "hey blockhead, you're not supposed to get caught. What's the matter with you?" (a couple seconds of silence passed) "I've never told anyone any of this. I wouldn't want my children in corporate sales or politics or possibly any other area of the like. The money is made the oldest, worst way in the world. Lie, cheat, steal."

Ed kept listening attentively then came back with, "The irony of it all."

"The irony of what?" Michael asked.

"You wouldn't want your kids in the life because you would be protecting *your* kids from people like ... *you*."

Michael just sat there staring. Ed then simulated a toast with his right hand (and no glass).

"Gentleman, good morning!" William walked in with his hands in his pockets as usual, a smile, and a look like *today is the day*.

"Morning Billy." They both said at the same time.

"Mike do me favor, please don't have another one of those until we get through here today."

Michael looked at him with a slight bewilderment,

"Okay sure, this must really be something important."

"It's gonna shake things up that's for sure." William replied, "I've recently been made aware of a technique that Russian coaches sometimes implement with their athletes. If the coach does not believe he is getting the peak performance from his team members or if he feels that another form of unity could be implemented to assist in the camaraderie among the members, he will deny food to the players before or after a competition."

Ed and Michael just looked at each other.

"It's highly unorthodox isn't it." William continued, "On the surface you immediately think how can an athlete perform on an empty stomach? The food is the fuel that creates the energy that is needed to perform. But what are some of the most highly influential variables in so many situations ... *the intangibles*. Are either of you familiar with Anatolei Tarasov, know who he is?"

"Not in the least," said Michael.

It rang a bell with Ed as he watched the winter and summer Olympics with a fervent passion.

"Is he the Russian National Hockey coach?"

"Yes, he is! (as William's eyes lit up). Here is a man that was chosen by the Soviet's military elite. Maybe even Josef Stalin himself or Vladimir Lenin who the heck knows, but they chose a man who had no idea what a puck was. No idea what a red line, blue line, or the difference to a clothesline. Knew nothing of a stick or goal net. And they specifically (and intentionally) select this man to be the founding architect for their nation in a sport (that prior to his appointing) had absolutely no presence in. What was it? Why did they choose him over anybody else? I have to believe that they had someone with even the slightest minutiae of better credentials than he had."

"Lemme guess, *intangibility*!" Michael spoke out while sucking on the last piece of ice in his glass.

"Tarasov believes in love." William replied.

At that moment Larry Bucyk the head of the Exchange Division and Janine walked in. They got there just when the *L* word was dropped. They both took their seats in silence as quickly as they could.

"He believes that love is the most powerful form of energy on earth. He believes that nothing can destroy love. He believes that only love can truly create. And look at what he has created, from nothing. Up until the 19—'s Russia was non-existent in the world of global competitive ice hockey. Canada was the country that set the standard. The United States (yes) we were in the mix along with Czechoslovakia, Sweden, Germany, Great Britain, and Switzerland. Now look at them, they are the dominant force to be reckoned with in international play. And why? Tarasov believes that when you step out on that ice that you are going out there with the love of your life. *No Michael, not to the extent of The Spartan Military.* Now don't get me wrong, they train harder, longer and more excruciating than any other country as well. There was a story of a Swedish player training with the Russians in the off season. He would end up lasting about two weeks. His heart rate got to 240 beats per minute one day. I guess he said to the press, *I love the game of hockey, but I don't want to die because of it.* It appears the players can't wait for winter to come so that the ice will freeze. Their training is easier for them when it's cold than when it's hot."

Michael raised his hand as if he were in a classroom but didn't want to be called on,

"So, does this mean that you love us but aren't going to feed us?"

William smiled then replied,

"Actually, I did inform the caterer not to come in until we were through here today, but don't worry, I won't let you go hungry."

Larry was sitting across from Janine and Ed across from Michael. William was still standing at the head of the table in front of the slide projector,

"Thank you all for being here today with such limited information regarding the design and on relatively short notice (William wanted to be semi-formal and professional at the beginning but didn't overextend with an introduction to everyone. He felt everyone knew each other well enough). I've called this meeting because we need to stay ahead of the curve in one distinctive very prominent area."

There was a moment of silence. The anticipation. William wanted to be as overly dramatic as he led up to it. He looked into each of their eyes individually with zealous excitement then,

"Communication! I know that word is vast, perhaps too non-descript (at this time) but in a way that's how I want you to think about it. The various forms and methods verbal, non-verbal, written, sign language, braille, morse code you name it. And then I want you to think about its effects. Effects on commerce (thus society), economics (micro and macro), discretionary inflation, social/professional even political interaction etc ... We need to think linear, microcosmic, infinite and transcendent on how we communicate faster, clearer, more concisely and ultimately in ways that are revolutionary, unprecedented and that will ultimately present a new platform."

William paused there and just let them digest it all. Yes, it was a leviathan size task that he just dropped on them. How would they first respond? William was observing each of their facial expressions and body language. Larry sat there with his arms crossed leaning back in his chair and legs extended. Michael was forward in his seat, arms in front on the table with fingers of both hands intertwined in front of his crystal glass. Janine was racing her pen back and forth in between her thumb and first finger. Her right leg going a hundred miles an hour under the table. You could faintly hear the sound of polyester rubbing against itself. And her eyes were fixated on the imitation Rembrandt mounted just slightly left of center on the west wall. Larry was a cucumber. Showed little emotion or body gestures of any sort. Ed asked the first question,

"How did this all originate? What was the source?"

William was willing to give full disclosure,

"I got a call from Major General Atkins not too long ago. The military is always looking for ways to stay ahead of the competition in this dynamic. New forms, how it evolves and in connection with the various applications. They look to people like us. I'm hoping we can get the contract before anyone else. I'm sure he has other sources considered. He knew I wouldn't ask such a question upon an initial outreach but I'm sure we can deduce a few just from process of elimination and historical outcomes."

"What time frames are they *realistically* thinking something of this magnitude could happen?" Janine asked this but tried to keep her assumptive tone to herself. Her prior experience with military requests was that they wanted it yesterday.

"We didn't get into that either." William replied, "I guess as a courtesy General Atkins felt it better not to mention it to me. I'm sure he is well aware of their reputation for *hurry up and wait* on so many levels."

"It's safe to assume a contract of this extent will be in the 11-figure range. What are the chances it could get to thirteen?" (Michael couldn't help himself)

"I'd say if we do this right and make it happen on (or close) to schedule it is a legitimate possibility." William confirmed for him.

Michael leaned back in his chair and folded his leg, so his foot was over his knee. William looked over and saw Michael's foot racing up and down (he never saw him do that before). There were another couple seconds of silence before Larry offered his first level of input,

"You know what Einstein once said?" They all just looked over at him. "He said, imagination is more important than knowledge. For knowledge is limited, whereas imagination embraces the entire world, stimulating progress, giving birth to evolution."

"Yes!" William chimed with exuberance, "That is exactly what I am talking about. We don't want to just think outside the box. We need to destroy the box, so it doesn't even exist. Void and formless. No boundaries, no barriers. Step on the shoulders of giants to soak in the view and get that perspective then jump off! Land on our feet and make our own unique path."

"Billy, I hate to bring this up at this moment but it's a real thing and if we're involved in something as big as what I *think* we are it's a factor at some future place and time."

"Michael, I want you to speak freely. Please continue."

"If we do accomplish this monumental task and create something so effective and original that no one has ever seen before (and it works), who owns it? The applications and industries are presumably endless. This would end up being a global interjection much like electricity and certainly much bigger than that guy from wherever that created that rubber."

"What guy with rubber?" Ed asked.

"There was a guy working for Ellis & Lilly years ago. He created a rubber of such high quality that (for the automotive industry) he placed a guarantee on every tire he would manufacture. His guarantee was that you would never have to replace your tires for as long as you owned your car. It didn't take long for the execs of Goodyear, Firestone, Michelin, Cooper and many of the foreign manufacturers to get wind of it. I imagine it got political as well. They all got together for a live personal consultation and decided they could not allow a product of this nature (of this quality) to enter the market of an industry so incredibly enormous and important. And I'm not even talking about the dollars and cents on the surface. The actuaries crunched numbers and evaluated numerous possible outcomes. One of which being a common theme was that of unemployment. On a global scale. Think about it. A guy buys a car that he knows he will never have to buy tires for again as long as he owns that car. He keeps it for 15, 20 maybe even 30 years if he knows how to turn a wrench. Eventually all the other manufacturers stop hearing their phones ring for orders. No purchase orders being placed. First the hourly workers are laid off to include the janitors, secretaries, and assistants. Then lower management and so on and so forth. Not to mention any associated industries like shipping and packaging supplies. It may take 30 or 40 years but eventually it would lead to hundreds of millions of people out of work across all the ponds."

Janine then wanted to know,

"What was their solution?"

Michael continued,

"They bought him off. They all agreed that society cannot afford to let this product enter the market. And I heard that the Japanese were instrumental in assisting with all of the decimal points. The Japs have every intention to be a major player in the automotive industry in the relative near future. They are watching us and working on ways to differentiate and implement themselves. They have taken into account factors for inflation, fuel surges/shortages and family size. They are developing engines that are more efficient, economical and more reliable than anything we have ever seen."

"Where do you get this stuff?" Larry asked him.

Michael just nodded raised his empty glass and continued,

"So from what I understand, due to economic measures and other various reasons this guy is sitting on a beach in Bora Bora for the rest of his life drinking mint juleps for breakfast and his children's children children children (not to mention all the generations to follow) will never have to work a day in their life because of what they pooled together and gave him. And now that chemical formula for the rubber is probably sitting right next to the ingredients for Coca-Cola in a vault made by the same company that secures the Declaration of Independence."

William knew where Michael was coming from, and he wanted to address his concerns with patience and understanding. "Who would own it? I've been thinking along these lines as well. If history has taught us anything from a business acumen, it's that it's best to get it taken care of on the front end because it's a train wreck to get it resolved on the back end. What I would propose to each of you is 2% ownership of any and all future royalties, monies, accolades, recognition, distinctions, acknowledgement or proprietaries of any kind."

The silence in the room was deafening. You could not only hear the pin drop, you could hear it bounce back and forth getting fainter and fainter. There were two in the room that knew better than to say a word at this time in the conversation. Both Michael and William were of the school of business where once you put your offer on the table, whoever breaks the silence loses. Larry was unaware of such policies and procedures,

"May I ask this (with all humility) and certainly no desire to offend in any way shape or form."

"By all means." William confirmed, "I assure you all that I will not be personally offended by any inquisition anyone may make here today."

"Would we be allowed to have our own personal lawyers draft our contracts regarding this and present them?"

"I don't see that being a problem at all." William assured, "I could provide each of you with the guidelines the board is looking for, an outline (more or less), and you could have each of your lawyers write up a contract for review. Please keep in mind (again), that time is going to be of the essence throughout this whole project. The sooner we create, test, confirm and apply the sooner we *own* (to coin a phrase). And that brings up another element I would like to address with each of you. You were all specifically chosen to be here today because you each have unique capabilities. Extraordinary talents that I believe when nurtured, encouraged, and allotted numerous resources can produce unprecedented results. One question I do have (and only time will tell how this will pan out) is how will any collaboration occur? I don't care to speculate right now. I simply want to discuss various options that will likely present themselves. We are all sensible, intelligent adults that co-exist harmoniously. I certainly believe we can collaborate on a project of this level without any he-said, she-saids. That was my idea, no it wasn't, etc ... etc ... I know we're way above that. For now, this weekend, I want you to digest everything we have talked about here today. Take it all home with you, every ounce of it because this is bigger than all of us. This is designed to change things."

William was trying his best not to repeat himself, but he was having a hard time due to the immensity of the situation. He looked up at the clock on the wall. "Wow, we've been here for almost 4 hours already. You all must be hungry by now. I guess I *should* let the caterer in."

As William walked over to the phone he looked back at Michael, "See, I wasn't gonna let you starve." They both gave each other a kind, approving grin.

"Where is it coming from?" Larry asked.

"Looks like The Gurus. That Mediterranean place off 3rd and Delano."

"I love their gyros."

Janine was encompassed in her thoughts throughout the entire meeting. Some of the topics they were discussing never crossed her mind once. Royalties, contracts, percentages? She didn't think that way. The creation is where she was glued. This is where she thrived. Overcoming obstacles. Being presented with a problem and then presenting the solution. The reward was in the recipient's eyes. Assisting where no one else could.

She flew home after work that day. Had no concept of anyone around her on the subway. No notice to any of her neighbors as she entered her apartment building. They knew she was a bit quirky as it is, so a greeting one day and no acknowledgement the next was kind of the norm.

Busting through her front door she threw her bag on the ground. As anxious as she was, she still had the presence of mind to lock the door behind her. Her coat and scarf were flung over the dining chair in a hurry. "Think, where are they?" She said to herself.

In a mild frenzy she took out every box in her closet that she kept all her college notes, papers, exams, reports, and thesis'. She was meticulous with saving and filing all her work (at every age level). Box after box, page after page she was reviewing material from 12 years ago. A report on non-trivial zeros where she tried to verify the statement is true for that concrete number. A thesis on fluid mechanics when she attempted to combine a simple mechanistic model with the additive of an in-homogeneous forcing term. It felt a little like going in a time machine to her. Thoughts and ideas she had been writing. The material was all coming back to her. The time of year and the fragrances of the seasons in which they were created triggered her as well. Being completely encompassed with the task at hand the hours flew by. She got home by 6pm and it was now after 9, but she had no idea what time it was until, *Ring! Ring!* It startled her. It brought her back to reality.

"Hello?"

"I thought you were gonna come over for dinner then stay the night. He's been asking about you."

"Hi Ma, I'm sorry. I completely lost track of time. There is a new situation at work and my mind is going in 8,000 directions. I hope he doesn't feel sad or disappointed."

"No, I covered for you. I told him something along those lines with work. He has no idea what you do. Both daddy and I don't even know what you do either for that matter. He just knows it's really important and he accepts that."

"Is he in bed now?"

"Yeah, he was tired. He spends so many hours in that basement shooting pucks, hitting pucks, slapping pucks. Now he's using me and daddy as ... what are those orange things called they usually put on the roads?"

"Pylons."

"Yeah, pylons. I'm down there making pasta and he's got his stick going left and right then around me one way then around me the other. I've got the damn dough going through the cutter turning the handle and to him I'm some defencer guy. Oh, and he got daddy on the shins the other day with his stick. Missed the ball he uses for handle stick."

"I think it's called stick handling."

"Yeah, that stuff. Missed it and whap! Got him good. Daddy didn't say anything at the time. He said he saw the look in his eye of how bad he felt, so he just smiled and went on doin' whatever it was he was doin'. He showed me the black and blue on his left leg and started laughing."

"Hey Ma, are my school papers still at the house there?"

"If you left them here then they still are. All of you and your sister's schoolwork is around here somewhere. I haven't thrown anything away in ages, I need to. Way overdue on a spring cleaning."

"No! Please don't!"

"Well, I didn't plan on doin' it tomorrow. That stuff would go way back to grade school for you, wouldn't it?"

"Yeah, it would, but I have a hunch on something, and you may have just given me the key to it. I'll be over tomorrow morning around 7am. Tell him I'll make him German pancakes if he wakes up before I get there."

"Okay I will. Oh, he woke up the other day in a strange way."

"What do you mean? In what way?" Janine asked her mother.

"It was odd. He looked confused, disoriented, or distraught in some way. When I asked him about it, he said he had a bad dream. I asked him what it was about. He said he was dangling in hell like a spider. There was just a long, tiny, thin string attached to his back and he was looking straight down. He said he was looking at the face of the devil and he had these huge fangs that were dripping, mouth wide open waiting to devour him. He said there was fire exploding everywhere as he was looking into his cat like eyes. Then he woke up."

"Ma, he's too young to be having dreams like that. What are they teaching in catechism right now? Where are they in The Bible?"

"He doesn't go to catechism yet. He's too young. They don't start that 'till later."

"Well, he must have got something from the catholic services. It can be fire and brimstone on steroids at times. In the Aramaic Bible it reads, 'The awe of God is the beginning of wisdom' in the King James Bible it reads, 'The fear of God is the beginning of wisdom'."

"Yeah, what's your point?"

"My point is that the Aramaic language was created before the English language was. Jesus spoke Aramaic. As the centuries continued and new languages were formed, man altered the word of God. Man varied their own interpretations. To keep people in line. Maybe. It certainly is effective. You put the fear of God into someone or a society to get them to walk the straight and narrow. And it works. The Catholic church certainly believes in fear as a tool for discipline (along with quite a few other forms of discipline Janine remembered the nuns administered to her when she was young). I just don't want him to have that level of fear at such a young age. I want him to have those visions of sugar plums for as long as he can because as we both know; the years go by quick."

"They sure do, which reminds me. I've got to get my blood pressure prescription renewed. I'm overdue."

"Please give him happy thoughts Ma. No morbid nonsense. Not yet at least."

"I ain't got no say in what the priests talk about when we go to a service. You think they consult me with their weekly regiments."

"I know I know; just please promise me you'll try your best" Janine pleaded.

"That's all I know how."

"Thank you, Ma."

"Alright, I guess I'll see you tomorrow bright and early."

"Do I need to pick up anything for the pancakes or do you have everything?" Janine asked.

"I don't think I have any nutmeg if that goes in those things. Those special pancakes were always your thing. You always made them come out good."

"Alright, I'll see what I have and pick up anything else at the grocers on my way over. Night Ma. Love you."

"Goodnight honey. Love you too. Bye."

Janine placed the phone down and returned to her sea of research papers, citations, and hypotheses from years ago. She only got a few hours of sleep that night as the adrenaline was running high. A few pieces of the puzzle were being put together, but she still needed something and couldn't quite put her finger on it.

That night she fell asleep on the floor in her work clothes, but still had remembered to set her alarm clock. She fell asleep in a bevy of papers filled with algorithms, unproven hypothesis and equations that were illegible to most. She got up that morning took a shower and put on some make-up to look as fresh as she could. The bags under her eyes were a little bit bigger than normal but nothing too noticing. She downed a cup of instant coffee and was out the door. It takes a good half hour to get to her parent's house from her apartment.

CH. 5

Saturday mornings have cartoons! Tom & Jerry, Bugs Bunny and The Flintstones. He got up a little after seven this am. Grampa was at his desk in the basement while gramma was washing a few dishes left over from last night's dinner in the sink. He went to the bathroom and came down the stairs still a little bit yawning. Just then Janine came through the porch,

"Morning Ma."

"Good morning."

"Is he up yet?"

"I'm not sure. Sometimes I can hear the upstairs floor crack and sometimes I can't. I've had the faucet going with these glasses, so I haven't heard."

Just then he poked around the corner into the kitchen,

"Hi Ma, mornin'."

"Good morning honey!" She said as she gave him a hug, "How about some German pancakes for breakfast today. Made from scratch."

"Yeah, that sounds good." He said while still getting some of the sleep out of his eyes.

Janine started to open the cupboards to get out the mixing bowl and special cooking pan needed for the pancakes. Then she asked him,

"How was school this week? What'ya learn?"

"Wednesday I was standin' in line in front of Miss Smith's desk waitin' my turn to hand in my assignment. There were a couple kids ahead of me and the line was movin' real slow. I saw her stapler on her desk, and I just touched it. I put my two first fingers under the square end and happened to lean down. I stapled my fingers together."

"You what! Honey, why would you do that?"

"I didn't think it would even happen. I figured my fingers were too thick to get stapled. I was wrong. The blood started to ooze out. When I looked up, Miss Smith just stared right at me and said, 'Do you want to go to the nurse?' I said okay. The nurse pulled the staple out of each finger then put a band-aid on each one. There's only a round dot on each one right now. Wanna see?"

He held his two fingers up to show his mother as she walked over.

"Oh yeah, I forgot to tell you about this one." Gramma said.

Janine looked at her son's two little fingers with curiosity,

"Well, I guess you learned that one the hard way. What did your friends say?"

"Brandon and Kevin were laughing their heads off. I don't think something like this has ever happened before. Even the nurse looked surprised."

Then gramma gave him what for,

"Of course, it ain't never happened before! Most people know to keep their fingers away from the staple machines. When you gonna use them brains the Lord gave ya."

He looked back at his two fingers again and thought, *I guess it will need to be sooner rather than later*.

The aroma of German pancake in the oven filled the kitchen and made its way throughout the house. The scent of vanilla blending with eggs, flour and butter permeated everywhere. When it finally reached the basement, grampa got a whiff and made his way up. He opened the door from the cellar to the kitchen. Janine greeted him with,

"Hey good morning Dad. How are you?"

"Good morning. Am I right on time?"

"Just a few more minutes. The sides need to rise and brown a little bit more."

"Okay. I'll make more coffee. You want some?"

"Yeah sure."

When the main part of breakfast was ready Janine slid it out of the oven and everyone took their prospective seats. Gramma always sat across from grampa and junior always across from his mother.

"How's work going?" Grampa asked his daughter.

"It's gotten extremely interesting and even more so just in the past 24 hours."

"Anything I could relate to?" He asked.

"Perhaps. Not immediately or directly, but certainly in the foreseeable future and his generation (as she points to the kid with two cheeks full of pancake) will be changed forever."

"Are you able to discuss it?"

Sven knew her security clearance and he certainly understood from his days in the war that sometimes not saying anything protects others.

"I don't even know if I can articulate it very well yet. We literally just had the meeting yesterday. William our CEO dropped it on four of us. No one else."

"What's CEO mean?" The kid asked.

Janine responded,

"That stands for Chief Executive Officer."

"What's that?" He came back with and then gramma chimed in,

"That's the boss!"

"The boss of what?" He asked again.

"Everything!" Gramma told him.

"Everything?" He said again, "I thought that was you?"

Janine lost it. Started choking on her food. Couldn't stop laughing. Her father had to pat her back a few times to make sure it went down. She slid down in her chair and could hardly breathe. The kid didn't know what she was laughing at. He just kept eating and taking sips of his orange juice.

After she regained her composer Janine came back to the conversation,

"So, there was just me, Ed Cheevers, Michael Bonfiglio and Larry Bucyk. William informed us of a conversation he had not too long ago with General Atkins in Washington. There is a need, and we have the assignment of solving this if we so choose or more to it, *if* we can."

Breakfast was winding down and grampa was almost ready to get up from the table. Janine always instinctively knew when he was about to get up so she said,

"Hey Dad, do you know where (downstairs), any boxes of my old papers and reports would be?"

"Yeah, we keep most of you and your sister's things on the lower shelves in the back corner."

"My stuff isn't mixed with hers, is it?"

"Of course, it is. You think I filed each of your childhood paraphernalia separately. Your mother and I collected all that was here from the two of you. Put it in a few storage bins and taped it up. It's been down there ever since."

"Okay, no problem. I'll be able to separate hers from mine as I go through."

Just then Janine looked over at the kid who had just finished as well.

"You wanna help me little Lum Lum?" She said with a smile.

"Ma, I'm too old to be a little Lum Lum."

"Not to me honey bear."

Then the three of them got up from the table and put their dishes in the sink. Gramma stayed there just thinking to herself. She was always extremely concerned about Janine's job and the role she played within the company. Diletta may not have known the details of her day-to-day activities. The sub particle fusion or anatomical weight of an atom, but she knew her daughter could be in harm's way of some highly influential individuals. Not knowing how to protect her always weighed a heavy concern.

Janine and her son headed downstairs together. His first instinct was to grab his hockey stick and puck, but he caught himself and kept walking with her.

"Now where did Grampa say that would be, back corner, lower shelf. Ah, there they are."

"What exactly are we looking for Ma?"

"Well, that is actually a really good question. I'm not quite sure myself, but I know I'll know it when I see it."

"Wait a minute Ma, I'll be right back."

He ran up the stairs as fast as he could. The kid has IBS, and it can hit him like a ton of bricks at a moment's notice.

Janine took each storage box off the shelf and placed them on her father's workbench that was neatly and recently cleaned off. There were four boxes total. Taped up just as Sven had told her with simply, *Delores and Janine* written in black marker on each one. The dust was somewhat caked on, and the tape had all but lost its adhesive properties. She unsealed the first box slow and delicately. At first glance there was a first-grade report card of hers. All handwritten by her teachers. She put that aside quickly. Whatever she was looking for, she knew that wasn't it. A few minutes later he came back down the stairs again to help her. He looked at the 4 boxes and said,

"Which one should I start on? That one?" And he pointed.

"No, let's go through each one together. You tell me, read to me what each piece of paper has on it."

"Okay." He replied.

"Promise you washed your hands?" She said sternly.

"I promise."

"Good boy."

He got an old wooden stool that grandpa had made many years ago so he could reach up and get to the task at hand. He outstretched his tiny arm and started to read the headings on each of the pieces of paper.

"Blessed Mary Elementary School. Delores Jalinski."

"That's Auntie's report card. We should keep both of our work in two different piles. First, we'll go through everything in this one. Anything you see with Auntie's name on it put it here."

"What if there is a paper with no name on it?"

"Put it there. We'll figure it out later where it should go."

The first hour and a half was just that first box. Not an iota of anything useful just the sentimental childhood awards, artwork, and photos. A perfectly flattened rose pedal that immediately crumbled when the light hit it. She opened the second one with the same gentle care as the first. A handful of drawings and notes written in the handwriting of a young child. The boy was placing everything in its proper location on the table just as he was told. He was no further along in knowing what they were looking for, but he knew to just keep doing it. Like that old saying, *we may be lost, but we're making good time*. This was that.

By the time they got to the third box the task had ceased to amuse him, but he kept going. Trying to read words he had never seen before. His mother corrected him on pronunciation and tense. He was good at school although nowhere near her ability at the same age. Even Janine was ready for another cup of coffee by now. She started to get up and make her way back to the kitchen.

"You want anything to drink? I think Grampa has cranberry and more orange juice in the fridge."

"Yeah, I'll have some orange juice."

Janine came back with both cups while he was still sorting.

"Promise me you won't spill any of this on our work here."

"I won't." He said softly, then she gave him the glass.

They came to the fourth and final storage box.

"Nothin' yet, eh Ma?"

"Nope, not yet."

She opened the last one slow and careful again. Here (once more) were report cards and award achievements. A few more documents into it and there was a note from a boy passed in class to her sister. As she was reviewing an old paper she wrote on gravity back in the 6th grade, the kid reached in and pulled out a very thin envelope with a foreign name on it that he had never seen before and couldn't read.

"Hey Ma, what's a pen pal?"

"What did you say?" She asked him quickly.

"This letter has *pen pal* written all over it. What is that?"

There was a long cease and desist that was ever so prevalent although nothing said. She placed her coffee cup down ever so slowly and turned her head to the left to see what it was he was holding. In his tiny clear fingers held an envelope and letter she had received dated 19--. The paper and envelope were extremely thin to ensure the least paid postage was necessary. The letter itself was extremely brittle with the envelope being ever so slightly more-sturdy.

"Oh, baby you did it! You found it!"

She hugged him longer, harder and in a more dissimilar way than she ever had before.

"This was, this was the beginning of it!" She exclaimed.

Janine could hardly contain herself. This was the happiest she had been in years. The term *glowing* doesn't do it justice.

She then very delicately took the items from his hands. She pushed the box and other papers away from her and placed the two in front of her on the table. Janine just stared at them with an immense feeling of joy that (once again) he had never seen her display before.

"This is where it all started." She said to him while keeping her eyes fixated on each piece, "Where it began."

"Where what began?" He asked.

"This is a correspondence. A conversation I had through the mail when I was a little girl. Not much older than you are now. My teachers (at the time) set up a pen pal event where we would write letters to other kids of our same age in another country."

"What would you write about?" He inquired innocently.

"I would write about my schoolwork. Projects I was working on and how much I enjoyed them. My pen pal was a girl named Kiara. She was from India. I would tell her about what life was like in the United States at the time. How things like the invention of the television had changed the way we got our news, information and entertainment. Where she lived, they didn't have electricity or running water, so she didn't even know what television was. I remember I had a hard time explaining it in written form in my letters to her. I had a hard time describing that there are people on a square screen in a box in your living room. They are not actually there, but you can see them. I can only imagine what she must have been thinking or wondering at the time. These crazy Americans watch each other at 9" high on a square box?"

"What do we do now?" Her son wondered to her.

"Let's get everything back in and taped up again. This time we'll keep my stuff separate from Auntie's. If she wants her P.E. reports from 2nd grade, she'll know where to find them."

They re-organized each of the boxes, taped each one up and put them back on the shelves where they were. Janine was eager to keep reviewing other old papers she knew she had tucked away in her apartment as well as her old bedroom of her parent's house, but she didn't want to show it. She knew she would be there for dinner and most likely overnight.

As she made her way up the stairs with her letter, she saw that he wasn't in back of her.

"Are you gonna come up with me?"

"Is it okay if I shoot some pucks for a while?"

"Sure honey. We'll have dinner in a little while. I'll call you then."

"K."

Then he started blasting them against the wall. Janine just stared at him for a couple seconds then made her way back up. *Let the games begin,* she thought to herself.

CH. 6

In the kitchen gramma was pounding the cutlets to tenderize them. Janine placed the pen pal letter on the liquor cabinet very quietly and unnoticed.

"These damn chickens should be more tender than this at $.19 a pound." Gramma said to herself out loud.

Janine started to set the table,

"What did you want to have with the chicken Ma? Potatoes, rice? I'll get them started."

"Oh, ask your father what he wants. I got my hands full with this bird right now."

An hour and fifteen minutes later, it was time to sit down for dinner.

"Call him up from his hockey rink." She told her daughter.

Janine opened the door to the cellar,

"Time for dinner!" She shouted down the stairs.

He threw his stick down and ran up the stairs as fast as he could. By this time, he was starving again. Gramma then reminded him,

"Did you turn off the light to Grampa's desk?"

He had just got his butt in the chair when he rolled his eyes and headed back down to get the light.

"Call Daddy for supper. He's either outside or in the garage."

Janine walked to the door that connected the porch to the garage,

"Dinner time Dad!"

Sitting at the table (again) Sven asked her,

"Did you find what you were looking for?"

"I didn't find it." She smiled, "Lum Lum found it!"

Grampa turned to him,

"What was it?"

"A letter. A special pen pal letter." He said while scooping up some rice pilaf.

Gramma came into it,

"You mean that pen pal project you had in school when you were his age? That's what you were looking for?"

"Well, that was the origin of what I'm looking for. Remember how frustrated I would get having to wait for the letters to get to school from Asia."

"Is that where you were writing to?" Her mother asked her.

"Yes, it was excruciating having to wait almost two months sometimes to hear her responses with everything I would write."

"Ma told her we had a tv."

"I even wrote in one of my correspondences how I enjoy hearing from her so much that I want to find a way we can communicate faster. I had so much to tell and ask her that a one-page letter never gives me enough room and a boat carrying the thing never moves fast enough. Not for me. I got so many ideas at the time, but as the years went on, I got distracted. I would come back to the thought process a bit here and there in high school and undergrad (somewhat). I still need to find my notes and algorithms from back then, but my inquisition on faster communication all began with my pen pal."

"So that's what the meeting was about yesterday."

Sven was wondering why she didn't just say that in the first place.

"Yeah, in a nutshell. As an overall heading, but we're supposed to think about it abstractly to come up with new forms and methods in diverse directions."

Her father was very intuitive and noted,

"So I'm guessing the pen pal letter helps you get the old scent back. Takes you back to your childhood and creative imagination."

"It sure does Daddy."

"I'm glad you found it. It looks like it could be really helpful in your work. Now I want to talk to you about something a little different."

"What's that?" She asked softly.

"Trust." He said in a serious tone, "I know you've known your business associates for years and I'm sure you feel you can trust them implicitly, but Janine, when the zeros start to increase people change or even worse, their true colors come out. What's the root of all evil?" (he was reminding her by asking her)

"The love of money is the root of all evil." She replied.

"That's right. *Not* the money itself. It's the part of a person you can't see. What's in their heart."

"It's funny you mention that." Janine continued, "Because one of the executives who was at the meeting yesterday asked if we could have our own personal lawyers draft our contract with this project."

"*See*, that's exactly what I'm talking about. He sounds like someone that got the short end of the stick at some time and place and is doing everything to prevent it from happening again. Janine, I know how passionate you are in your work. I know that you're a purist with it all. Promise your mother and me here and now that you'll get your own lawyer too."

"Okay, I will," she assured him.

Dinner finished up just in time for The Lawrence Welk Show. Grampa and the kid went into the den while the other two cleared and cleaned the supper dishes. Both ladies were at the kitchen sink washing and wiping.

"He worries about you very much you know. It may not seem that way at times if he doesn't show the emotion, but he does."

"I know he does Ma. I know you both do. It's interesting what you say about emotion there. I've been accused of the same things throughout my life. I know I don't open up to people very easily and when I do, I often don't mean the things I say to be taken the way they are interpreted. I have a handful of regrets in that department. I know I am not the same person outside that front door than I am inside here. I'm never as comfortable. Never as at ease. I just try to adapt."

"I wanna ask you," (gramma stopped for a second) "is there ever a level of physical danger in the work you do?"

"It's highly unlikely. Sure, I have top security clearance and access *to* and *with* high level military personnel, but as a civilian in the private sector. The risk of harm is extremely minimal. I don't even travel outside the country."

This put Diletta's mind at ease (at least for the time being). They finished with the dishes and gramma went to lie down on the couch to watch television. Janine headed upstairs to her old room that she used to have to share with her sister. It was left exactly the same as the day she left for college. No pictures of boys anywhere or music people. She had her cross on the wall and rosary beads hanging over her bed post. An imitation Van Gogh painting that she liked out of the Sears and Roebuck catalog faced from the east side wall. The room had a tight slanted ceiling from the roof angle of an oversize Cape design. A small little red two-person love seat that looked like it was imported directly from London circa 1783 with carved wood trim, beaded stitching and velvet fabric stood in the back of the room near the wall and the closet. Right behind it was a door, only about 3' high with somewhat the aesthetics of a barn door but painted perfectly to align with the wall. It led to the eaves of the house. When she was a little girl, this was her sanctuary and playground. No noise to cause distraction. No interruption to break the train of thought and no one to poke fun of her. Only thing was, in the summertime, she would cook in there. Sven put the insulation in when they first bought the house. He packed it tight and applied more than usual. Trying to keep as much heat in and cold out in the winter. She would be in there so long sometimes that she would come out pale and sweating. Completely dehydrated. It would drive Diletta crazy, and she would make her drink four full glasses of water one after the other,

"You're gonna make me put a lock on that door one of these days." She would tell her.

"No please don't! I'm close to a breakthrough." Janine would pledge.

"Breakdown, breakthrough, break up, you're breakin' my heart." As she wiped her daughter's forehead and dried her hair.

Janine slid the love seat to the left and bent down to undo the latch that was never locked. She opened the small door and was immediately reminded by the hint of must mixed with insulation and moth balls. Diletta had moth balls all over the house and apparently even took the time to throw a few in the attic for good measure. Going in she was extremely careful to place each foot on the crossbeam member. As a child she could easily tip toe like a cat across them to get to the area she made. If she slipped now, she would go right through the ceiling and never hear the end of it. When she first started making this her private area all she had was a piece of cardboard she got when one of the neighbors threw out something. As time went on, she strengthened the area with particle board and some 2x4s. Not much for decorative nuances. No potted plants or picture frames (they wouldn't last in there anyway). This was solitude and a spot specifically chosen by the octagonal window placed in the middle of one corner attachment to the roof. This is where (as a child) she first came to the realization of frame of reference. Although she didn't know how to quite verbalize it at the time.

She would sit by the window and lie down to look through it. From this view all that would come into focus would be a tree leaf blowing in the wind ever so gently. A cloud moving at a different speed than the others in the background and with various degrees of thickness. The wavering shades of the sky depending on if it was raining, sunny, fog heavy or simply overcast. To move ever so slightly upward would bring the branch of the tree into view and then just ever so slightly more upward there was unbound life. The smallest little robin would rest on the part of the branch that it knew would support itself and as if to say, *I can stay over here and not get bullied by Mr. Big Crow.*

Then slowly edge her way a little bit higher and the body of the tree came into focus along with the very top of Mr. and Mrs. Gilliam's house next door. If she closed one eye she could focus on the detail of the bark of the tree. The patterns it made along with the unorthodox shapes. When she stood up and looked through the window in its entirety, she noticed that a level of attention to detail is possibly misplaced but gives exponentially more impetus to the whole picture. In it there is the trunk of the tree (some roots showing), a green lawn that is well kept with bushes neatly trimmed and a realization that you wouldn't expect from a young child. She noticed that when you look down from here, more life is prevalent. A car driving by on the narrow road that cornered her house. A dog lifting its leg on the mailbox post. Mr. Millbury trying to unravel his garden hose so his wife can plant more wild blue lupins 'cuz apparently 25 isn't enough. Anything can be how you look at it.

Janine reached her old familiar place and just closed her eyes for a moment. So many childhood thoughts raced back to her triggered by the aroma and touch of the wood. She stayed there for a good 45-minutes decompressing. Then she heard the patter of someone coming up the stairs at a faster pace than anyone else could in the house. She knew this solitary would be short lived. When the bathroom door next to her room closed, she figured this was a good a time as any to get back to reality. Carefully retracing her steps, she closed the door behind her. Put the room back the way it was and waited for him to come out.

"Wanna play scrabble?" She asked him.

"Yeah, sure."

They played until she saw his eyes slowly close every few minutes.

"Tomorrows another day. Why don't you brush your teeth and I'll tuck you in."

"Yeah okay, I'm tired."

"I know honey, me too. You were so helpful to me today you know. Thank you."

"Welcome. Night Ma."

He didn't hear the part where she was going to tuck him in.

The next day started with breakfast and then,

"Get dressed quick! We got to get to church service a little early. I need to see Sister Vincent before mass today."

Gramma was talking to both Janine and junior with this one but grampa leaned over to them,

"What do you think it is this time, the bake sale or the clothing drive." They both just grinned.

Almost nobody was in the parking lot when they got there so a close spot to the entrance was easy this time.

"I'll meet you two inside after I talk to Sister. She's usually on the side of the altar preparing for the service."

"Okay."

Janine and he just stayed in the car for the time being. He sat there in the back seat just staring out the window. After a little bit of calming silence, she turned around to face him,

"Should we walk around a little? We got about 20 minutes before it starts."

"Sure." He smiled to her.

They got out and walked along the perimeter of the parking lot, near a path by the woods.

"What are you thinking about?" She asked him.

"Why don't you and dad live together, and I live with the both of you?"

"Well honey, we're not married anymore. It didn't work out between the two of us. God wanted you, so he brought your father and I together. I guess he just didn't want your father and I to stay together. You were the reason he and I met."

"Oh." He said.

"I know it's hard to understand and believe me there are many days when I don't understand the whys. We just have to keep trusting that God is in control, and he knows what's best. Especially when we don't. His will be done."

"What don't you understand about the letter Y Ma?" Janine chuckled,

"Come on Lum Lum let's go see what Gramma's doing."

They walked back to church in their Sunday best and up the stairs to the main entrance. The two main double doors were carved meticulously with patron saints, martyrs, Christian and Catholic symbols. This entrance was huge to the kid and perhaps somewhat intimidating. He wasn't tall or strong enough to open either door, so she had to do it. When they walked in, the stone floor and molding accented each other throughout the structure. The long straight crimson walk rug led its way to the grand altar demonstrating a size and scale unsurpassed by any other residence in town. It delivered and included statues with the finest bronze commemorates as well as a two-foot-thick marble mensa. The generous allotment of funds kept the location in complete compliance with the Vatican council. Behind the altar was a raised eleven-foot wooden carved crucifix trimmed with strategically placed palms and depicting the emotion of the Lord at that moment in time. The medieval stained colored glass was prevailing and continually receiving the gaze of worshipers. The Bible verses and hymns of the day were illustrated in big script letters on a handmade board placed to the right side of the altar. As the two walked down the middle of the main entrance the sea of wooden pews were on both sides of them.

While holding his mother's hand he looked straight up at the massive hemispherical ceiling directly above. Immersed by all the light colors prudently portraying a heavenly sky within the dome ceiling to include sacramental scripture in a divine banquet of majestic imagery. He got what I can only describe as reverse vertigo. Taking it all in he was about to lose his balance and would have gone face first to the floor if his mother didn't get a sense that this was happening and just raised his arm while she had his hand. A little *whoop* up from her and he was back to ground zero again.

They went into the pews about 10 or 12 rows back from the front. Janine kneeled down to pray, and he mirrored her as best he could but didn't think of anything to say in his mind. He just knew he had to be extremely quiet from this point on.

A few families started arriving and took their seats arbitrarily. With ten minutes left before the beginning of the service, gramma found the two and took a seat next to Janine. The church was soon filled with worshipers and the giant bells' ringing had ceased. Father O'Malley was led out by his entourage and commenced the morning proceedings with his infamous,

"The Lord be with you!"

Followed by the ritually ceremonial response,

"And also with you."

The kid was too young to know that these were habitual to the service (although he soon found out). At the end of the ceremony Father O'Malley concluded with his,

"The mass has ended. Go in peace."

And would meet his flock outside the main doors (weather permitting). When they got home, junior ran inside to get his collar shirt and hush puppy shoes off as fast as he could.

"Janine, did you plan to stay for dinner?"

"I don't know Ma. I've got a lot of work to do, and I need to prepare for Monday. Can we eat early so I can get back at a decent time?"

"Sure," her mother replied.

They had Sunday dinner earlier than usual that day and Janine packed up her pen pal letter along with a few other school experiments notes she had recorded.

"I'll see you the week after next honey, okay. Your father will be picking you up on Friday for your weekend together."

"K Ma, see you then."

"I love you Lum Lum."

"Love you too."

Janine said goodbye to her parents and was on her way back to her apartment. The kid made his way down to the basement as usual. Grampa had just turned on the tv and gramma stood outside the porch door that led to the driveway. Her concern was still intense, but she didn't want to overreact.

CH. 7

Monday morning bright and early Janine got to work with a new breath of fresh air. The current research she was doing on binomials as well as utility was still on her mind, but they certainly weren't the level of priority she had with her new endeavor. She set up her area as she always did, had some coffee brewing and was about to begin when storming through her door there was,

"Hey Janine. Good morning! How was your weekend?"

"Morning Michael, very good how was yours?"

"It was a low-key, a more relaxed weekend than usual. Stayed in on Friday night. Didn't even leave the house, then went to a show on Saturday."

"Oh, what'd you see?"

"It was an old Hitchcock suspense thriller. Kept me on the edge of my seat the whole time. What did you end up doing?"

“I was with my son mostly. We were all together at my parent’s house for the weekend.” (she didn’t know if Michael knew that she had a son and thought never to divulge that information unless completely necessary or unless she trusted the individual implicitly. Needless to say, she wasn’t going to give Michael Bonfiglio that bit of intel)

“Oh yeah? What does he like to do?” Michael asked, “What are his interests or hobbies right now?”

“Hockey ... *hockey, hockey, hockey, hockey, hockey*. He eats, sleeps, and dreams hockey. His father got him on skates at a young age and he took to it like bees to honey.”

“That’s fantastic! Hockey’s a great game. I loved to play a little as a kid too. Just had the hardest time stopping, or turning, or skating. I basically lacked all of the attributes necessary for one to play the game.”

Janine smiled as he showed a side of diffidence that he rarely lets out.

“What’s up?” She asked him.

“I’ve been going over and over in my head what William gave us on Friday. Especially the voidless and formless direction or origination he was alluding to. It was almost Biblical in content.”

“Yes, there was an element of Genesis Chapter One wasn’t there,” she confirmed for him.

Michael continued,

“As I went back and forth in my head regarding everything we talked about, there was one thing that hit me that I couldn’t understand.”

“What’s that?” She asked him.

“Why was I invited? Why was I there? I certainly don’t have the resume that you have. And on your worst day your technical acumen is 100 points higher than mine. Why bring me into the mix on this one?”

“Why Mr. Bonfiglio, is this you at your most humble?”

“I will be the first to admit, it’s not a side I like to show too often. I’ve had experiences in the past where humility was interpreted as weakness. I would then reverse said humility and project strength and confidence. Only to soon be interpreted as arrogance, I'm sure. It would be a case of win some lose some, but I guess it has been my experience that the best defense is a good offense. It's not the same for women, is it?"

She looked at him,

"No, it's not the same for us. Most of us are just happy we can vote now."

"I didn't mean it like ..."

"I know, I know. Just messin' with ya."

"Wow, I guess I have to make another confession. I didn't know you had such a good sense of humor."

"Miguel, there's a lot you don't know about me. But as far as *why you* regarding Friday, I haven't a clue. Your guess is as good as mine. We all know you're talented. We all know you're intelligent."

"Yeah, but everyone in the room there that day is."

"True, but maybe ..." She paused.

"Maybe what?" Michael asked.

"I only caught the tail end of it when I got there. That part William was talking about how the Russian military elite chose a guy that had no prior experience in the game. No knowledge of the tools used or required to be successful. They still picked him specifically and intentionally. They saw something in him on the inside. Perhaps in the same fashion, that's what William sees in you. Even if *you* don't know it yet. You didn't even know I could bust your chops so easily, did ya."

"Ha! You got that right!" Michael expressed with laughter, "I gotta say, you never cease to amaze me. You're able to come to conclusions of various degrees (perhaps even simultaneously) regarding topics that are more or less mutually exclusive. I don't know how you do it."

"Have no social life for the first 30 years and submerge yourself in theoretical physics, sub-atomic particles, radioactive isotopes, fusion and you'll get there."

"Yep, I hear ya. Oh, I almost forgot. If you ever want Bruins tickets for you and your son just let me know. I can get you seats right behind the bench."

"I appreciate that. Thank you."

"Thank you, Janine. Take care. See you later."

Michael then walked out of the room and down the corridor with a level of perplexity he hadn't felt before. He had walked in that day in hopes to get some insider information on how he could excel with what is in front of him. Instead, he got a pep talk. And what's more, it felt good. He didn't have to read between the lines or look over her shoulder for some clue. It was more genuine than he was used to.

The noon hour was fast approaching, and Janine was more hungry than usual. She arrived at the cafeteria a little before the rush crowd came through. As she slid her tray down the stainless-steel tubes of the orderly assembly, she heard a semi-familiar voice from over her right shoulder.

"Hi Janine, how are you? Missed you Friday. How've you been? Have a good weekend?" Ted didn't realize he riddled her with so many questions in a row.

"Oh hey, hi! Nice to see you again. I'm good. Busy weekend. Actually, busy from Friday to Sunday, but yeah back to it again on Monday." She forgot his name but saw his ID tag and the small *TED* on it that saved her.

"Would you be able to have lunch again together today, if you're not too busy?" He asked and followed it with, "My treat!"

"Yeah sure." She said, "But you don't have to do that."

"I insist. My pleasure."

They continued down the line choosing carefully which entrée to select. Ted was deliberately avoiding the spaghetti and meatballs since his white shirt would certainly be a magnet for the red sauce. When they arrived at the end of the line the cashier said,

"$.65"

"For both please," Ted assured her.

"$1.37"

She took his two dollars and gave him back the change all the while looking at them both as if to say, *too cute*.

Making their way to two empty seats across from each other Ted had to break the silence,

"Were you in the office on Friday or did you take the day off?"

"Yes, I was here but we had a meeting that started at 9:30am and went 'till 3 or 4pm."

"Oh wow. I hope they let you grab a bite somewhere."

"They had it catered."

"I had no idea."

"No idea about what?" She inquired.

"That you were VIP."

"I'm not. (she found his idiocy to be refreshing and fun) I just happened to get included to this one, but it doesn't happen very often. Come to think, I can't remember the last time I was at a work function where they expensed catering."

"What was the meeting about?" He asked gently.

"I'm not at liberty to give the details, but I can tell you it was highly productive."

This had Ted's curiosity peaked. He thought to himself, "What was it did she say she did again?" He could not remember specifically. All he could recall is that she used some technical jargon that he had never heard before and had no idea what it meant. The proverbial wheels started turning in his mind. He said to himself, *This girl is in a whole different league than I am. What can I do?*

He didn't want to pry too much, be overbearing or show that he was overanxious to know more details of what was going on, so he just came back with,

"Well, it sounds like there is never a dull moment."

"You can say that again."

"Well, it sounds like ..."

Janine gave a grin and smiled.

"What did you do over the weekend?"

He quickly downshifted to less personal small talk although was worried that it would get too mundane. She told him bits and pieces about her personal life. The main things like she was divorced and had a kid. She wanted to get that out of the way quick and see his reaction. Ted didn't act surprised or aloof. He liked her more and more the more they spoke. When it was his turn to respond he told her how he had a brother and a sister but had never been married. His father was in WWII as well but was killed in Normandy on D-Day. The fact that they both had parents in the war gave Janine a little more of a connection toward him.

As the lunch hour was coming to a close it was apparent the two had hit it off. She was involved and eagerly engaged in his conversation, and he was more besotted with her every second. She cleared the corners of her mouth with her napkin, looked at his plate and gave a little giggle.

"What's so funny?" He asked her smiling.

"I noticed you ate each section on your plate separately and you saved your steak for last. Then had your salad with no dressing and finally dessert."

"Uh oh, I hope that doesn't mean anything bad." He was briefly worried.

"No, not at all. It's very cute actually."

That sealed it for him. When the lunch hour was near to end, he went full force.

"I'd love to see you again if you have the time. Perhaps lunch again this week or even dinner Saturday night if you would like to?"

"Let's meet here again on Thursday. See how it goes then we can discuss Saturday." She replied.

"Fantastic! I love Thursdays. Thursdays are the greatest next to Fridays and Saturdays. I will be here Thursday! Thursday yes!"

She laughed at how giddy he seemed. She hadn't felt this way in a long time. No one had paid this kind of interest in her in a while (or at least she did not notice it). He returned her tray for her. They said goodbye and went to their opposite workstations within the organization. When Ted got to his sector his face was flush. He couldn't remember where he put the LDF file. He spun around in his chair. Once again, Al Burke walked over to ask him a question,

"Hey Ted, what are the ... awe man not again. That cafeteria dame? I thought she gave you the brush?"

"She likes the way I save my steak for last!"

Al just shook his head and kept walking. *He'll be back to earth in a couple hours,* he thought to himself.

CH. 8

That evening Janine reviewed some old notes and formulas she had tried to calculate and prove back in high school. Computer Science was in its infancy at the time and even her advanced classes would just touch upon it briefly. Never enough for her inquisitive appetite. She saw the mistakes she made in the math. Errors in the algorithms. It made her say things to herself like, *How could you* and *You really missed that?* None of this work was part of her core curriculum. This was all leisure activity that she knew would best point her in the right direction for what lay ahead. She reviewed old possible rotor sequences and decipherment models. An old theorem of conjecture as it applied to decidability. There was an old summary of a proof that converted numbers, only to be left blank at the end of the page.

Getting ready for bed that night she took a few old notebooks in with her. She had seven to ten storage bins filled with material from high school, MIT and graduate school. She knew that some of the pieces to the puzzle would be in there somewhere or at least help to give new ideas. She fell asleep that night holding one from junior year when she was fourteen years old. The ink was a little faded but all still legible. She forgot to turn off the light on the nightstand next to her.

The next day was more research in the lab and personal review in the evening. Thursday came and went. Lunch with Ted was a success, so they confirmed plans for Saturday night. He was scheduled to pick her up at seven right outside her apartment.

Friday afternoon William stopped by her office to chat.

"Hey Janine. Good afternoon."

"Hi William. Good to see you again. How are you?"

"Good. Good. Is this the Denaris you've been working on?"

"Yeah, I'm just finishing up the illustrations to send it over to the team."

"Wow, that was fast." Complimenting her as he tried to make heads or tails of what he was looking at with the equations on her chalkboard.

"Thanks, I wanted to get it out of the way as soon as possible. I want to give our new issuance my full attention as I believe it will require."

"I'm so glad to hear you say that. My sentiments exactly. I hope I'm not being too pushy by saying this so please forgive me, but I just wanted to ask in the most general sense (extremely high level with no details), have you given any thought to possible procedures or directions? Once again, I apologize. I know it has only been a week and a thing like this will take years possibly decades to launch. I just wanted to ask ... *ever* so gently."

He ended this by looking up at her and adjusting his watch before folding his hands.

"Well, Mr. William, it's funny you should ask. To answer your question ... yes. Yes, I have begun to contemplate possible avenues regarding last Friday. And you're right! It has only been a week. And you're right! Something like this will most likely take a decade or more to come to fruition but yeah, I can't help myself. This is really something I have waited my whole life to be a part of. The potential here seems almost infinite."

"My sentiments exactly!" William let out with a boyish charm he couldn't help. "I knew you would have already begun. You have a dedication, passion, and work ethic (not to mention one of the highest intellects) I have ever seen. I will certainly waste no time in taking all the credit for hiring you."

"I appreciate your vote of confidence and exuberance. Please keep in mind we are at the bottom of Mt. Everest. Only touched the tip of the iceberg. And be prepared for setbacks. I can't tell you how many times I thought I was taking five steps forward only to realize I was actually taking seven steps back."

"I know, I know."

William replied wanting to reassure her he knew exactly where she was coming from,

"But in those six steps back I've never seen anyone slingshot eleven steps forward like you do."

"Well, thank you again." Janine replied.

"May I ask one more itsy, bitsy, teencie, weencie little thing?" He said this with a winced look that he hoped was taken jovially.

"You sound like my kids' pre-school teacher. Go ahead, don't worry about it."

"Which direction were those neurons, protons and neutrons of yours headed?"

"Really it wasn't like that. I wasn't thinking that far ahead yet. I'll tell you a brief story. When I was a little girl, I had the same dilemma that you, General Atkins and I'm sure countless others find themselves in today. Grant you it's night and day different comparing an 8-year-olds frustrations with a global communication quandary, but in a weird way the concept is the same. All I've done so far is trace a few steps from a long time ago. Take where I am now to where I was then and see what I come up with. That's really all I've done so far."

William was blown away,

"Are you kidding me, all you've done? You get it. You understand it. You take it to heart. And what's even better, I know you are just being you. Not trying to be something you're not. I hear you say something like that, and I have all the confidence in the world that we will get this done and probably sooner than anyone expects. All you've done, can you imagine."

"Okay, okay. I hate to cut this short, and you can feel free to write down all the good things about me you would like to, I just have some work here I need to continue to finish up."

"By all means, please continue. As always Miss Janine it has been a pleasure and a privilege. You have a magnificent afternoon, evening and ... weekend. Good day."

"See ya later Willy."

Janine went back to her work and William made his way up to the top floor of the executive suites and into his office. His professional residence was a grandeur in and of itself, illustrating what was deemed befitting a stark CEO. He sat down and picked up his phone to dial,

"Hello, General Atkins please."

"May I ask who's calling."

"William Bourque from Ratheon."

"Yes sir, just a moment."

"William hello, how are you?""Good afternoon General. Just fine thank you."

"I must admit William, I didn't expect to hear from you so soon. It's only been about two weeks since we last spoke."

"I know General, it's so true and I must certainly admit that I didn't expect to be calling you so quickly either."

"What can I do you for?"

"I just wanted to ask if you have any other prospective players in the mix that first started working on this type of solution when they were eight years old."

"I officially don't follow you, William."

"I've got a team member that has been thinking about ways to solve this situation since she was a child. It appears that ..."

"A she? That's interesting."

"Yes, sir. A she. Is that a problem?"

"I don't think it will be, at least my instincts tell me that it won't be, but I have been wrong before. More than once. People react differently to various uncommon presentations, surroundings or introductions. Do you know what Freud said about the uncanny?"

"No Sir."

"He defined the uncanny as the class of frightening things that lead us back to what is known and familiar. He said that it undoubtedly belongs to all that is terrible. To all that arouses dread and creeping horror. It is equally certain, too, that the word is not always used in a clearly definable sense, so that it tends to coincide with whatever excites dread.

"If I may ask a question General."

"Please do, William."

"Would I be correct to think that an individual's definition of uncanny is an underlying variable here and more often than not there is a fear of the unknown (of the unfamiliar)."

"Precisely."

General Atkins confirmed to him and then continued,

"All I am saying here is that I have no idea what anyone else's definition is. When I hear the word uncanny, I think more odd or peculiar. I don't associate horror or terror with it. I lean more toward remarkable as a synonym. Isn't it interesting that Freud associates the word with something negative. I associate it with something positive. More along the lines of 'he or she has the uncanny ability to play the piano upside down'. But like I said, I don't think it will be an issue. I just can't say for certain."

"I understand General. And you presented an interesting psychoanalytical scenario. I had no idea you were so well versed in psychology."

"I'm not my friend. I'm certainly only a layman in the field. It's more or less a hobby of mine. One that I would starve to death if I ever tried to make a living doing. I fear that I have taken the wind out your sail William. You started off sounding like a proud papa and I apologize for the reduction in your exuberance. Please tell me all you can about this fantastic protégé' of yours."

William proceeded to describe to General Atkins the exceptional perhaps 'uncanny' qualities that Janine was true to possess. He emphasized those unique intangibles that Atkins agreed isn't something you can teach. There was a slight change in William's tone. He truly believed that at this level topics of their prior discussion were completely irrelevant. But no doubt, he knew he had an advantage with her that no one else had.

Saturday night arrived, by 6pm Janine was still getting ready for her date with Ted. She had made a point to sleep a little later than usual so that her eyes wouldn't have deep circles under them or show any puffiness at all. As far as extensive preparation, that's as far as she'd get. She was light years more practical than extravagant. And in the dating world she was the opposite of most. There was no trying on a closet full of clothes and seeing which shoes would match. There were two ensembles of evening attire and that was it. There was no hour for hair and another for make-up. Hair quick. Make up went on one way every time. As much as she enjoyed Ted's company on their cafeteria lunch rendezvous, she wasn't that nervous or excited like a lot of people get. No wondering, how will it go? Where will he take me? What will we talk about? As far as she was concerned if the night was a total bust so what. Doesn't matter. *Got a lot more on my plate* is the way she saw it.

Ted (on the other hand) was talking a mile a minute (to himself) while getting ready. It was like there was another person in the room but knowing there was no one else there and then again thinking is there someone he is talking to? "I think we're gonna have a good time. Do you think we'll have a good time? I like this suit, it's a nice suit, fits good this suit, you like this suit? Man, I'm hungry, you hungry? I'm starvin' gotta get some of that food food food." And on and on and on. All to himself and wicked fast.

He knocked on the front to her apartment at seven on the dot. She was all ready and waiting by then and opened her door with a cheerful grin and accepting eyes.

"You look fantastic!" He immediately complemented her before even saying hello.

"Thank you kind sir, you look very handsome this evening as well."

"Shall we?"

He extended his arm to her so she could wrap her tiny forearm around his. He escorted her through the hallway down the stairs and outside to where he was parked. He drove a very well-kept Plymouth Valiant and opened the door to allow her in. She unlocked his side, and they were off.

"Where are we going tonight?" She asked him.

"I hope you like Italian. I have reservations for us at Lombardi's and then there is a special concert that the Boston Pops is having. They are giving a performance of The Magic Flute I thought you might enjoy."

"Did you have spies or detectives tail me to find out everything that they could? Did you call and talk to my mother?"

"Ha! I was thinking about it. Why? Does it sound like a good evening?"

"It certainly does! First, my mother is 100% Italian, so I've grown up with it and continue to."

"I'm sorry." Ted got worried, "I was hoping to show you something different and new and maybe ... maybe I can get us into the Hong Kong Gardens, or maybe a Thai or Indian restaurant?"

"No no, sorry. I didn't mean it that way. I was trying to express my love for Italian food and how I'll eat it forever. Please don't think otherwise."

"Whew." Ted expressed his relief.

"Second, I absolutely love, love, love the Boston Pops and Mozart. I've never seen a performance of The Magic Flute. So, I'm tickled pink right now."

"Oh, what a relief! I don't think I could have got us in to the Hong Kong Gardens anyway."

She laughed so boisterously as they drove through the cobble stone streets of Boston on a beautiful clear evening.

They arrived at the restaurant and were seated immediately with Ted's reservation. A very romantic table for two with candlelight and a delightful little view of the Back Bay with outside streetlamps accenting the scenery. The waiter arrived promptly,

"Good evenin' Sir/Madam. My name is Bennett, and I'll be your waiter this fine evenin' together. You are in for a delight as our chef is experiencin' an extremely diversified medley on his menu this weekend. He is includin' a robust magnificence with *khan*! We have creamed *khan*, grilled *khan*, sautéed *khan*, boiled *khan*, poached *khan*, fried *khan*, freeze dried *khan*, pureed *khan*, minced *khan*, distilled *khan*, smoked *khan*, elevated *khan*, overturned *khan*, metabolic *khan* and the always beloved, *khan* on the cob. Howeva' ya take ya *khan,* our chef is up to the task. Special orders are gladly accepted. May I start yas off with a cocktail?"

"Ladies first." Ted said.

"I think I'll have a bourbon Manhattan. No wait! A bourbon old fashioned please."

"And for you sir."

"Coca-Cola, no ice."

"I'll be right back with your drink orders." The waiter then turned and left the two.

"No ice. That's interesting."

"Yeah, it's usually kept cold, so the ice just ends up being a filler then watering it down."

"How efficient of you." She said with an approving glance.

"Can I make a confession of sorts, no one has ever paid so much attention to my dining habits before in my life. No one has even commented to me regarding it. I find it extremely flattering."

"Since we're making confessions, I guess I'll make one of my own. When I was a young girl, I would notice and divulge myself to the unobvious. At first in animal behavior, then in human behavior. As an adolescent it can be extremely detrimental to one's social life, and by that I mean making friends. Young girls are not very receptive when their distinctive behavioral patterns are noticed. Regardless of the fact that you're only looking at it from a clinical point of view."

"Why Miss Janine, did you just confess to me that you didn't have any friends growing up?"

"Oh, I had many friends. Too many. It was hard keeping track of them all and they never left me alone. They would follow me wherever I would go. Some of 'em even came with me here tonight with you. What's the matter? Can't you see them?"

Ted chuckled and sat back in his seat just staring at her. She grinned and looked back at her menu.

"You mentioned your interest in bizarre animal behavior a moment ago. What did you find in your studies?"

"Hmmm, let me see ... *zebra finches!* The birds. They have a peculiar reproductive habit."

"Is this another one of those where the female devours the male after mating types?"

"Not exactly. If the female believes her mate is unattractive, she will lay a slightly larger egg. This bigger egg has extra nutrients that she hopes will 'help out' the father's bad genes. The levels of antioxidants are 2.5 times higher in eggs sired by unattractive males than those sired by good-looking ones. It's fascinating and still unknown yet how the female perceives male attractiveness and translates it to chemical concentrations in her eggs."

In his attempt to be witty and charming Ted replied,

"I've always had a fascination with birds. As a child it was with the most obvious, their ability to fly and the fact that their bones are hollow. Then as I got older it was so interesting how an eagle has such immense strength in their their ... feet, claws ..."

"Talons." She said softly to assist.

"Yes, talons. Such immense strength in their talons to grab and carry fish and yet still have the care and attention to transport their young or even the fragile eggs in those same claws."

"Would you consider yourself an ornithologist of sorts?" She asked politely.

"In the most basic sense perhaps. If there is a level below amateur, then I might reach that category. Why do you ask? I feel like there is a test coming up." He offered still grinning.

"A test perhaps. With no negative repercussions if a wrong answer."

"Okay. I'll play. Let me have it."

"Can you name the fastest member of the animal kingdom?"

He thought about it for a second. His first instinct was to say *cheetah* or *sailfish*, but that would have been too ... *eh. We're talking about birds* (he said to himself), *could it be a hawk or the eagle that he just mentioned?*

"I'm guessing that it is a carnivorous bird since we are on the subject, but for all intense purposes I have no idea which one it could be, I'm gonna go with the eagle."

"Bravo! Bravo! That was an excellent choice!"

"Was I right?" He asked with excitement.

"No, but the Golden Eagle is number two on the list, so you were very very close. It is the Peregrine Falcon."

"That was my next guess!" He said hoping she would laugh (and she did).

Continuing to play the game she added,

"They are absolutely amazing, aren't they? They can reach speeds of over 240 mph when they go into a nosedive. They even have a clear membrane that serves to protect their eyes when they make their descent. Any debris particles in the air could act as a bullet to their sight if they didn't have this extra layer at such speed."

"Here we are, one bourbon old fashioned."

"Thank you, sir." She said to their waiter.

"And one coke no ice."

"Thank you."

"Both, very welcome. Have you had a chance to decide on some appetizers?"

"Oh wow! I've been so captivated by the lady's conversation I haven't even looked at the menu yet. Just a couple more minutes please."

"Of course, sir."

Dinner went on as a complete preeminence. Ted's efforts to be witty and charming were making headway. She was receptive to his glances and never made him carry the weight of continuing the conversation. One aspect she internalized but wouldn't mention (not yet anyway) is that she was just fine with the silence (and with him as well). She learned over the years through trial and error that telling someone, *it's okay if you don't talk* isn't quite the same as, *I appreciate and enjoy how we can both comfortably share silence.*

They finished their entrees when Ted noticed the time.

"Oh wow! The performance starts at nine. Would it be alright if we ordered one dessert and shared it? I'd hate for you to miss the beginning."

"Was this your way of being cutesy romance man with me? One dessert with two spoons *hmmmmm*?"

"I cannot tell a lie, absolutely! I only wish I actually planned it this way."

At the completion of dinner, they drove over to the Hatch Shell where the concert was being held. She was enthralled by the energy of the performance. Ted would sometimes lean back and glance at her noticing how much she enjoyed the music. At the end of the evening, he drove her back to her apartment and walked her up the stairs to her door.

"This has been the most fun, wonderful evening I've had in years. I sure hope we can do this again." He said with a level of puppy dog eyes.

"I would like that." She replied.

He leaned in to give her a gentle hug. As they began to separate, he snuck in a quick kiss on her cheek.

"Nighty night. Sleep tight." He said to her then went back down the hallway to the stairs leading to the outside.

He looked back and saw her standing in front of her door sort of sideways with her keys and arm at the top lock. Her shawl still covering her shoulders and her eyes looking toward him. He gave a slow wave with his fingers and went out the front door of her building. The picture of her standing there looking at him that way was etched in his mind forever.

Sunday morning Janine was reviewing old notes and various unproven hypothesis' she had done in her senior year of high school and freshman year at MIT. She was reviewing a theory of *time-sharing* and how or if it could be created, implemented, and applied. Some of the research material was still organized and aligned while a few pieces were in fragments and somewhat discoursed. *How could I have let this happen?* She told herself.

While continuing to review and put some particles together her phone rang,

"Did you go to mass this morning?"

"Hi Ma, no I didn't make it today. How many Hail Marys is that?"

"I don't know, I stopped countin'. It's between you and the Lord now. Watcha doin'? Watcha do last night?"

"Well, actually last night I went on a date ... actually."

"You did? With who?"

"His name is Ted. We work together. I mean, we work for the same company. He works in data processing. Completely different aspect of the company."

"Isn't this just the latest development. How ironic."

"What do you mean?"

"I was just talking with Farina after church today, when we all went to the Mug n' Muffin. Her niece has a boyfriend who has a friend that she said would be perfect for you. They wanted to ask you if you would be up for a double date with them sometime."

"Oh, I can't Ma. I have too much work to do and he'll be back with us next weekend and ..."

"And what? I already know. You like this guy don't ya."

"Yeah, I do."

"Ah ha, I knew it. So, where'd ya go? What'd ya do?"

"We went to Lombardi's in the North End."

"What'd ya have?"

"I had the mushroom risotto, he had the veal carbonara."

"Better than mine?"

"No, of course not." Janine smiled to herself on the other end of the line.

"What else?"

"He doesn't put any dressing on his salad. You ever known anyone to not use any dressing or at least oil and vinegar? I've never seen that."

"Yeah, there was a friend of your fathers years ago that was the same way. I can't remember his name, but he did no dressing too. What else?"

"He doesn't drink. He ordered two cokes with no ice. I didn't ask him about it. I just thought it was interesting he didn't order a beer or scotch or something."

"It's 'cuz he's a recovering alcoholic! Don't you know that?"

"Ma, just because someone doesn't drink doesn't mean they are a recovering alcoholic. I'm sure lots of people don't drink. We just don't know any."

"The people that don't drink either can't see over the steering wheel yet or their finishing up one of them twelve step programs."

"Not necessarily. How did Daddy quit?"

"He just stopped. Cold turkey. He saw what it did to Morris Flynn. Had him bed ridden. Couldn't move."

"Yeah, I remember poor Mr. Flynn. He lost two wives to cancer, didn't he?"

"Yes, he did (poor thing). So, what else you do after?"

"He took me to The Boston Pops. They had a concert of The Magic Flute. The brass section was amazing, the violins were on fire, it was a magnificent show."

"He certainly pushed all the right buttons. How did he know?"

"I asked him that. He said he just got really lucky. Took a shot in the dark with it all. Did Alfredo pick him up on time Friday?"

"Yeah, he was here for a second then they were off. You know he doesn't stay long to chit chat when he comes to get him."

"Yeah, I know." Janine confirmed.

"It'll be the same story where he'll bring him back late and he'll be tired for school tomorrow."

"I know it. I wish we could get him to break that habit, but I'm sure they both want to spend as much time together as they can."

"Oh, hey honey I gotta go, your father's calling me. Probably can't find a fresh pair of drawers.

"K Ma. Bye."

Janine immediately returned to her pre-professional notes to recall which direction she was taking at the time. She had collaborated with professors and other students on various data and statistical analysis. They bounced ideas off one another and took turns trying to prove them mathematically. There was one idea she had at the time that she didn't have the confidence to articulate to her peers. *Would it be possible to achieve the idea of time-sharing over a wide area of networks?* She lacked the conviction at the time because it took her back to her pen-pal days of unbridled awkwardness. Now she knew how to use that negative energy and turn it into positive.

Sunday afternoon quickly turned into evening and late evening. She didn't hear from her mother, so she assumed the kid got home alright that night. In more than one instance and on more than one occasion she took the path of, no news is good news.

Monday morning William Bourque asked to have an unscheduled meeting with the team. Larry, Ed and Michael all arrived together and a few minutes earlier than requested. Janine had to close her research office unexpectedly, so it took her a few more minutes to get there but she still arrived on time. William was sitting to the right of three dark suits who were the company's private legal team. William didn't lead with introductions. After everyone took their seat, he began with,

"When I was fourteen and a freshman in high school, I had a little chip on my shoulder (at times). I look back at it now, I see I was angry at this or that or whatever else there was. I played JV Baseball. There was another kid on the team, Robby O'hare. We knew each other since seventh grade and played on teams together. He was admittedly a better player than me. Better hitter, better pitcher, fielder, and he had the ego to go along with it. Off the field or in the classroom I could be the butt of a few jokes of his. It wasn't ever over the top, but there was certainly a degree of separation with us and by now we had known each other for a few years. I got to the point where I would play the antagonist with him. I look back at it now and I realize this is where and when I started to develop such a lack of respect for insolence. I would intentionally push his buttons just because of this and he would give it back to me in some way shape or form. One day in Phys. Ed. class we were playing tennis. He was serving on the court to the left of me and I was busting his chops about something. He dropped his racket and said, *That's it!* And came running at me. I dropped my racket and we squared off. He got one shot at my ribs, and I completely missed with my right. I probably moved like I was in slow motion. My friend Donny jumped the net and got in between us to break it up. Good thing too 'cuz Robby would have fed me my lunch. When gym glass was over, Donny and I were walking back to the school building from the tennis courts. I got this immediate, very peculiar feeling inside and I just happen to look back at our P.E. teacher Mr. Schmidt. He looked me right in the eyes and started laughing. It took me a second, but then it hit me. That was the exact instance that Schmidt sold out. I was wondering why Robby and I *weren't* sent to detention. If I had got into a fight with anyone else that day we would have been in detention for a week. Automatic. No questions asked. But you see, Robby's mom was a teacher at the school. She was very well liked. Robby was also a promising athlete. Mr. Schmidt wasn't going to send a fellow faculty member's kid to detention. To this day I regret not calling out old Stan Schmidt. I had the words too. I was going to yell out, *Remember this day Stan! Remember it for the rest of your life! Today is the day you sold out!* But I still had that part of me where you don't speak to your elders that way. Ed, Larry, Michael, Janine this is Mr. Lamar, Mr. Akoya and Mr. Rainey from our legal team. They have contracts for you to review regarding this project. If you have consulted with your own private attorneys already, I completely understand. If you have a copy of any drafted contracts, we can simply exchange documents here today. What I want you all to understand is that I will *never* sell you out."

William went silent as the three lawyers passed out copies of the agreements they had drafted. After receiving them Michael, Ed & Larry each gave a copy of their personal contracts that each of their lawyers had written on their behalf. Janine just sat and watched the presumably 'legal formalities' take place as she remembered that she promised her father.

After pleasantries continued to exchange and smiles were worn by everyone William said,

"That was really all I had today. We can reconvene on this subject in the next few weeks either collectively or individually. I don't want to keep everyone away too long especially since this was called on such short notice."

Then each member got up from their seats, said their goodbyes and went out the door. Janine stayed back to talk with William.

"I'm so sorry." She said, "I had no idea this part of it all would have taken place so soon. I'll have something for you within the week."

"Quite alright Janine, please don't feel over pressured with this stuff. These guys will take a look at whatever you have, whenever you have it."

Janine said goodbye to everyone again and left to return to her workplace. Lawyer number two, Mr. Akoya turned to William and said,

"I'm a bit surprised. Who wouldn't have consulted with an attorney by now?"

William turned to him with a straight face,

"One who eats, sleeps and breathes her work." He simply stated.

When Janine returned to her area, she immediately called Larry,

"Hi, Larry it's Janine."

"Hey, what's up?"

"I'm a little embarrassed to say the least. I haven't consulted with an attorney yet. Haven't even researched one. May I ask, who did you use?"

"I went with Marshall Leibowitz over at Klein & Leibowitz. He of course being one of the partners. Ed and Michael went with Philip Hodge simultaneously. I think they've had history with him, so they were comfortable giving it to him. I've seen what Marshall has done in previous litigations and depositions. He's expensive, but you get what you pay for."

"Would you mind if I gave him a call? I'll understand if you prefer I don't. I'm sure a desire to remain separate or single in this area can be a measure of appeal."

"No, not at all. Let me get his number for you. Here it is, it's 508-555-1247. His secretary is named Pamela. I'm sure he won't mind taking on another client under the same pretense. In fact, tell him I referred you and tell him I said we want a group discount."

"Oh, I didn't know lawyers offered such things."

"Ha! They don't! When he told me his hourly rate, I nearly hit the ceiling. When he saw my reaction, he offered me a drink as consolation. He'll get the joke when you call him."

"I appreciate this, Larry. I'll call him now to set an appointment."

"This should be easy money for him. All you have to say is, I'll have what he's having."

"Ha ha! Exactly!" Janine replied.

"Oh hey, I've got a call on another line I've got to take. Give a ring back if you need anything else."

"Will do. Thanks again!"

"Bye." -click-

CH. 9

Ted started each day with the usual morning ritual. Wake up, have some sort of grained cereal with a banana. Juice (never coffee) then take a shower get dressed and commute to the office. He arrived at the same time every day. 8:30am. Never earlier. Never later. He had only been with the company about seven months. Originally came in under contract for a specific project then hired full time shortly after. He just got a new boss that was from England, Edgar Lewis. Edgar was no nonsense. Didn't believe in or much less acknowledge *esprit de corps*. Didn't care about high morale, low morale or no morale for anyone he managed. There was a level of contempt for Americans that Edgar embraced, and he wasn't the least bit concerned if you were offended.

Edgar Lewis made it a point to give Ted every mundane and mediocre task he could think of. In Edgar's eyes all his subordinates were beneath him and he let them know it. Edgar's requests were anything but. They were demands. Demands that had timelines shorter than anyone prior. But Ted never complained. He never argued. He never expressed an opposing opinion. Other team members would boisterously voice their disdain for Edgar (to each other). Ted wouldn't engage in those conversations. A handful of others reportedly used the phrase, *I don't know how much more I can take with this guy.* Ted never said a word.

The following Friday Edgar called Ted into his office at 4:30pm. With his heavy British accent and an emotionless tone he said,

"Theodore, we need the reports from the geological data of Alledum completed by the end of business today."

And then silence. Not the slightest movement made by Edgar. No response yet from Ted, just an expressed look of ... *what*?

Ted took a moment then,

"Sir, those aren't due for another week and a half. I just received the updates on Alledum."

"If we stay late Theodore, can you have them completed by Monday?"

Edgar had no issues staying beyond normal working hours. He had no family in the States and no obligations to attend to. He expected the same from his team and had no empathy for anything otherwise.

"Mr. Lewis, it's my mother's 79th birthday. Tonight, my family has organized a party for her. We have cousins coming in from out of state. It has been planned for months. I'm supposed to pick up the cake in forty-five minutes on my way over there."

Edgar simply stared at him while Ted tried to plead his case. Edgar blinked once,

"So, is that a no?"

"Unfortunately sir, I will be unable to stay late tonight, but I will be happy to come in tomorrow and Sunday. I honestly don't know if that is enough time to complete this, but I am willing to try with best efforts."

"I see." Edgar replied while looking down at his paperwork, "No, that won't be necessary Mr. Sullivan. Good evening."

Ted didn't know what to think. He just stood there for seven seconds. Kind of sideways towards the door with his head a little bit down still looking at Edgar Lewis. "Good evening sir." Is all he could say then walked out of Lewis' office. Completely dazed and confused he finished his remaining work for the day and left the building a little after 5pm. He picked up his mother's birthday cake and completed other preparatory work expected of him for the festivities. Then went to his mother's party.

Sullivan arrived at the restaurant still a little distraught from the earlier events, but he did his best to hold it together. He kept his spirits up as he was walking toward the entrance. Cousin Maxwell was coming out of the double doors to have a cigarette. He was a beer and blue jeans kind of guy. Worked in the autobody shop as a primer in Franklin. Not a care in the world.

"Ted! What's shakin' my man! How you've been?"

"Hey Max. How are you? Good to see you."

They caught up on a few things then Ted let him know he had to get inside to set the cake.

"Sure thing!" Max said, "I'll see ya in there. Just gonna finish this up quick."

Ted got to their reserved section of the restaurant to find numerous nieces and nephews either sitting down or running around the chairs playing tag. He set the cake on the table when his sister Monica walked up to him,

"Hey!"

"Hey Mon."

"Everything cool with the cake?" She asked.

"Yeah, I guess. They spelled her name correctly and got the right numbers. I haven't dug into it to see if the flavor is what we ordered, what did we order?"

"I don't know, just cake. Hey, did you see Max outside?"

"Yeah, he was having a smoke when I walked in."

"Have you *ever* met his girlfriend?" Monica asked with great enthusiasm.

"I don't know. I don't think so, why?"

"I have to introduce you 'cmon."

"Okay wait. Let me make the rounds, say hello to everyone then I'll come find you."

He re-acquainted himself with numerous relatives he hadn't seen in a while. Some for years, others since last New Years. A few faces he didn't recognize but gave a polite hello and nod. His sister came back to him,

"You done. Ready to go meet her?"

"What is going on? What is the big deal with her? Why is this so important?"

"I can't explain it. You just have to experience it for yourself, 'cmon."

Monica grabbed her brother by the hand and led him to a table that was occupied by one single solitary woman. She was sitting completely upright with the most perfect posture of anyone in the room. She would glance from left to right staring at anyone or anything for just a brief inkling then avert her attention elsewhere. She was dressed extremely proper with a lace collared blouse and large rimmed glasses. Her shoes had a similarity to that of the Pilgrims which landed near Plymouth Plantation but with a hint of modern trace. Monica walked right up to her with a giant smile,

"Elaine, this is my brother Ted. Ted, this is Max's girlfriend Elaine."

"Hello Elaine, nice to meet you." He said while extending his handshake in friendship. With a brief pause and an ever so slightly pursed lip Elaine returned with,

"Charmed Theodore. Won't you sit down."

She extended her right arm and hand which for a second Ted thought she was expecting him to kiss her two middle fingers. This caught him off guard, so he just gave her the most gentle handshake of his life. He sat down at the round table in the seat to her immediate left. Monica plopped herself right next to him.

"How long have you and Max been together Elaine?" Ted asked her in hopes of making a good impression.

"Maxwell and I have been in commence for approximately four months now."

Ted nodded politely to be courteous as well as waiting to see if Elaine was going to contribute to the verbiage. She continued to look to the left and right when she spoke. Not overly obvious. Nothing as fast as a grandfather clock pendulum bob going back and forth. More like an owl searching for a varmint to devour.

"What do you do for work Elaine?" Ted asked her.

He was beginning to wonder why his sister was so intent on him meeting her. She seemed to be only responding to whatever he said. Monica was almost biting her nails in anticipation as if she was saying to him 'just wait for it'.

"I am the Head Librarian at the Sharon Public Library."

"Oh, how nice." He replied cordially.

And then, out of nowhere like a comet racing through the sky with the utmost sophistication and a little rolling of the tongue Elaine stated,

"Theodore, I certainly hope that you are *brrrushing* up on your vocabulary in expectation that we might have some stimulating conversation."

Monica almost fell over. She grabbed her brother's leg under the table as if to say, *That's it! There it is!* She was about to burst out laughing, but she did her best to hold her composure.

"Elaine, I have a confession of sorts (I suppose). I haven't picked up a dictionary in well over twenty years, maybe longer. I imagine my homework for next time is to learn a few new words. Make sure I get the proper tense, frame of reference and be able to apply them in our next dialogue, whenever that will be."

"That will be adequately sufficient Theodore."

Just then Max came back reeking of cigarette smoke,

"Hey! I'm so glad you all got introduced. I was hopin' as much. Makin' my girl feel part of the family."

He sat down on the other side of Elaine and put his arm around her.

"Maxwell! Your melodious air is protruding my person. What say you to this?"

"Awe, hey baby I'm sorry. I ran out of gum and that special smell good deodorant stick."

Ted was now intrigued by the supposable couple he had just encountered.

"So how did you two meet?" He asked them.

"I was requesting petrol from the attendant to be administered into my automobile when Maxwell stopped and noticed that my bonnet had become ajar. He was *grrracious* enough to secure it."

"Yeah, after that I asked her where she was from since I never heard some of these words she'd been usin' this way. We struck up a conversation and then I just figured I'd ask her out. Here we are."

"I must adjourn to the loo Maxwell. Theodore, Monica, if you would kindly excuse me for a brief duration, I shall return momentarily."

Elaine very refinely arose from the table and proceeded to the bathroom a few feet away. Just then Max blurted out,

"Don't forget to mind the gap baby!"

Elaine looked back disapprovingly (rolled her eyes) and said,

"Maxwell! You know that does not apply at this juncture." Then she entered the restroom.

Monica was chomping at the bits. As soon as Elaine was out of sight, she burst out hysterically,

"Max, she kills me! I get the biggest kick out of her. She's so proper and dignified. And she's so serious that I feel bad laughing. I know she's not doing it on purpose, and I certainly don't want to offend her so I just have to hold it in, but sometimes I think I might pee myself from how funny it is."

"I know what you mean." He replied, "A couple of weeks ago we were out and about running a few errands. She said her car was *completely filthy* and needed a good *scrubbin'*. I said hey, there's a good car wash right off of 1A here by the exit. Let's go. I'll take care of it for you. We get there and have to wait in line a little while. There were a couple cars ahead of us. The first guy (as you know) takes our order, we pay him, and he gives us a ticket. We drive a little further, get closer to the wash. This young kid musta been 15 or 16 years old at the most. He takes our ticket, looks at the order of what we are getting then gives us the instructions, *pull up behind the car in front of you, when they exit proceed thru* etc..., etc.... There was no one ahead of us at this point. She put the car in drive went straight through the wash and never stopped. When we got out the other side she turns to me, *Maxwell! What kind of scrubbery device have you brought me to?* She drives back around to the entrance of the drive thru. The young kid is standing there with his jaw on the ground and the most dumbfounded look on his face because nobody has ever driven straight through the car wash ever before. She rolls her window down. *Young man! I must certainly anticipate a complete refund if your scrubber is out of order! What say you to this?* This poor kid, it took him a couple seconds, *Uh, ma'am. You have to stop in the middle to allow the soap and brushes to go over your car.* I have all I can do to hold it at this point. She just turns to him, *very well.*"

Both Monica and Ted were cracking up uncontrollably as Max felt the need to order a drink.

"Well, my friend." Ted wanted to show his approval, "I for one am extremely happy for you. You look happy. She seems happy and what's more, I'm guessing there will never be a dull moment.

"I'll drink to that!" Maxey proclaimed.

The following Monday Ted arrived to work business as usual. There was an eerie quietness he noticed. Got his papers out of his briefcase and prepared the work area for the day. Still no noise. No conversations going on around him about their weekends. No keys heard typing or coffee pouring. Just a subtle murmur from the electrical appliances. Ted picked up where he left off with his last report. He had worked at home on Saturday and Sunday to be further along than he originally anticipated or expected to be. By 10:15am he saw his other team members coming back to their areas collectively. Nate Gross was the first to see and greet Ted.

"Hey, Ted my boy! We thought you were out sick today. Why weren't you at the meeting this morning?"

"Hi Nate. It appears as though I wasn't invited. When was this one called?"

Nate looked stunned. He had worked with Ted for a while now. He knew he was proper, diligent, and competent.

"Uh, last Thursday." Nate said somberly.

Ted thought to himself, *okay, the day before Edgar even called me into his office.*

"I see," was his only response.

The rest of the team filed in and gave their good mornings. Work resumed, but there was an unspoken feeling of unease. Everyone felt a certain level of ferment, but no one said a word. Colin Deveraux an equivalent associate would look over occasionally, just to see what he was doing. Phillip Lindey asked Ted a question just for the sake of saying something to him.

"Hey Ted, was the projector we used on Delaney in high resolution?"

"Yes Phil, it sure was."

"Thank you, sir!"

It was there. Something. Nobody knew what, they just knew.

The next week Ted was called into Edgar's office early in the am.

"Theodore, I am pulling you off of Alledum and re-assigning you to Baxter. If you could please forward all of your current progress to Howard Exeter that would be greatly appreciated."

Ted was dumbfounded. He couldn't believe what he was hearing.

"Sir, with all due respect, is this about last Friday?"

"Absolutely not. This is about allocating the proper resources accordingly."

"Mr. Lewis, I have worked on Alledum since its inception. I've edited and stored all the programs line by line on the cards. I stacked all the elements and based it on the principle of last in first out. I have it almost completed and prepared to hand in by end of business today. Two days earlier than the deadline."

"I'm sure Howard will be most grateful to you," Lewis replied.

"Not to mention that Baxter is out of my scope. I have no training or affiliation with the Baxter file in any way."

Edgar finally stopped writing and took off his glasses to look Ted in the eye,

"Mr. Sullivan, I have read your job description, Mr. Lindey's job description, Mr. Devereaux's job description and numerous others that I'll spare you at this juncture. One characteristic that is listed on each and every one of them is *having the ability to deal with ambiguity*. Now I'll ask you again, kindly sir, please forward all of your current work to Mr. Exeter and align yourself with the Baxter file."

Ted's ears were smoking as Edgar put his glasses back on and simply went back to writing at his desk. He walked out of Lewis' office and did as he was told. He didn't know where to start on the Baxter file. It was completely foreign to him. He literally didn't have the vocabulary for what was required. He was in unchartered territory.

That week Janine and Ted were having lunch together every day and speaking on the phone at night. Their fondness for one another was growing more and more each day. Ted was doing his best to suppress any emotion of angst or anxiety over his job, but a woman's intuition is very astute. She could tell he was distraught and wanted to help him in any way she could.

"Are you alright?" She finally asked, "You seem to have something you're thinking about and perhaps don't want to burden me with it. If that's the case, please know I'm here. I want to help in any way I can."

"Thank you very much," Ted replied with a grin. "I'm not as good at hiding it as I thought."

"You don't have to. Not with me."

Janine wanted to reassure him as much as possible.

"I got a new boss not too long ago. In a noticeably short time frame my work life and environment has changed 180 degrees. I have always been prompt and concise with my reports. Haven't had any push back regarding my competency. I'm well liked among my peers (or at least, I think I am). No one has ever sent me to the principal's office for bad behavior. My quarterly to annual reviews have shown I do well. This new manager of mine seems to be wanting me out of here and for the life of me I can't figure out why."

"Who's your new manager?"

"Edgar Lewis. Do you know him?"

"No, never heard the name. Do you think that's his plan? To get you fired?"

"It sure seems that way."

"Would you like me to talk with William Bourque and get you re-assigned?"

"Mr. Bourque. The CEO? I knew you were higher up on the food chain than me. I didn't know you rubbed elbows with the brass."

Ted's amazement made him forget all about his situation at the time. Then she tried to calm him further,

"It's no big deal. I can make a phone call and you'll be all set. New division. New area. New team."

Ted's astonishment grew more and more, but he tried to appear ever so composed in front of her. Couple minutes on the phone and your whole life changes at the blink of an eye (he thought to himself).

"I appreciate that, thank you, but how would it look to people knowing my girlfriend not only saved my job, but she also got me to here, there, wherever."

This was the first time an official label was mentioned. The butterflies started to flutter in Janine's stomach and Ted just realized that he used the term *girlfriend* with her. There was silence for a few seconds then with a twirling of her fork and a cute little beam she said,

"So, am I your girlfriend now?"

Without hesitation he replied,

"I sure hope so."

For the rest of the week and throughout the weekend the two were inseparable. Flying on air and never coming down. Ted forgot all about his problems at work and Janine didn't review one theorem. Like two kids in junior high. Almost made you puke.

As the weeks progressed Ted tried everything to adapt and conform to the Baxter account, but to no avail. He simply did not have the background or experience. He was given his two-week notice and let go immediately at the end of it. At the final out brief meeting with human resources Edgar Lewis had the audacity to shake his hand and say, "I like you Theodore. Best of luck to you."

Ted was escorted back to his area to clear out his personal belongings. His closest associates and friends provided as much consolation as they could. Al Burke was especially empathetic as he had been in Ted's shoes before.

"Hey man if you ever need anything you've got my number. Don't hesitate to call."

"Thank you, Al. I appreciate that."

"I've been right here more than once in my professional career. I'm guessing that they didn't give you a hug at the end. On two occasions they gave me a hug as they were sending me out. It was bizarre. It's like they just wanted to turn the knife while looking at me with a smile."

Ted got a little laugh from it,

"I'm sure if Lewis produced estrogen, he would have hugged me at the time. He just shook my hand and told me he liked me."

"Did you step back to avoid the lightning?"

"Ha, I sure should have. It almost seems like they hire you just to fire you."

"I know it. And then when they realize all the costs associated with having a high employee turnover rate, they change their tune."

"And Al, for the life of me I haven't been able to figure out the why. There literally has been no substantial reason as to why this has happened."

Al stood there, arms folded as he watched his friend pack up. He debated with himself if he should tell this to Ted. He didn't want to make him feel any worse than he already did, but he decided he had a right to know.

"Amigo, please know there is no way that I would be the one to *want* to tell you this. I had no clue you didn't know."

Ted stopped what he was doing completely. Al looked over at the escort then back at Ted and moved in closer to speak quietly.

"You're a casualty of war my friend. You're an example. What Lewis is doing, he's saying to everyone. None of you are safe. Work harder. Do more with less. Don't complain about a thing. And on and on, all that stuff."

Al leaned back to where he was with even more empathy than before. He knew he had just shown Ted a side to the business that he had never seen before. Ted sat back down in his (for all intense purposes) *ex*-chair.

"Al, is that how naïve I am? I never put two and two together and got that."

"Don't put yourself down my friend. Don't look at it that way. They will behave so unethically when they want to. Intentionally use words that have multiple meanings for a given situation. Mix lies with the truth to purposely coerce and influence. I got fired by a manager one time that had different facial expressions and tones of voice depending on which lie he was saying at the time. You know that test you can do?"

"No, what test?"

"There's a test you can give people to know when they are lying. Ask someone a question or make a statement that you know the answer to. When they give you an answer that you know is not the truth, that is what they look like when they lie. This guy was so deceptive he had many different versions of himself when he lied. It's a level of evil I want no part of."

"Is that why you keep getting fired Al?"

"Ha ha! Yes, most likely. That's the Ted I know. That's the man that will roll with this easy."

Ted finished packing up his things and was escorted out of the building. Al walked along with him to the end.

"Remember, you need anything just call. And let me know where you land."

"Thank you so much Al. I appreciate all your support."

"You got it my man. Take care!"

As Ted made his last step out of the building, he was just a few feet away from his car as Al called out to him,

"Oh hey! One more thing! Don't believe anyone that calls you *buddy*. They never mean it!"

Ted gave him a thumbs up and thought to himself, *that too?*

CH. 10

The kid had to have his wrestling fix every Saturday morning on the tube. Flying into the turnbuckles. Double suplexes. Pile drivers. Sleeper holds. He was into all of it. Grampa walked in one day while he was yelling at the tv,

“You know that’s all fake, don’t you?”

“No way! It ain’t fake. It can’t be. Look at him fly from the top rope! Watch him give the big leg, slap the chest, then boom! Down he goes. No way fake!”

“It’s all choreographed. They know how to hit each other so it doesn’t hurt.”

“What’s calelograf?”

“They know where each other is gonna move before they do it. They practice their sequences and timing.”

Grampa knew he didn’t want to believe him, so he left it alone. He figured let him enjoy it. A few Saturdays later gramma was getting ready to make lunch. She opened up the fridge,

"Where's the butter? I had a whole stick of butter still!"

She heard the tv on in the background. All she heard was, *Killer King Fish is about to drop the elbow on Leapin' Leopold The Unscrupulous!* She walked to the doorway of the den. The kid was standing on the arm rest of the couch all greased up and as shiny as someone who just got out of the pool. Talkin' to himself as the announcer and wrestler all in one and ready to jump off and deliver the big elbow to the pillow on the other side of the couch. Gramma turned back to the kitchen just shaking her head. As she passed the door to the basement grampa came out and into the kitchen.

"What's the matter?" He asked her.

"Just when you think you've seen everything. You get reminded you haven't."

"Heh?"

"He took a whole stick of butter, rubbed it all over himself and is jumping wrestling moves on the couch in his underwear."

"At least he kept his drawers on." He assured her.

"You goin' grocery shopping today?"

"Yeah."

"Add butter to the list. We're out."

Grampa got in his beat-up old car and headed out to the grocery store. On his way he saw a man at a stop with a sign around his neck that read, *Hungree. Pleez Help*. When he got to the market, he picked up everything on the list plus an extra sandwich to give to the guy. He drove back to the same stop. No bum. He looked around, saw people walking along the sidewalk, few cars around. No bum. He decided to take a few passes around the blocks to see if he would show up. Five, ten, then after fifteen minutes of looking for him, the guy was nowhere to be found. Gramp decided to head home. He started to get a little hungry himself and opened up the sandwich. The store cut it in half so while he was eating one part, he just closed the rest. Two stops later he came across another guy askin'. He rolled his window down and shouted over to him,

"Hey Mac! You want the other half of this? I just bought it."

The guy turned to him,

"No thank you. I don't eat pre-opened food." Then he walked further down the line of cars asking.

That was a change in society Sven had never seen before. Any food during the depression was sent from heaven. When they ran out of MREs during the war they had to butcher a calf out in the woods. Now here's a guy who won't touch an untouched half of sandwich. He thought to himself, *if you were hungry enough, you'd eat it ... (bum).*

Sven got home about a half hour later to find a strange automobile in his driveway. One he didn't recognize from any relative or neighbor. As he pulled in next to it a man stepped out with a giant jovial simper and a very friendly look.

"Good afternoon Sir!" He said.

Grampa had his window down, but he wasn't out of the car yet,

"Good afternoon. What can I do you for?"

"My name is Dennis Lane, and I am with the Kingdom Hall of Jehovah Witness, would you have a moment to converse kind sir?"

"Sure, why not."

Grampa got out of his car and went into the trunk to get the groceries.

"Would you be able to take one of these Dennis? That way we can bring it all in in one trip."

"Absolutely! Your first name sir!"

"Sven."

"Pleasure to meet you Sven."

Dennis eagerly grabbed one of the grocery bags. He was wearing a very conservative brown suit and dark tie on this Saturday afternoon. His shoes were nicely polished, and he was clean shaven. A hint of Old Spice was in the air which was all too familiar. As they walked up the steps to the breezeway door they heard,

"Did you remember to get the ... oh, hello." They caught gramma by surprise.

"Good afternoon ma'am."

"This is Dennis. He's from the Kingdom Hall Witness protection. Givin' me a hand with these bags. Set 'em down right there Dennis and please, have a seat. Can I get you something? Coffee, juice or water?"

"A glass of water would be just fine sir, thank you."

Grampa got two glasses and filled them with ice. Got the water from the tap and gave one to his guest then sat across from him at the kitchen table and said,

"Please continue Mr. Lane."

Dennis took a drink of his water,

"I thank you kindly for inviting me into your home Mr. Sven. I would like to take this opportunity to talk to you today about the glorious attributes that coincides with the congregation of the Jehovah Witness. We are a Bible based denomination that come from hundreds of different ethnic origins and language backgrounds, yet we are unified by similar, common goals. First and foremost, we want to honor Jehovah, the God of the Bible and the creator of all things. We initiate every effort to emulate Jesus Christ and we are honored to be called Christians. It is part of our daily mission to spend quality time assisting people learn about the Bible and God's kingdom, and his heavenly throne."

"Mr. Lane, I sincerely appreciate your enthusiasm and I'm so glad to hear we're on the same team. The only thing is I would hate to waste your time here as we are long time members of a different denomination. We as a family have been a part of Blessed Sacrament for many many years. Our two girls were baptized and went to catechism there. All of my wife's friends are there. Our newest addition is being groomed similarly. He's somewhere around here, I can't keep up with how fast he moves anymore. I just don't want to be misleading to you in any way sir."

Dennis smiled to him,

"I appreciate your hospitality Mr. and Mrs. Sven." Diletta was chopping onions at the counter the whole time pretending not to listen. "You both have been extremely cordial, and I as well am so pleased to hear that we are on the same team. Thank you very much for your time."

Dennis Lane rose from his seat. Shook hands with Sven. Waved to Diletta and was on his way. Sven looked over at her,

"By the way, where the hell is monsignor junior?"

"Where else," she replied. "He went to play hockey with some friend of his."

He rode his bike over to a new friend's house. It was a cottage settled in the woods with a long 850-foot driveway that dipped down at the very end. In the late 1800s it was rendered as the servant's quarters to the manor, but as time moved on and additions were made it now stood as a 3,500 square foot domicile on 25 acres. The kid hadn't seen a home like this before. He walked up to the front door with some reservation. He heard of rich people, but I guess up until now had never met any (or none that he knew of).

Only his new friend Sammy was aware he was coming over. Sammy didn't have the same stringent rules that all guests be required pre-authorization.

The kid knocked on the main door at the same time Sammy's father opened their side porch entrance to let out their dog Oliver. Junior stepped back to wait for Sammy to answer when from his right ear he hears the loudest, deepest heart pounding *woof* of his life. As he turns his head, he sees a giant black 200lb. Newfoundland running straight at him. He froze. Time stood still at that moment except for the mammoth behemoth running full steam. Being about six feet away from the door his only thought was to get inside the house. He ran full throttle into Sammy's front door. Knocked himself out cold. Flat on his back, eyes closed he was brought back to consciousness by long wet licks and drops of drool falling on his cheek and nose. The massive k-9 stood over him in silence and rendered aid as best he could. When he was finally able to open his eyes, Sammy was standing over him as well,

"I see you've met Ollie." He said laughing uncontrollably.

When the kid got his bearings back, he stood up. Almost eye to eye with the largest animal he'd ever been in the presence of.

"Is that? Who is this?" He asked in astonishment, "He's the most beautiful thing I've ever seen. Can I pet him?"

"Sure." Sammy replied, "Oliver's very friendly. And gentle too. He's protective of me and my sister which is why he barked, but once he knows you, he'll love you."

Sammy's dad came running around from the side of the house,

"Hey kid, are you alright? I'm sorry, I didn't know Sammy was having anyone over and I didn't see you at the door otherwise I wouldn't have let him out yet."

"Yes sir, I'm fine."

"We're gonna play street hockey dad."

Sammy walked to his garage to get his sticks and goal net. The kid walked with him gazing at Ollie from a low-angle view and petting him as much as he could.

CH. 11

February 29th of that year General Atkins is briefed by his secretary on his agenda for the day.

"Sir, you have a 9 o'clock with Joint Staff Grogan to go over updated policies. You have a quick 11 o'clock with Mr. Fabersham from ABC news as a follow up to last quarter and a lunch with everyone regarding Avianet that will most likely take you through the rest of the day."

"Thank you, Margaret. What time is it now, almost 8am? Alright, can we get Benjamin on the phone before 9am? He tends to be long winded so *if* you can get him by 8:45am otherwise I'll try again later this evening. I've never had a conversation last only 15 minutes with Benny."

Atkins fulfilled his first two obligations that morning and returned to the oval office for his assembly with the Secretary of Defense Evan Sweeney, the White House Chief of Staff Nells Peeters, the National Security Advisor Owen Nilan and the President of the United States Lawrence

Huntington. He walked into the President's quarters and placed his briefcase alongside the chair he had chosen for the day.

"Good afternoon Mr. President."

"Good afternoon General, please have a seat. The others should be joining us shortly."

"Thank you, sir."

Just then Nilan, Peeters and Sweeney arrived to make their courteous greetings as well. After the President closed the double doors, everyone sat down. He began the day's business at hand.

"Gentleman, shall we. What is our latest update with Avianet? Where are we?"

Atkins was taking lead point on certain measures of this project, so everyone instinctively looked to him first to respond.

"We've presented it to Alan Morris at Vell Labs Tech., Xaviere Lynch at Beacon Development and William Bourque at Ratheon. All have incredibly talented, capable teams. One that has an anomalous flare to it."

"Which one is that?" Sweeney asked.

Atkins continued,

"William says he has a troop that blows the competition away and leaves them in the dust. Unparalleled in intelligence, dedication & instinct."

"I'm glad he's on our side." The President chimed in whenever he felt necessary. "Who is he?"

They all turned back to Atkins again.

"Not a he. A *she*. Her name is Janine Jalinski and I've read the dossier on her."

Atkins gives them the greatest hits that he can remember off the top of his head. Nilan was slightly impressed,

"Don't they all have those credentials. Aren't all those guys (and gal) of that to some varying degree?"

"Yes, to an extent. And then you have to say if there was a league higher who would play in it? The answer here is, *she* would. It's fascinating to read her on the page. You get the same feeling that William talks about. There's a persona there that you can't quite put your finger on. Can't quite verbalize what it is. You just feel it and know."

The President sat back in his chair and listened as the other's discussed Janine's past present and future. Then he interjected with,

"We have to consider our other *friends* across the pond. Their reaction. How will they instinctively respond and if there is any skepticism or negativity how we will address it."

General Atkins concurred with him,

"Yes Mr. President, I've thought about this as well. I think the best (most cautious) approach would be to keep this under our hat for as long as possible. Even as the research and development progresses. What we have here is commonly referred to as a 'little sister' situation. Being that she is a female we have a heightened level of awareness regarding security and safety issues to consider."

"Does she have a family?" The President was first to ask.

"Yes, she has a son. Mother, father and sister. She's divorced and the grandparents have custody of the boy."

"That's different. How old is her son?" Nilan inquired.

"Kindergarten, first grade, what is that? I think 5 or 6."

"That young?"

"Yeah, I know."

That piece of intel was a factor beknown to everyone in the room and did not require any further comment. The President stepped in again,

"I certainly agree with you General. Let's not make an issue of something that isn't currently an issue, and we don't know if it would be."

The rest of the conference commenced as routine. By 4:30pm everyone had dispersed and returned to their prospective offices or homes. President Huntington was staring out of his window by himself concerned with how much more delicate operation Avianet had just become. He didn't let on that he felt this way to the others.

William Bourque went home that same evening and was greeted by his beautiful bleach blonde wife and their housemaid Valencia. Their home is everything you would expect of a CEO. Five massive pillars in the front that were led by a set of stairs that extended over twenty-five feet out. The frontal landscape of the mansion could be a view taken from a picture of a plantation owner in the 17th or 18th century. Precisely landscaped grounds encompassed the residence. One of the first in the area to implement a three-car garage to be built detached and on an angle from the main entrance. Inside the 9000 square foot decadence was Greek marble throughout the entire manor. The residence (and neighborhood for that matter) was intentionally created to mirror that of the Newport summer dwellings of the Carnegies, Mellons and Rockefellers. Only on a slightly smaller scale.

Artwork from the Renaissance period was strategically placed along the hallways. An individual Elizabethan chair or love seat placed in the corner or along the wall would accent the artwork and cathedral like crown molding. Although these seats would never be used functionally. They were strictly aesthetic value only.

The kitchen was equipped with state-of-the-art appliances that provided the most modern room in the house. The living room did have the most sophisticated television and entertainment system to date, just not in line with the décor of the rest of the house. The furniture was kept to the period of the structure, William couldn't stand it. It wasn't exceptionally comfortable to watch television or movies, but he didn't say a word about it. He couldn't (he felt). When they bought the place, he told his wife she could decorate it any way she wanted.

William made every effort to keep his hypocrisy in check. He knew he was just that. Like every other person who breathed oxygen, but he didn't want to be. He didn't enjoy it and to some extent he wouldn't just blow it off depending on the circumstance. He had a level of remorse no matter what. When reflecting upon his life he once thought about what he would do differently if he had the chance to do it all over again. Sure, he was wealthy. Yes, he was powerful and influential. He had a beautiful family (the 2nd time around). He traced his steps, the decisions he made which brought him to where he is today. Graduate school, then a transition to law school. Finishing a law degree only to return and complete a doctoral in business administration. It never hit him at the time, but now he was saying to himself, *What am I? What would Srinivasa Ramanujan say about me? A man who recovered from a case of smallpox at the age of two. Then independently compiled almost 3,900 mathematical identities and equations. Had unconventional and original results in the Ramanujan Prime, Ramanujan theta function, mock theta functions, Ramanujan sum, theorem, and series. All while living under British rule in India and having no formal training in pure mathematics.*

There was a part of William that was unfulfilled. He wanted to create. His entire life, he always reminded himself that he had a finite number of days. He acknowledged the fact that he *allowed* himself to be seduced by the promise of wealth and prosperity. In his mid-twenties, the bright future that was presenting itself was very enticing. People were impressed by his acumen as well as his ability to close a deal. One thing William never did was panic. When the heat got turned up, he would focus. Not allow emotion or surrounding circumstance to cloud his judgement. The powers-to-be took notice of this and groomed him at an early age. It's understandable how he went along with it all. He'll even admit that he wanted it ... then. Only to himself will he now say, *What if? What if I pursued, what if I tried, what if I decided to?* He felt it was too late for him now. Too many people depended on him. Too many expectations of him both professionally and personally that he knew he had to live up to. And he knew he could. He makes every effort to express confidence without seeming haughty. It's a rare breed. So many people feed off their own abilities and talents then grow immodest. They appear to use it as fuel to keep progressing. Especially those in high profile positions. William was making every effort to acknowledge humility when and where he could. And he looked at it as a delicate balance. Too much in the board room and they might try to take advantage of him. Too little at home and he might be on his third wife at some point. His first marriage failed as a result of infidelity. They were married almost twenty years. When it came time to sign the papers it was just a formality by then. His current wife Elisabeth is a striking ornament twenty-five years his junior. They met at a charity event that Ratheon was having when William was a Vice President of the corporation. She had him in her sights and he was completely smitten by her beauty. Another one of those fine examples where there is no correlation between emotion and intelligence. They've only been married about three years. No kids yet and William doesn't know how long he can hold that off. He has four from his previous wife.

The two sat down to dinner together that night in a picture of elegance that few ever experience. Never mind the fact that this was just another Wednesday night. Elisabeth noticed the concern on his face,

"Darling what's troubling you?"

"I want to make sure." He replied.

"Make sure of what?" Elisabeth asked.

"I want to make sure that I am doing enough for our company, our people, our stock-holders our partners of all kinds."

"Oh, I'm sure you are darling. Everyone looks up to you. Everyone admires you. Everyone wants to be near you. They all look to you for direction. You're their leader."

"Yes, but how much of it is real and genuine? I was listening to one of our Vice Presidents give an address to about 70 or 80 employees regarding stream-lining our processes, implementing efficiencies and protocols that will boost productivity."

"Isn't that a good thing? Isn't that what you want dear?"

"Yes of course (if it actually works), and then he called his assistant (I guess you would call him that). That's certainly not his title and pay grade more like an elevated ... *whatever*. The assistant merely repeats everything the Vice President says, *We're going to stream-line our processes and upon stream-lining our processes our processes will become more streamed and thus more aligned.* I sat there thinking (a). is this blatant redundancy a colossal waste of time, energy, and resources? Having someone paid so much money to simply come out and repeat what was said right before them. Are we (I) the fools for paying such a high salary for such a lack of individual thought? And (b). is there a certain element that they, we, I could be insulting the intelligence of our audience? Kind of the way those humanoids insult us on the radio when they ask for money. Do they really believe their audience does not know what a matching donation is? Why do they feel the need to say the words, *Due to a generous benefactor we have the opportunity to match any donation given. That means a $5 donation becomes a $10 donation, a $20 donation becomes a $40 donation.* Last Tuesday I heard one of them use the word *double* instead of *match* and then had the audacity to give monetary examples of what doubling means!"

"Darling, what's really bothering you? You can tell me."

William sat there and looked at his wife. He certainly wanted to be careful with what he said next.

"How much positive effect have I ever really had on people? In a most general sense Elisabeth, have I had an actual positive, lasting impact on any of our 60,000+ employees worldwide? I know I haven't on the one's that have been laid off during my tenure. I'm sure I've created more animosity than I realize. Especially the families that relocated themselves from different states only to be terminated six months later due to a last-minute variance. When poor decisions are made by executives, you know who pays the price. Did you know that laughing (humor) can add time to your life? Think about that. Something that doesn't cost a thing. Makes people feel good, can add to the longevity of your life. Comedy has a medicinal value. A comedian has a similar trait to a surgeon in that aspect (and doesn't risk bankruptcy to his client if he doesn't have insurance). Nine times out of ten the recipient of the comedic stimuli has no idea this is even happening. They only know it's funny. There's a beautiful innocence there. I have a responsibility to shareholders. I have a responsibility to the board. I have a responsibility to the employees. There's a bottom-line factor that is a constant variable. Okay, no problem. Accepted. And then ..."

There was an even longer pause as he stopped eating. Simply held his fork looking at the table setting. Elisabeth was slowly, gradually realizing how important this was to him. Her first responses of commonality were insufficient. Her concern drew more intense,

"And then what William?"

"I can do more. I can do better. I can go further for people. On their behalf. And here's the key, not in a conventional way. Not in the typical, expected business model or behavior that everyone has seen a thousand times over. I'm not talking about the things that work. I'm a huge advocate for the *if it ain't broke don't fix it* mentality (when it's ethical). Also, the *kis* method. Keeping it simple seems to get lost and forgotten daily. I bet Einstein wishes he could stamp that one on the forehead of every ceo, president, dignitary or czar there ever was. One aspect of what I'm talking about right now, encouragement. Encouragement, realization and recognition. Recognition which is authentic. Do you know how many people take what somebody else says and use it as their own to make *themselves* look good. I see it all the time in corporate America. Have for decades. And to be truthful, I've been guilty of it as well on more than one occasion. But can I tell you how much I dislike that behavior (myself included). It lacks any sense of originality. It's rooted in greed and self-absorption. I've turned a blind eye to it my entire professional career. Now here's a question, how do you get people to *want* to give proper recognition? Even harder, how do you get people to *want* to tell the truth. To create a virtuous culture where everyone believes that they *are* their brother's keeper. Think about the psychological difference when you want to see someone else recognized and not yourself. And then, take it to where you're happy if they get the credit for something you've accomplished. How many have ever done that? In our world, they'll (we'll) only do it when money isn't involved. Another aspect, people are so afraid to disagree with one another. Why? Two of our national account sales reps were having lunch together one day. I overheard their conversation. They were discussing their automobiles. One guy said he likes to drive a luxurious Cadillac. He believes in projecting a sense of wealth and success. He said that successful people want to do business with successful people. The other guy drove an old Pontiac. He said it ran fine. Got him to see his clients and then he mentioned the real reason. He said (in not so many words), that he believes people don't want to make a rich person richer. Sort of like, this guy already has it. Why get him more of it. Now here's the most interesting part of the conversation. The two were never willing to disagree with each other regarding their philosophies. It was all that, *Yeah right exactly! Oh, me too! I know it, I know it I'm the same way*. But they weren't the same way. Not on this topic. They had two different beliefs on how to conduct themselves doing the same exact job and they were too scared to say, *I disagree*. As if it were taboo or something. Two grown men should be able to maturely, reasonably disagree and not be afraid that the other will think, *whatever*. Do you agree my love?" He asked his wife playfully.

"William, do you know what you're talking about right now? You're talking about very common human behavior. You walk into any American high school cafeteria what will you see. The jocks sitting with the jocks, the greasers sitting with the greasers. The Latin club members sitting with ... nobody. Why? Because they want to be accepted. It's part of our human make-up. And people are comfortable around other people that are like themselves. Those two guys might have completely different backgrounds. They might have similar backgrounds (who knows) but they have a need and desire of, *I'm like you and you're like me.*"

"You're absolutely right Elisabeth. I couldn't agree more. My question is why. Why does a situation such as this, with the demographic that it is, regress back to adolescence? Why do two grown, educated adults act like children (and not in the innocent virginal way)? It seemed to be a high priority of the popular crowd back in those days. Very conscientious of what to say, how to dress, where to go, who to be seen with. You know that is an inhibitor of creativity. Confining your mind to such will put chains on your potential to create, invent and contrive. But I must admit, we're certainly effected by what our parents simply say to us aren't we, both good and bad. Let's face it. They're people too. They make mistakes. It's how we internalize the information that shows the difference. During the formative years, kids are like a sponge. The mother and father are everything to a child. Their whole universe. Some kids will take everything to heart. Some won't. Are you familiar with Major League Baseball's stolen base leader of all time?"

Elisabeth didn't even stop chewing her food. She wasn't going to even acknowledge that one.

"His name is Raymond Hillandson. He has more stolen bases than anyone else who has ever played the game of baseball. The man is fast. The man is agile. The man is electrifying, but it didn't start out that way. He came from a modest upbringing. An honest, working class family. When he was old enough, he asked if he could play little league. His mother agreed so he was allowed. When the season started, she noticed that he would come back from every game as clean as when he left. He rode his bike home after a Saturday afternoon game and his mother said to him, *You didn't play baseball. No one comes home with a clean uniform if they've played the game.* That was the beginning. That's where it started for him. He cared so much about what his mother said to him. He internalized it. That was the spark that put him on the path (no pun intended)."

"Heh, what?" She asked.

"There are lines from one base to another, they're called the base paths. He would run in between, never mind. That one second of what she said to him and his pure reaction to it took him all over the world. Made him a champion. Provided inspiration and motivation to countless other young aspiring athletes. Think of what wouldn't be if he didn't care about what she thought of him."

"Darling you're putting way too much on yourself. You've hardly touched your food. Please eat before ..."

"You want another one! How about this."

Elisabeth just rolled her eyes and kept eating.

"How do you get people to see past the immediate. As an undergrad I had a few marketing classes. This one professor walked into the classroom one day with a coat hanger. A common everyday coat hanger from the dry cleaners. He said, *I know you all know what this is, but what I want each of you to do is tell us another use for this item.* He handed it to the first kid in the first row and it went to each student one by one. I felt bad for those sitting in the front of the class. They had to think so quick on their feet."

"What did you say when it was passed to you?"

"I got fortunate. When it came to my turn I stood up and said, 'It just so happens that I have this very same device holding up the muffler of my automobile at this very moment'. He and the rest of the class got a kick out of it. Necessity is certainly the mother of invention. The task I place before myself is how do I bleed that into our people. How do I encourage them so that they believe what one person can do another can do. I've got one on my team. She embraces resistance. Most people fear change and adversity. She expects it."

"She? What's her name?"

Elisabeth tried to be discreet, but she was unable to be as subtle as she had hoped. Her eyes widened and she stopped movement.

"Yes dear, she is a she. Please don't think there is anything ..."

"I didn't say anything like that."

"You didn't have to. What's funny is I've been dealing with this issue in some way shape or form for some time now. General Atkins addressed somewhat of a concern. I can only imagine where your mind will go with it, but please know there is nothing, absolutely nothing going on."

"I apologize if I gave you that impression William. I trust you completely."

"Thank you, sweetheart face. No, it's just a matter of fact that she is smarter than everyone else and she incorporates the unfamiliar and the unusual. She thinks in a way that most people don't while having the tools to create and accomplish what has never been done before. What I place before myself is how do I get others to believe that they can accomplish the extraordinary as well. A lot (or maybe all) of what this woman has is what people will say can't be taught. And I'm sure to some extent they're right, but what if we can tap into just another 1% or 2% of our capability. It is believed that the average person uses 4-5% of their brain. Einstein uses 6-7%. If we can find a way to tap into just one more percent or even half a percent. We could be that much closer to a utopian society."

"You're impressed with her William. I'm actually extremely proud of you for that."

"And I'm impressed with you, my love."

The two had a thing where they would talk to each other as if they were in a Mumphrey Boogard movie.

William didn't want to go on and on about another woman to his wife, so he gradually changed the subject and asked Elisabeth about her day's events. She got into specific detail of what happened at the homeless shelter where she volunteered. He tried to pay attention and appear interested as much as he could although his mind was elsewhere. Elisabeth could sense this, although she didn't want to push him too much, so she let it go. Dinner ended with a creme' brulee that was given the attention of vanilla seeds at the bottom of the ramekin. The two retired for the evening as the staff diligently scurried to clean as fast as they could and reach their families at a decent hour. That night in bed William was watching his wife brush her velvet hair at her personal vanity. The soft glow of the dimmed light from the mirror gave her even more beauty as the shadows reflected her cheek bones and profile. She knew he was waiting for her. The anticipation was part of the fun for both of them. When she finished grooming herself, she would intentionally flutter across the bedroom floor to turn the ceiling light off. She knew how much he enjoyed seeing her silk pajamas and robe trail in the wind when she moved. Sometimes she would go into the adjacent bathroom again just to give him a little more.

“Good night honey."

"Good night darling. My sweet prince, until the morrow."

Then they giggled like school kids and went to sleep.

CH. 12

President Huntington had an earlier than normal wake up call to provide a courtesy and allow for the time difference for his telephone conference with Chairman Zhangwei of The People's Republic of China. Ever since his Vice Presidency he had made it a point to learn as much Chinese as he could. After his election to the Presidency his technique for doing so made the first lady completely irate. He would tape Chinese words that had their definition and pronunciation on an itty-bitty piece of paper and have them up all over the White House. There were words taped to the light switch of every bathroom in the East wing. The Oval Office, Cabinet Room, Situation Room and Roosevelt Room each had these words scattered throughout the nooks and crannies. They wouldn't be noticeable from far away, but up close they were apparent. It wasn't until the second time he was entertaining dignitaries from a foreign country that he was tightly reminded to at least remove his words temporarily at the risk of appearing rude to their guests. His wife said it in a way he could understand,

"Lawrence. You can put your words back up after they leave. It looks terrible that you have guests and are not putting forth any effort to learn *their* language."

He agreed with her so after that he had to make a special request that someone take his words down and then put them back up again. He hated to ask such a thing of his staff so whoever did it got a little extra in their stocking at Christmas.

The President continued to prepare and at the beginning of the call it was,

"Dongshi zhang ni hao Zhangwei (hello Chairman Zhangwei)."

"Zong tong ni hao Huntington (hello President Huntington). Ni de zhongwen Yue lai yue hao (your Chinese is getting much better)."

"Feichang ganxie ni (thank you very much)."

After a few more pleasantries were exchanged, and courtesies provided the President asked that the interpreter be brought in to assist.

"Chairman Wei, I consider it a privilege to be able to speak with you again. It is my sincere hope and desire to resume harmonious relations between the United States and China after an all too long venture of diplomatic separation between our two nations." The President's interpreter clicked on the line and spoke his words in perfect translation and accent. Upon return with Chairman Wei's response he replied,

"I couldn't agree more. Any suggestions you may have I am more than open to."

"With your permission Chairman I would aspire to meet with you in your beautiful country and discuss such matters in person."

Wei replied, "I and my associates will welcome you with open arms. Whatever dates and times you request I assure you our staff will be prepared to accommodate."

"Once again, Feichang ganxie ni Chairman. I look forward to meeting you and your colleagues. I'll have my secretary coordinate the arrangements with your staff."

"I as well President Huntington. Very good sir."

They each hung up the phone at the same time. Owen Nilan had been briefed about this call prior and was requested to attend.

"How'd it go?" He asked.

The President paused for a moment then,

"Someone else be the first to tell my wife, we're goin' to China!"

Nilan had been prepared for such an event for quite some time. He was there when then Vice President Huntington first insinuated to establishing a new relationship with the People's Republic of China. Over the years Nilan had flown on secret diplomatic missions to Beijing.

"We're making progress toward your vision aren't we Mr. President."

"I certainly hope so my friend. Shirley, do you have a minute (he hit his phone buzzer). Could you come in here please?"

"Yes, Mister President."

The President's personal secretary walked in with pen and pad in hand and an unsurpassed attention to detail look about her.

"Shirley, could you please coordinate a conference with General Atkins, Mr. Sweeney, Peeters and Manchaca. Just to give you a heads up we're going to be coordinating a trip to China sometime in the next few months. Please don't mention it to anyone on the phone when you call. I want to see the looks on their faces when I spring it on them."

"Very good sir," Shirley replied while writing her notes down then returned to her desk.

The President's personal secretary coordinated with each member and two days later they all reconvened. The President kicked off the proceedings with,

"Gentleman, we shall begin to prepare for a week that will reshape *the everything*." They all looked at one another. Atkins being of a genial spirit smiled and said, "Again?"

"Yes sir. I want you all to be the first to know. We're coordinating a visit to China. I want to know all your thoughts, hesitations, reservations, enthusiasms, predictions. Everything that comes to mind with this."

There was a slight pause in the room until Sweeney broke the silence,

"This will end over two decades of no communication or diplomatic ties with us and them."

"Yes, it will. It's been something I've been thinking about for years ever since the cold war started. I kept it to myself back then. Heck, I'm sure no one would have listened to me any way as a fledgling. Now it's come to discernment."

Atkins knew the president well and he knew how intelligent Nilan was. He saw the writing on the wall.

"This will attain more influence with the Soviets. With our best form we could change the trajectory for numerous future generations."

"We've worked together so long now we start to think alike don't we General."

"We certainly do sir."

Nilan then added,

"The American public hasn't viewed images of China in decades. Will the First Lady be willing to tour schools, factories and hospitals to promote cohesion?"

"She better! If she doesn't, I'm cutting up her Macy's and Bloomingdale's cards."

They all gave a little laugh then,

"Sir, may I ask?" Sweeney always asked permission before presenting a question, "would this visit be a time to or not to present our global communication initiative?"

"I've thought about that extensively as well. And to answer your question right now, I don't know. Is it too soon, possibly. Is it the perfect time, possibly. Do we present just a taste, possibly (keep it at the 50,000-foot-level). I would request each of your input regarding this issue. You're all involved and have valuable recommendations."

Sweeney contributed by saying,

"The Chinese economy is dominated by state ownership and central planning. Their GDP per capita is growing at a rate of 2.9% per year on average. They have neighboring capitalist countries in Japan and South Korea. If we hint to them to turn toward a market-oriented reform, possibly the de-collectivization of agriculture and opening up to foreign investment. We won't even mention avenues with privatization and contracting out the state-owned industry. What we look for is their reaction. Will they have a willingness? If so, perhaps we mention it abstractly or obscurely. The slightest breath of what we hope to provide for all citizens."

"Why Mr. Sweeney that was much more dramatic than usual. I enjoyed both its content and presentation, *Bravo!*" Atkins voiced his genuine appreciation.

"Thank you. Thank you. I felt the need and desire to stay within our theme of changing everything in a week."

The whole room was laughing so hard the military guards outside the doors just looked at each other as if to say, *here we go again*.

After the volume level returned to its original state President Huntington turned to his security advisor and said,

"Mr. Nilan, your thoughts if you please."

Nilan re-adjusted himself in his seat to provide his reply,

"I'm sure you all know by now I believe it is our responsibility to provide our people from where they are to where they have yet to be. For some, an unfathomable advance. If we're too ambitious in our responses, we will pique a curiosity and then risk being thought of as untrustworthy. If we don't give disclosure, I don't know. The Chinese are very astute as are the Soviets, and they might even be a bit more intuitive. I've always veered toward the side of caution and sometimes it has been to my detriment."

"What would Immanuel Kant have to say Owen?"

Mr. Peeters knew that Nilan was a voracious reader and philosophical views were a special forte of his.

“Ha ha, in his essay Perpetual Peace he argued that it would eventually come to the world in one of two ways. Either by human insight or by conflicts and catastrophes of a magnitude that will leave humanity with no other choice.”

"Are we at such a juncture Owen?” The President asked.

"I believe we are, sir. Blessed are those whose leaders can look providence in the eye without recoil but also without attempting to play God. And isn’t it one of history’s tremendous ironies that communism, advertised as a classless society, tends to breed an entitled class of feudal proportions. I certainly hope that their tumultuous history has taught them that not every predicament has a solution and that too great an emphasis on total mastery over specific events might upset the harmony of the universe. A lesson I would have thought was learned with the sparrow incident not too long ago.”

Sweeney needed a refresher,

“How many did they lose during that one?”

“The numbers we got were never confirmed, but that ecological unbalance resulted in somewhere between 15 and 45 million of their people dying from starvation.”

“Man, that’s a lot of people and an exceptionally hard way to go,” Manchaca came in with. “So slow and painful. Watching it happen day by day. I want to go quick, fast in the blink of eye.”

“Don’t we all.” Huntington confirmed.

When he felt he wouldn’t interrupt, Nilan continued with his synopsis,

“Information is continually becoming more and more accessible and with the implementation of Avianet, communication will be instantaneous among the masses. There appears to be a diminution of focus on its significance, or perhaps even on the definition of what is significant. This dynamic may inspire their policymakers to wait for an issue to present itself rather than anticipate one, and to regard moments of decision as a series of isolated events rather than part of a continuance. When this happens, manipulation of information replaces reflection as the primary policy tool. What I suggest is that we prolong the inevitable from occurring. And keep in mind. The Soviet Union will never be constrained by agreements. It only understands the language of counterpoised force. In effect, none of the more important nations which are to build a new world order have had any true prior involvement with a multi-state system. Never before has a new world order been collected from so many various perceptions or on such a large scale. Knowledge from books provides an experience different than any other. There is no interference. Both China and The Soviet Union have highly regulated the literature it allows its population. That which we propose will be monumentously more difficult to govern. Reading can be very time consuming. To be more enticing, style is implemented and valued. Due to the fact that reading all of the books on a given subject is not possible much less the entirety of books, or to easily organize everything one has read, learning from books places a premium on conceptual thinking. The ability to acknowledge comparable information or events and project patterns. Style being the ingredient which propels the reader into a relationship with the author. The acquisition of our agenda is exceedingly contrary to their centuries of format."

Arrangements were requested and confirmed for the United States dignitaries to meet with the Chinese regime. Itineraries were set and the departure date was close at hand. President Huntington gave a formal announcement to the American media two weeks prior to the scheduled egress.

"My fellow Americans. It is with great pleasure and fulfillment that I inform you that members of the White House staff and I will have the distinct privilege to meet with Chairman Zhangwei and Premier Li Wei of the People's Republic of China. We will do so in their native country as they have been gracious and receptive to our request to converge. Our desire to improve relations with the People's Republic of China has been met with mutual eagerness as well as optimistic overview. It is believed by both parties that this rendezvous is long overdue. The Chinese military and political embodiment have extended courtesies and hospitality to our staff and I, for which we are extremely grateful. The United States has and always will go to great measures to ensure, promote, and protect a global standard of peace and civility. These proceedings have every expectation of continuing and embracing this standard. As a prelude to our forthcoming departure, I sent Dr. Owen Nilan. The director of National Security Affairs to Peking amidst his recent world tour for the basis of having preliminary in person communication with both Chairman Zhangwei and Premier Li Wei. The assembly with the leaders of China and the United States is to seek the normalization of relations between the two countries and to exchange views on questions of concerns of the two sides. In expectancy of the assured conjecture that will accompany this address, I want to put our policy in the clearest possible context. Our measures in seeking a new relationship with the People's Republic of China will not be at the outlay of our old allies. It is not governed at any other nation. The United States seeks companionable relations with all nations. Any country can be our ally without being any other countries' enemy. I have taken this action because of my profound conviction that all nations will benefit from a reduction of tensions and a better relationship between the U.S. and China. It is in this essence that I will undertake what I deeply desire will become a journey for peace. Peace not just for our generation, but for many future generations on this globe we share together. I thank you. May God bless you and may God bless the United States of America. Good night."

When the Huntington administration was met in Shanghai, they were greeted with a fairly small crowd to include a few members of the Chinese honor guard. After so many years of hostilities the anticipated reception was admittedly greater than its actuality. The first few days were spent socializing with mid-level notables of the Chinese government. The American entourage was taken to the

Great Wall, The Forbidden City and Emporer Qinshihuang's Mausoleum Site Museum.

As soon as President Huntington arrived at the Chinese capital of Beijing Chairman Zhangwei invited him for a quick meeting. Zhangwei was never a man of elegant, elongated conversations. His tough and ruthless upbringing from peasant decent came through in his vernacular. Short, non-descript responses while varying from topic to topic proved to be a very skillful performance. In an easily misunderstood and unorthodox way he had set forth the main lines of Chinese policy. He had made clear the features that he considered most important, and that other ideas and hopes could fall into place.

Most meetings throughout the venture were held with Chinese Premier Li Wei who presented a persona in significant contrast to that of the Chairman. His refinement and Mandarin quality were apparent in both his speech and mannerism. He was more versed in English than Zhangwei and even made an effort to tell a couple jokes during their time together.

The first lady was escorted with great care and attention during the entire trip. In the course of a few of the President's political summits she was individually accompanied to the nearby primary schools of China where six and seven year old's curriculum was principally focused on the big two, Chinese and math. The children often sat and stared at her in fascination as if to be saying, *who in the world is this and why is she here?*

CH. 13

Upon Ted's first invitation inside Janine's apartment, he found the usual items and appliances. Television, couch, coffee table and refrigerator. He also paid attention to the artwork on the walls and the pictures strategically placed. No pictures of a son anywhere.

"Can I get you something to drink? Juice, water, coke no ice?" She said with a convivial tone.

"Coke would be great. Thank you."

"Have a seat, make yourself at home. I'm just going to put the pot on for tea. I'll be over in a minute."

Ted sat on the end of the couch. His head was at the same height as the lamp on the end table. When the tea was ready, she presented the beverages on a delightful floral pattern tray she got as a wedding gift so many years ago. She smiled so contently as she placed the tray on the little coffee table.

"This is a swell apartment you have. Did you decorate it yourself?" he asked her.

"Thank you. Well, kind of but not really. I don't have a flare (or much interest for that matter) in interior decorating. I got a couple of magazines, looked at complete rooms that were decorated and just bought it. I can't take any credit for any mix n match décor."

"Well, it's all very pretty. I just have one question." Ted paused as he poured his drink into his glass. "What in the world is that?"

Ted pointed, but Janine's eyes didn't follow his finger. She knew exactly what he was asking about.

"Those are my little soldiers." She said while taking a dainty sip.

"Little soldiers, an ant colony? Okay. Rock n roll! Quite a few questions come to mind, but I guess I'll start with the most obvious. Why do you have an ant colony in your living room?"

"I study their behavior."

"You study their behavior? Alright, I'll bite." (they were both still twinkling at one another) "Why do you study their behavior?"

"I've done it for quite a few years now. Ant behavior has proven to be quite inspirational in both computer science and operations research. The Ant Colony Optimization algorithm is a probabilistic technique for solving computational problems that can be deduced to finding good paths through graphs."

Ted got that feeling again that he was simply in an all-together different association intellectually, but he was determined to give it that 'ol college try and stay in the game.

"I'm gonna do my best here to keep up with you. Please forgive me where I go astray, make a mistake or flat out have no clue what I am talking about."

Janine smiled cute and softly at him as she took another sip of her tea. She knew he was making every effort to contribute on a highly technical plateau.

"I understand that probability is a numerical description of how likely an event is to occur or how likely it is that a proposition is true. I believe the probability is characterized as a number between 0 and 1 where, (generally speaking) 0 indicates impossibility and 1 indicates certainty. The higher the probability of an event, the more likely it is that the event will occur. How am I doing so far?" Ted knew he was right; he was just doing his best to keep things light and social.

"You are absolutely correct."

"Whew, okay and a graph (as it pertains in mathematics) is a structure amounting to a set of objects in which some pairs of the objects are in some sense 'related' to one another."

"Precisely! The objects correspond to mathematical abstractions called vertices and each of the related pairs of vertices is called an edge."

"You lost me at abstractions, no pun intended." He said seriously but she got a kick out of it and started to laugh. When Janine realized this, she immediately took another sip of tea to cover up her grinning.

"So, I guess my first set of questions begins with, why ants? What is it about the way they perform that ignites inspiration?"

"Excellent question." And she was being sincere (not in the same way some greasy insurance salesman tries to stroke the ego of a client). "The main quality of the colony of insects, ants or bees lies in the fact that they are part of a self-organized group in which the key is simplicity. Everyday ants solve complex problems due to the sum of simple interactions. They lay down pheromones directing each other to resources while exploring their environment. Their behavior has proven instrumental in some metaheuristic optimizations."

"Yep, that's where I need help again." Ted knew better than to bluff at this point. "What are metaheuristic optimizations?"

"A metaheuristic is a higher-level procedure or *heuristic* that is designed to find, generate or select a partial search algorithm which may provide a sufficiently good solution to an optimization problem. It's especially useful with incomplete or imperfect data or limited computation capacity."

Ted looked down at his glass and reached to take a drink,

"It's amazing." He said.

"What's that?"

"The core of it. The whole reason why they are studied and used in the first place is because of their simplicity. As we progress in our example (here it is our conversation), we get more and more complex. I imagine in your research it gets exponentially more compounded as you dive further into it and then at some point revert back to some trivial component that provides a breakthrough which then starts on another path of complexity until a final outcome is reached."

"You get it! You understand it completely!"

"Oh, I understand it alright. I understand that after about one week of me trying to do what you do, I would be in a rubberized room in a straight jacket."

"Would you pick up drinking?"

"Heh?"

"Never mind."

"So how do you keep from getting discouraged?" Ted continued, "How do you manage the set-backs? I'm guessing that the re-sets are in overabundance and progression can be painstakingly slow."

"That is very true." She confirmed for him. "And to answer your question, it took me years to come to grips with it. As a child I would get easily frustrated or disappointed regarding problem solving. I must confess I would sometimes express my frustrations in an immature manner such as throwing my chess pieces across the room or dumping my GO stones in the trash. Only to sift through discarded banana peels and apple cores a half hour later."

"Ha! I bet your mumma and puppa chuckled seeing that sequence, *pun intended*!"

"Hee hee! Yes, they did! It wasn't until after freshman year of college that I made (more or less) a paradigm shift."

"How did you do that?" Ted asked.

"I was so terribly homesick that first year. I remember vividly the anxiety the second we pulled up to the campus parking lot. I held it in for as long as I could. My mother and father brought me to the orientation bureau to get my dormitory keys and itinerary. We followed the map to its location. My father took all my luggage and personal items into my room. My mother started making my bed up and then I just lost it! I cried and cried and cried and cried, for what seemed like forever but was probably only 45 minutes. I literally just sat there and cried like a baby in the middle of the floor. Exactly the way parents just let their kids get it out because they know there is nothing really wrong. They just need to get it out of their system."

"So, let me see if I have this picture correct, your mumma is fixing up your room (fresh sheets, pillowcases, dusting etc...), puppa is standing there, by now watching you not knowing what to do for you, and you're just sitting there (presumably criss cross apple sauce) bawling your eyes out."

"Close. By this time my father walked outside into the hallway and was chatting it up with all the other kids moving in. Everybody loves my father. When you meet him, you'll see why."

Ted loved hearing that. He tried to play it cool, but his face got a little red. His pupils dilated and his grin went from ear to ear.

"I had boogies all over, my mother would stop decorating to wipe my nose then go back to it. I didn't socialize with anyone. I hardly said fifteen words to my roommate at the beginning. My awkwardness reared its ugly head from my adolescence. It wasn't until after the fact that I found out there was this other student apparently even more shy and cumbrous than I was. I never knew his name. Never spoke to him once. He rarely ever left his room (at least that's what I heard). Like I said, I was so homesick I would make my way back to my parents' as often as I could. It wasn't until after I started to come out of my shell that I heard this story. From what I understand he insisted upon a single room. I didn't even know it was an option at the time.

Apparently, he would only come out to eat at the cafeteria, attend his mandatory classes or to use the restroom. Other than that, he wouldn't leave his room. No social interaction of any kind. Then one day seemingly unannounced to any faculty member, two long black Lincoln Continentals pulled up to the dormitory. Five men wearing dark grey suits, dark grey coats and dark sunglasses entered the building. They took possession of the young man along with all of his computer hardware, personal items and led him out of the building and into one of the cars. Never to be seen or heard from again."

"What was the reason? What was going on?"

"It appears (by all accounts) that he was trying to penetrate the computer security walls of government entities. Rumor has it he was of the mind (that he believed), they would hire him if he was able to show them that he was able to break through. Thus, being more sophisticated than their current dominion."

"That was his reasoning for doing it?"

"That's what I heard. Funny thing is, he has a point."

"How so?"

"If you do something so creative, so original, so perplexing that they don't know how you did it, yeah they'll probably ask you to come work for them. But if they know how you did it, you're just going to jail. Anyway, that's how it went for most of that first semester. The pain inside was so much that I would skip many classes to go back home to feel good. After that first semester I realized that I could use that pain. That it didn't have to go to waste. To find a way to channel that negative energy into a positive. I sat there in my dorm room. Alone as usual. No one ever preferred to be around me since I was such a kill joy. And I went back to an old equation that at the time I still had not proven. I did everything to embrace the hurt I felt inside. I took that old equation of impedance and I solved it in half an hour. What I couldn't see so many times before became crystal clear. I completed that one and went on to another and another. That day I had solved seven equations that up until that moment had only served as roadblocks. As I continued my studies, I repeatedly worked at trying to perfect this technique. I'm certainly not there yet, but I believe with each trial and tribulation I encounter I can use that to move forward. I guess to answer your question, now I try to use discouragement as motivation. Use a set-back as a set up. Take what appears to be time, energy loss and re-direct it to gain. Look at it as a shame to waste all that negativity. I'm sorry if I got long winded there. I can have a tendency to do that."

"No, no. Not at all. I find it fascinating. Which is to say I find *you* fascinating."

The inculpability of newfound love was apparent although neither would have the forthright to mention such a thing so soon. They continued to talk over short bread cookies, tea and cola. Ted had been holding off on telling her about the loss of his job. And the way things were going this day he didn't want a change of direction. He was worried such news might cause her to re-evaluate him as a prospect. In hopes of avoiding this level of uncomfort, he made an attempt to impress.

"May I ask, are you familiar with Herman Hollerith's application of the punched card equipment used for the 1890 United States census?"

Janine being well versed in all aspects of I.T. she was more than familiar with the origins of data processing and its evolution. Knowing this was Ted's area of expertise and getting the feeling that he wanted to spread his peacock feathers, she downplayed her knowledge of the field.

"I vaguely remember hearing something about it in college. Please, refresh my memory."

"Oh, it's especially interesting. Herman Hollerith was ahead of his time. He was a businessman, inventor and statistician who developed an electro-mechanical tabulating machine for punched cards to assist in summarizing information."

"Really? That is interesting. He seems to be a pioneer for his day." (She was making every effort not to sound condescending, and it was working)

"Yes! Using Hollerith's punch card equipment, the census office was able to complete tabulating most of the 1890 census data in two to three years. Comparatively, the 1880 census took 7-8 years to complete and there were twice as many questions. It is estimated that using Hollerith's system saved about $5 million dollars in processing costs."

"It sounds like Herman had vision, intelligence and guts."

"Yes, he did."

"And the latter being the key to it." She said while taking another sip of tea.

Ted was surprised that she would say such a thing. Even the fact of acknowledging courage as a virtue was extremely rare among his male counterparts. Here was a woman saying how important it is to face your fears.

"That's why we can't be afraid to fail." She included, "And to the contrary, we should expect it. Learn from it. Use it. Take an appreciation of the humility that is derived from failure and use it to move forward. That's what it appears your Mr. Hollerith did. That is certainly what our Mr. Edison and Mr. Lincoln did."

"Didn't Edison have over 10,000 attempts before developing the light bulb?"

"It's unknown how many attempts he made, but it was certainly over 1,000 and that on its own is a definition of persistence."

"I'm unfamiliar with the failures or setbacks of Lincoln. I'm guessing they were in abundance."

"Yeah, it's amazing. Here's a man who in 1831 loses his job. In 1832 gets defeated in a run for Illinois State Legislature. 1833 fails in business. 1834 he gets a little taste of success as he's elected to the Illinois State Legislature. In 1835 his sweetheart dies. In 1836 he has a nervous breakdown (and understandably so). 1838 he's defeated for Illinois House Speaker. 1840 He's defeated for Elector. In 1843 gets defeated in a run for Congressional nomination. 1846 has another little snippet of success where he is elected to Congress. 1848 it's back to reality when he's defeated for Congress. In 1855 he gets beaten again in a run for the

Senate. In 1856 he gets defeated for the Vice Presidency. 1859 one more beating in a run for the Senate. But then, finally in 1860 he's elected as our 16th President of the United States. And he's known (remembered) as one of our greatest leaders of all time."

"Let me ask you this." Ted wanted to get dynamically philosophical. "Do you believe we choose our destiny, or our destiny chooses us?"

"Are you familiar with the Old Testament?" She asked in sincerity.

Ted knew that this was neither the time nor the place to tell her his theological posture. The challenge he felt was to make sure he didn't say anything decisive. He didn't want her to think *he believes this, it will never work.* He came up with the most generic response he could think of.

"I believe the Old Testament and The Torah are the same book. Judaism and Christianity separate at the New Testament."

"The Torah does contain the first five books of the Hebrew Bible. As it applies to destiny I think of the story of Joseph."

Ted just kept sipping his drink to make sure she kept talking.

"Joseph was a young son of Jacob and Rachel. Jacob displayed additional affection to Joseph which prompted feelings of jealousy within his brothers, primarily the sons of Jacob's other wife,_Leah. These ill feelings were exacerbated when Joseph told his brothers two dreams he had. Dreams that portrayed him governing over his brothers. In the first, the brothers were gathering wheat in the field. The brothers' bundles had bowed to Joseph's bundle. In the second dream Joseph envisioned the sun, the moon and eleven stars symbolizing his parents and brothers bowing down to him. Soon thereafter when Joseph was seventeen, tensions with his brothers had come to a summit. One day, Jacob directed Joseph to visit his brothers in a town called Shechem, where they were tending their sheep. Joseph, always abiding his father's instructions did as he was told. The brothers viewed this as an opportunity of dominance over Joseph and threw him (unsuspecting of it all) into a pit. A short time later they spotted an Arab caravan passing by. His brothers sold Joseph to the traders. He was eventually ushered to Egypt where he was sold to Potiphar, one of Pharaoh's ministers. For a while, things started looking up for the young lad. He had experienced what is referred to as *Divine Success*. By this I mean he had the talent to read dreams. He read the dreams of Pharaoh's ministers and Pharaoh himself. This brought him favor in his master's eyes and he was eventually appointed head of Potiphar's estate. Unfortunately, this didn't last very long. Joseph had more hardship on the horizon. You see, Joseph was devastatingly handsome."

Ted had to chime in at this point to make sure he was paying attention. "So, this guy's got the ability to read dreams of the most authoritative figures in the land. Now you tell me he's extremely attractive. I can see where this is going."

"Oh yes." She took another sip of tea, "Potiphar's wife had a strong desire to be intimate with him. Here's where it gets worse for Joseph, he turned her down. Continually refused her aggressions towards him."

"He's a stronger man than most."

"Yes, and he didn't want to betray his master either. One day when no one was home (other than the two of them) the mistress seized Joseph's robe demanding that he consent to her. He slipped out of his garment and ran outside. Everyone must have known all that he was going through as this self-control earned him the appellation, *Joseph The Righteous*. Of course, Potiphar's wife did not handle this rejection very well and she lied to her husband telling him it was Joseph that tried to entice her. An angry Potiphar reacted by placing an innocent Guiseppe in prison."

"Guiseppe?"

"That's Italian for Joseph. So, while he's in prison his charm and charisma followed him along and the warden took a liking to him making him his personal assistant. Shortly thereafter his unique capabilities expressed themselves once again. The King's royal cup bearer and baker were amazed. Joseph successfully interpreted the dreams and was able to correctly forecast that the cup bearer would be released, and the baker hanged. Two years later the King Pharaoh visualized 2 dreams himself. None of which his own advisors were able to decipher. Remembering the youth from when he was in prison the cup bearer suggested that Joseph be summoned. Joseph, I believe to be thirty years old by now, interpreted Pharaoh's dreams as being a Divine prediction for seven years of abundance followed by seven years of famine and advised Pharaoh to prepare by storing grain during the first seven prosperous years. Pharaoh was so impressed by Joseph's wisdom that he appointed him as his Viceroy. Second only to the King himself and tasked with preparing the nation for the years of famine. The effects of the famine were extremely prevalent in the nearby town of Canaan. Hearing that there was grain stored in Egypt, Joseph's brothers proceeded there to buy food from the Viceroy, having no idea that it was their brother."

"How the tables have turned for Mr. Joseph." Ted wanted her to hear his voice.

"Oh yes."

Then he made his best attempt to provide a moment of levity, "Reminds me of that old adage."

"What's that?" She asked.

"Be good to the people you meet on the way up, 'cuz you're gonna meet the same people on the way down."

Janine giggled politely then continued,

"So Joseph decided to use this as an opportunity to see whether his brothers had any remorse for having sold him. He tests them by having a silver cup planted in the youngest brother's (Benjamin's) grain sac. He has his servants run out and accuse him (them) of stealing the cup. At this point none of them know that the Viceroy is their brother Joseph. He has them all brought before him and he is witness to the loyalty his brother's have toward Benjamin. It is then that Joseph finally reveals himself to his siblings to their astonishment. Jacob's family finally settled in Goshen, Egypt. This all served as the backdrop of Israel's ultimate enslavement in Egypt and the ensuing Exodus."

Ted was blown away. "Your attention to detail is remarkable. If I was telling that story, it wouldn't have been nearly as descriptive."

Then Janine tried to dial it down a notch, "I guess my point here is that (in this scenario) Judaism instructs us that divine destiny and free-choice both exist and that they are not mutually exclusive. Do you enjoy sports? Specifically, football?"

"Yes, very much."

"Are you familiar with the player Beldin Sorensen?"

Ted's ears and eyes light up,

"Beldin is considered to be one of the greatest of all time if not *the* greatest at his position."

"I'm not surprised, and I'll tell you why."

This had Ted's attention 10 times more than the Bible story of Joseph. Janine continued,

"I happened to watch his Hall of Fame speech he presented when he was inducted. He said something so interesting at the beginning of it. He was talking about his childhood and how (technically) he was forbidden to play football by his father. His father believed he was too young at the time. Beldin rebelled and decided to play any way. His words have always stayed with me. He said, *I didn't want to play. I had to play.* At that young age of five or six he had an absolution. A definitive internal direction to the game of football. I'm sure at the time and throughout the years you couldn't have got him *not* to play (sort of like my son with hockey). As the time continuum occurred this man obviously progressed in an exemplary way. His performance earned him a decision to be inaugurated into the highest fellowship for his sport in the land. Here's my question to you, do you believe he was destined to be there, or do you believe the conscious choices he made (hard work ethic, determination, persistence, all of it included) is what got him there?"

Ted took another gulp of his drink because he didn't have an answer right then. He paused for another second and an obscure thought came to mind that he deemed applicable at this time.

"You just made me think of another athletic situation which on the surface appears to be just what we're talking about, but with a twist."

"Please, do tell."

"There's a professional hockey player. Your son may know of him. That is known for his exceptional skating ability. He is often and continually praised for his long strides on the ice, his finesse. He makes it look so effortless when he's out there. The radio or tv announcers will describe him as gliding on air. His skill and agility are unparalleled. The man is also a fantastic goal scorer and play-maker. He plays defense so he has the full ice in front of him whenever he makes a rush. He's certainly *destined* for The Hockey Hall of Fame. Sorry I couldn't think of another word to use there right now."

She smiled, "Quite alright."

"I viewed an interview with this man, and he was specifically asked about how he became such a proficient, efficient and picturesque skater. His response was that it was a, *God given talent*. He said it simply came naturally to him. His own words were that he could sit there and tell you he worked hard and had dedication, but no, it was God given according to him. Not only is this man able to prosper financially from what seemingly comes natural to him. He is the recipient of numerous accolades, awards and recognition. All of which opens doors to a multitude of various opportunities to explore as well as continue to be able to prosper at levels most never reach. This allows him to provide for his family and friends (and whoever else) at such rare levels. And it gets better."

"How so?" She asked.

"He's part of a franchise that has won four Stanley Cup championships in a very short amount of time. Under 10 years I believe. They refer to them as *dynasties* within certain circles. Anyway, this team is loaded with talent. The names on their roster are so deep and wide it's truly remarkable how they put this team together. Then I saw another interview with a player from this same team that was talking about a third member. His own exact words verbatim were, 'he was *born* to be great'."

Janine started to analyze the dichotomy of the statement then said,

"That is extremely entrancing. Here is a man that is exceptionally close to the subject he is referring to. This isn't a case of a fan in the stands or a statistician or even a reporter who follows the game intensely and for many years. Here's an individual who practices with him every day. Presumably rides the train with this man to every contest. Spends multiple hours in hotels, locker rooms and I even imagine at each other's homes during the off season or in social settings. And he is somewhat indirectly acknowledging a deity has pre-ordained this independent for success."

"Not merely success." Ted added, "A level of success that a fraction of a fraction of a fraction ever achieve. How many generations of their offspring will be immune to layoffs or gas shortages or food prices or the economy as a whole. All because they can put a puck in a net better than anybody else."

"Perhaps this could be another way for them to see."

"Who?" Ted asked.

"The atheists." She replied, "Many atheists don't acknowledge God until they're on their death bed. Considering the extreme popularity of sports (athletics in general), this could be a fresh way to get those who deny, to acknowledge and repent ... sooner."

She sensed a feeling of unease in his posture and had to ask,

"Do you have anxiety regarding the future?"

"Wow, that's a new one for me. Nobody ever asked me that before." Ted felt vulnerable, but he didn't want to project weakness in front of her. He knew she was obviously thinking this, so he couldn't lie to her. "Yes, I suppose I do at times. I know how expendable I am so every now and then I think about it. I guess you're gonna be my therapist today."

"Only if I can help." She said smiling, "My mother and father are devoutly religious, as I am as well (I believe). My mother once told me that worrying is an insult to God. I know it's an instinctual reaction at times. We get bombarded with negativity. Just watch the news for ten minutes. That's enough to depress Bozo the clown. We can't let it consume us. Can't let it have room for vacancy. I think of Genesis 4:7 – 'If you do what is right, will you not be accepted? But if you do not do what is right, sin is crouching at your door; it desires to have you, but you must rule over it'. Some versions state 'you must master it'. I think we can take that process and apply it to anything. Sorry, do I sound too over the top right now? I didn't mean to..."

"How do you remember facts and figures so well? Some days I have a hard-enough time remembering where I put my car keys."

"I see it." She said.

"You mean like a photographic memory?"

"My parents had me tested as a child. The analysts referred to it as an eidetic memory. I saw the report that they gave to my mother and father. It stated that, 'Janine appears to have an eidetic memory with traces of hyperthymesia and mnemonism."

"What did they give you for that?"

He was expecting her to say penicillin as he was completely serious, but thinking he was joking she gave a cute cuddly laugh to brighten his mood.

"You have more ability in your little pinky than I have in my entire body." He said to her while looking down and holding his glass.

"No, I don't believe that," she replied with conviction. "We all have special and unique capabilities. To have faith and trust in one's ability you'll just start to scratch the surface of what you can accomplish. To have the faith of a mustard seed."

The last thing she said soft and quietly before finishing her tea.

Ted felt the risk of bringing down the mood, so he quickly switched gears,

"Hey, how about we grab some dinner and maybe a movie?"

The two finished their drinks and had an evening on the town. Not another word like previous was spoken. *It was too good,* he thought.

CH. 14

It was a beautiful Autumn afternoon. The patterns on each leaf were as unique as a snowflake. Multiple shades of yellow, brown, red, amber, and orange. And then when you look closely, the texture and blends of each one displayed their own personality. The smaller ones look like they are the offspring of the larger. Having a distinct similar characteristic on a petal and then showing how different.

This Saturday grampa was in the cellar with his tackle box and a couple of rod and reels leaning against his work bench. The kid had just finished breakfast and saw that the door to the basement was slightly open. Gramma was cleaning up the first round of dirty dishes and then turned to him,

"Finished yet?" She said, not seeing that he had already left the table but forgot to bring his dish, glass, and silverware over to her. "He's determined to put me in an early grave." She said to herself.

He stumbled down the steps after three pancakes, four strips of bacon and cranberry juice. When he turned the corner, he saw Grampa sorting out some lures, hooks, and lines. Right away it was,

"Hep Pop! What's the plan?"

"Well, let me tell you. I just read in the paper that they stocked Elgin Pond not too long ago. What'ya say we go down there and see what we come back with."

This is gonna be one of those good days, the kid thought to himself. He loves to go fishing with Grampa. Everything about it. The preparation. The anticipation. Finding the right spot at the pond and then watching that red and white bulb go under the water because the official war of man vs. fish has begun.

"Oh yeah!" He yelled out, then ran up the stairs to change out of his pajamas and into his dungarees and flannel shirt to match his senior. As he flew past Gramma still at the kitchen sink. She asked, "What's the hurry?"

"We're goin' fishin'!" He exclaimed.

All the gear was set to go and sitting at the foot of the basement steps. The kid flew down there as fast as he could (and almost took a header ... again) and once more made his feeble attempt to carry Grampa's tackle box up the stairs. It's almost as if he doesn't even remember that every time he tries to lift the thing it doesn't budge or he's spazzing out so much that he can't help it. Gramp was right behind him, "Here, you take the rod and reels for us this time. I'll get the box. It's like it has a mind of its own sometimes."

Now I mentioned how much he loved the preparation. That includes putting everything into the car. They had an old Dodge Dart that just wouldn't quit. This thing had that workhorse slant 6 engine (the one that eventually ruined Chrysler because they made it so good no one had to buy a new car). The body of the coupe was rusting out from all the New England winters, but the heart of it was fully intact and purring like a kitten.

As the kid opened the door, the old weathered, ripped, and torn seats had an aroma (to him) that was exponentially better than any other day they were going to the boring 'ol grocery store or old folks' home to visit relatives. This time it had purpose. This time it had spice. This time it was meant for one thing and one thing only, to catch fish.

Gramma had to quickly get some sandwiches together for the two to take.

"Why didn't you tell me yesterday yous was goin' fishin'! I coulda had it all ready by now." She demonstratively proclaimed.

"Musta slipped my mind." Sven said then winked over at the boy.

Now keep in mind, the kid can barely contain himself. He can't get the poles in the trunk fast enough. He's like a dog that jumps into the car and circles around five times then looks at you. Waiting for you to get in and take him, wherever. The sandwiches ain't on his mind. Lunch doesn't exist right now.

They got everything together and started backing out of the driveway. As they pulled away in the faint distance they heard,

"And don't come back empty handed!"

They drove through the back roads of the quaint little town at a blistering 22 mph (no seatbelts for either). The air was cool and crisp. Just a few more miles and they parked along the woods' dirt road that led to Elgin Pond. It's actually more like a lake in size, but for whatever reason it's only been deemed a pond. They got all of the gear out of the car and started walking down the trail.

"What kinda fish we gonna catch today Pop?"

"Only the wet kind."

The two arrived at their spot and began the preliminaries. Night crawlers, the Cadillac of worms appear to be in glorification this day. Gramp got the boys pole set with a bobbin, weight, and worm. The kid planted himself along the banks of the water by the rocks and attempted his first cast. Locked and loaded he drew back his weapon and with a mighty thrust he projected forward a shoulder of iron in expectation of reaching the middle of the entire body of water. The line plopped right in front of him.

"Don't forget to turn the bail over!"

Bail, Bail, Bail, Bail (he thought to himself), *what's the bail?*

"The thin silver handle!" Grampa instructed.

Oh yeah, he finally remembered. Take two. Ready, set *boom!* It's out there.

This is the hard part for the youngster. The wait, and wait, and just a little more ... waiting. What feels like 2 ½ hours (but in reality, is only 5 minutes) makes it a form of torture for the child. And then, just as he's about to put the reel down to go pee in the woods the red and white bulb dipped below the clear fresh water for just a second. A few seconds pass, same thing. It dipped below for just a fraction. Then a third time, *bam!* "Hey Pop! I got one!"

Then with a mighty pull from his 55lb. frame he tried to sink the hook. With all his power reeling back and envisioning landing Dicky Moe to shore on the end of his hook was ... nothing. Not even the night crawler that was baited. He looked over at grampa.

"You gotta give the fish a chance to get it." The senior said.

"I thought I did."

"Ha ha! It's alright. We've got plenty of fat juicy worms." Pop assured him as he re-set his pole.

As the afternoon progressed, it proved to be a productive outing. They each caught a couple of perch, one or two trout and a few crappies. The trophy so far was a 1.25lb small mouth bass that came in towards the end of the afternoon. The sandwiches were long gone, and it was getting close to dinner time. They rustled up the tackle gear and the boy left his line out there unattended for a few minutes. His pole was leaning against the rocks, and he heard the scraping of his reel as it headed toward the water. Jumping over to where it was, he grabbed the handle and started (or rather attempted) to bring this thing in on his own. He fought the beast with everything he had. Grampa had all the gear packed up and the fish in the bucket ready to go home. Junior was sweating profusely trying to get the ornery brute on land. Ten minutes go by, fifteen.

“Think he can break my line?”

“I doubt it. What’d we put, 10, 12lb. test on yours.”

Twenty-five minutes of stop and re-starts got the fish within. Grampa got the net out and walked into the water to get it. The kid looked at the first catfish he ever caught in complete amazement. It almost didn’t even look like a fish to him. To him it looked like a deep, out of space, overturned, hyperventilated, alien monster. They put it in the bucket and headed home for dinner.

Pulling into the driveway and walking into the porch they could smell what gramma was cooking on the stove.

“Everything I got going now goes with fish.” She said, “The vegetables, mashed potatoes. Show me what we got men.”

They planted the bucket of water with creatures in front of them.

“Oh, how beautiful!” Then she reached into the bucket to begin scaling and gutting them for the frying pan. The only one still alive was the catfish.

The following weekend he was scheduled to be with his father. Another late Sunday night was staring at Diletta and Janine. The semi-kidnapping fiasco was still fresh on their mind. Janine decided to stay this time to see when and how Fredo was going to drop off their son. It was long past sundown and Sven was tired. He went to bed around 9:30pm. The two ladies were sitting at the kitchen table when the glare of a pair of headlights shined through the windows and into the house. Fredo went quickly back to his traditional tactics of returning him when he felt like it. This time he brought his new girlfriend with him just because.

“Do you want me to go with you to get him in the house?” Diletta asked her daughter.

“No, I’ll deal with him.” She exhaled.

Janine walked to the porch screen door and stood inside with her arms crossed. Fredo turned the engine off to his van but left the headlights on. As the three of them slowly got out of the vehicle Janine opened the door and stepped outside.

"He still has school bright and early tomorrow morning you know." Janine said to Fredo while returning her arms to the crossed position.

"Hi, Ma!"

"Hi honey."

"Janine, I'd like you to meet Audrey. Audrey, this is my ex-wife, Janine."

"Hello Audrey." Janine replied briskly.

Audrey just nodded in a manner of, *there's no reason for us to be cordial.*

"What's it gonna take?" Janine proclaimed louder than usual, "What's it gonna take to get you to see that it's detrimental to him when you bring him home this late! The teachers have expressed their concerns. It's obvious how tired he is, and it's noticeable in his behavior up until Wednesday. What will it actually take to make you see!"

Fredo didn't say a word just had his hands in his pockets waiting for her to finish. He didn't even have any interest in acknowledging her when out of nowhere,

"Look here psycho!" Audrey yelled out, "You weren't woman enough to keep him and you ain't woman enough to get him back! I see right through this little charade of yours. Fredo is with me. He doesn't want nothin' to do with you no more! Got it! I don't want to hear you flap your trap to him ever again! Understand!" Then Audrey went back into the van staring straight into Janine's eyes.

"Does she think ... she actually believes I want to get back together with you?"

Fredo didn't even look at her,

"I'll see you in two weeks son."

"Okay Dad."

They hugged each other then Fredo and Audrey backed out of the driveway and drove back to Rhode Island. Janine tucked him in and woke him up as best she could in the morning for school. A couple of days later Janine was back at her apartment in the city and had just got home from work. She retrieved her mail from the complexes' community drop box. Walking up the stairs toward her place there was a faint yet odd aroma. One she never encountered before in her building. She entered her apartment and closed the door behind her. Threw her jacket on the couch and the mail on the coffee table. That faint smell had followed her. She sifted through her mail. There was one white 5x8 letter with no return address on it. Just a name ... Audrey. She opened the envelope and took out the card that was inside. There were no words written. Just a thin smear of excrement strategically placed on this inside of the card.

CH. 15

As Ted continued to search for gainful employment, he was met by more resistance than he had anticipated. The interview process was proving to be an exercise in futility. The standard questions were getting more and more mundane and tedious. 'What's your communication style? How do you interact with a manager? How do you deal with stress? What are your problem-solving skills like? Are you organized? Are you good at multi-tasking? Do you work well on teams? Do you work well on a deadline? Where do you see yourself in five years?' On and on, over and over. It was a revolving door that never quit. Finally, at one interview he just snapped,

"In five years! I expect to be president of this entire corporation! Have you ever had someone work their way from lower management to CEO? No? Well get ready 'cuz it's in full effect in this seat! The man with a five-year plan is in hand! Yes sir, cut and dry easy as pie! Just don't tell the current chief I'm gunnin' for him will ya? He might not take it too kindly knowin' that I've got his job in my sights. I'll wait to hear from you with your offer! Please keep in mind what the board intends to provide as stock options in five years as well. With a TTM of a hundred million and an average annual rate of return I intend to double in five years. Year over year. What we have heretofour is an unprecedented growth percentage! It will be often imitated but never duplicated! Inspiration and perspiration! I have nothing to offer but blood toil, tears and sweat. Keepin' body and soul together. Noses to grindstones! We will *be* the Jones'. Loose lips sink ships. The frying pan *and* the fryer!"

After as much animation as he could create, accentuating his voice and timbre. Feeling like he was on stage. Then, he stopped. Picked up his briefcase, jacket and walked out.

It may have turned into a suicide mission, but he felt better than he had in a long time. While walking to his car in the parking lot, he knew this type of behavior was not sustainable in this environment, but why not just enjoy this one a little. What he didn't consciously realize, at this precise moment, was the *ever so slight* chip on his shoulder that he was allowing to form. For so much of his life he was quiet, reserve, and non-confrontational. He had a breath of fresh air and he liked it. Somewhat euphoric. He stopped into a local bakery and picked up a few honey-glazed, a Boston cream and two crullers to go. With an 8oz. carton of milk he took a drive to Harrisville, Rhode Island. The home of one of the greatest penny arcades in New England. He played the Three Wise Owls 10 times. He played Rawhide Pinball 20 times. He even played an original Jennings one arm bandit too many times to count. Never got three in a row and never let his grand demeanor diminish.

On his way back he felt a transition. Nothing extravagant that hit him like a beam or a bolt of lightning. It was slow, subtle and ever so slightly seductive. He was going to make up his own rules now. What was once may or may not be again. If there was a need for the old way sure, it will be utilized. If not, there is a new process and procedure to follow. One question he asked himself, *Why is it so easy to lose money comparatively to making it?* He was asking this both in a general sense and in his personal finances. He was asking, 'What does it seemingly mean when someone can work, save and scrimp for years then make an investment in say a stock, bond, precious metal or real estate only to have it lose 50 or 75% of its value in a couple months. Not talking about fly by night companies that have no history. Solid blue chips that have sound fundamentals and continuous year over year growth. Or precious metals like gold and silver. What does it mean that for 70 years the gold to silver ratio was 20-1 and just in the past three years it expanded to 100-1 where silver takes it on the chin. Who's pulling these strings? Losing it happens so quickly. The road to recovery (if it ever does) takes so long. For the longest time people say to buy real estate, it *never* goes down! That's the kiss of death when you read that in a prominent investment publication. Don't they know you never say never? That's like the year Sports World, Inc. magazine predicted the Boston Red Bombers to win the World Series. Nobody that was a Bombers fan wanted to see that in print. They put the whammy on it before the season even started. Or what about the fact that 95% of the world's population makes less than the equivalent of $10,000 a year. Why is it so lopsided? And what about the dog track? Or gambling in general? It's so much easier to lose comparatively to win. People study their programs to try and handicap the field at the track. *This dogs' a banker. She's got good run-ins. Gimme a dollar tri-key, 3 over 2, 4 and 1.* Or a casino. The forever motto being *the house never loses.* And businesses, what about how quickly and easily it can be for a business to fail versus being a success. Ask that one to anyone who tried to open a restaurant. Then there's those days like an auto repair. It can set a person back five, six or seven months when they are trying to save for retirement. And certainly, the current situation, how is it so easy to lose a job comparatively to getting one.'

He kept asking himself these questions from what he thought was a completely analytical viewpoint and not noticing the intense level of his emotions as he drove home. Over and over in his mind, 'There are the haves and there are the have-nots. Is it time to be on the other side, to be immune to such turmoil as an *economic turndown* or *price fluctuation*.' He saw the pictures and heard the stories of what the Great Depression did to his family. His father's unemployment. The bank foreclosures on his mother and father's home. His uncle's suicide. Relatives' alcoholism. This led him to research other notable depressions throughout history. Starting with the General Crisis of 1640. He read Thomas Hobbes' *Leviathan* regarding how the Ming Province of China went bankrupt and the Stuart Monarchy was in a civil war on three fronts in Ireland, Scotland, and England. Being a history buff, Ted was fascinated how Hobbes created the first recorded explanation of the need for a universal social contract since his book was based on the general misery within society at the time. He went into both the Great Depression of 1837 as well as the Panic of 1837. Finding it interesting that in the same year this depression ended in the United States due to the California gold rush and its 10 times addition to the US gold reserves subsequently followed by a thirty-year period of an extremely prosperous economy. While the panic was a financial crisis built on a speculative real estate market with once again a failure of banks and a record high unemployment level. For some reason, the Long Depression from 1873-1896 didn't have as much interest to him even though many who lived through both the 1930s and it, regarded the Long Depression to have been worse at times.

All of Ted's studies on the subject were leading him to answer one question, *do I want to be subject to the decisions made by those pulling the strings?* His answer was an astounding, *no*.

He got home that evening to look in his refrigerator. Half a quart of milk, 1/3 pound of bologna, pickle jar of mostly juice, two bottles of cola, jar of mayonnaise, and a half a loaf of bread. The pantry had a couple cans of beef stew, corn beef hash, and a bag of rice. His bed wasn't made. The laundry basket was full. The windows of his apartment had dirt and crust of grime on them. The bathroom shower just started its second layer of soap scum and his toothbrush had lost all uniformity within the bristles. He simply thought, *enough is enough.*

He empowered a recruiter to set up interviews for him and hopefully provide insight into the job market and its tendencies. His new best friend was Gus Graham. A fast-talking fast-moving heavy-set associate who never stopped eating. Even in between breakfast, lunch, and dinner he would have twizzlers, pretzels, peanuts, and lollipops. Sometimes even a sandwich to get him through till dinner. He wore the best suits and was always groomed flawlessly. His hair had a luster and shine to it that was noticeable immediately and from across a room. He wore a larger than normal gold pinky ring and drove a silver Coupe de Ville. Their first conversation didn't leave Ted with the highest level of optimism.

"Teddy my boy!"

Gus was the first person to call him Teddy in decades. He didn't care one bit. He figured you can call me Agnes or Muriel if you get me a decent enough job. "I'll shoot ya straight, as I do all my clients. Your resume is nice. Bachelor's degree from Curry College. Multiple years data processing experience. Even experience with Zilker."

Ted couldn't help but ask, "I feel like there's a *but* coming here Gus."

"But you're not currently employed. Many recruiters won't even take on new prospects if they don't have a job."

"I don't understand, why wouldn't they want to work with someone that is actively and eagerly searching for work? If there is a pool of people and 50% currently have a job, the other 50% don't, but are looking, those guys only focus on the 50% that do?"

"Yep. It's the image. They believe that since someone has already hired them, there must be a good reason why. Also, there is an underlying connotation that companies like to take their competitor's work force away from each other. Funny thing is they just end up exchanging employees for a certain amount of time then go back and forth. Not to mention all the ones that end up just strengthening their position with their current employer. That's where guys like me lose big time."

"Let me see if I understand. Is this like those crazy dames that look to see if a guy is wearing a wedding ring?"

Gus took a second then,

"I'm not sure I follow you."

"There appear to be women that will only date married men. They look to see if the man has a wedding ring and they view it as a challenge. Sort of, *I can do better than she can*. They also believe that if someone was willing to marry him, he must be good (at something)."

"I've never heard that analogy Teddy, but yes you are correct."

"Wow, it never stops."

"What's that?"

"The crazy. The crazy never stops."

"Hey, I'm not saying that I won't be able to get you a job. I'm just saying it's going to be a lot harder and will take more time."

"I hear ya, and I don't mean to sound negative. I assure you I don't portray any negativity on an interview. It just seems that I have been surprised more than usual lately. Anything you can do is greatly appreciated."

"You're welcome Teddy. And don't worry, we'll get you somethin'."

Ted left Gus' office that day no more optimistic, but it added a little more gravel to his eye. He was thinking the unprincipled tactics within the corporate world are profound and extensive. There seemingly appears to be no end to it. In every form and in all directions. That old joke, *how do you know when a politician is lying ... his lips are moving*. Does it apply to every office setting as well? How many elections throughout history have been rigged? Maybe the better question is, how many haven't. How easy is it for them when there's a manual count.

In the following weeks he had an interview in which he gave a stellar performance.

"Good morning, Miss Bla ..."

"How do you do Mr. Sullivan?"

"Thank you for meeting with me Miss Bla ..."

He answered all her questions with accuracy and enthusiasm. He prepared well for the meeting so his questions to her were thought provoking, original and creative. He had reviewed the history of the organization and applied it to his process. By the end of the interrogation, he felt confident with his performance. And Miss Bla gave every indication that he would be a perfect fit for the role. Ted did his best not to give any indication of, *I'm probably the most overqualified candidate you've seen for this position.* He knew that it was about three degrees below what he was used to doing, but at this point a job is a job. Two days later he was offered the position and accepted.

CH. 16

Early Saturday morning Ted went to his favorite diner for breakfast. He had been going there for years as he was a creature of habit. Often, he would recognize a few faces just walking in. A few other locals that were known acquaintances but nothing beyond that. He was much more familiar with the waitstaff. As a regular he was always greeted with a friendly word. He got there this Saturday a little later than usual. The breakfast crowd was in abundance. When he walked up the steps to the entrance there was a relatively calm, cool breeze outside. Faint sounds of motor vehicles in the background and a baby crying in a stroller 500 feet away. Nothing overly boisterous. The second he opened the door, *boom!* "Table 4 needs a wipe down!" "Pickin' up an eggs benny!" *Ding!* "Short stack is up for the corner!"

The place was moving in high gear. He walked up to the seating arranger.

"Morning Ted! How are you this bright and shiny day!"

"Good morning Florence. Just fine. How are you?"

"Another day another fifty cents my friend."

"Ha ha! You and me both, sister."

"I think your usual booth is filled right now. Did you want to wait for it or another? Maybe the counter has something right now."

"Yeah, I can read the paper at the counter. Whatever is available."

"Please help yourself."

Flo always enjoyed Ted's company. She would pay him extra attention on more than one occasion.

He walked up to one of the three available stools at the counter service area. He wasn't fond of the swiveling pivot seats. They hurt his back a little, but he had to make do. When he put his neatly folded newspaper in front of him on the counter he was immediately greeted again.

"Mornin' Mister! What'll it be ... the usual?"

"Morning Miss Angela. Yes please, with a side of hollandaise for the fries."

Angela yelled to the kitchen,

"Two over easy, side of beef and a big little big little stack!" (just to play with the cooks). She knew they didn't take verbal orders anymore, but she couldn't resist. She ended it with a softer, "And one tall oj."

Ted smiled and unfolded his newspaper with care. *A wouldn't have it any other way Saturday morning,* he thought.

The headlines on his Boston Globe stated the current unemployment numbers and interest rates. He perused through story after story although couldn't help to be bombarded by the conversation the two-gentleman next to him were having. It was almost as if they were including him, but not.

"These types of people live and breathe under the notion of perception is reality. Live and breathe, heck. Live, breathe and prosper at unprecedented levels. These are people that have a blatant disregard for the truth. Or worse, will mix truth with lies so that they and theirs will benefit. And that's exactly how they justify it. They'll say things like, *This is how I feed my family.* Say it with a smile because in their mind they believe they are noble. Their friends and family think they are superheroes for all they have accomplished and acquired. Especially in business. But here's the kicker, all those friends and family don't know the how."

"What do you mean?"

"They don't know *how* they do it. And what's more, they probably don't even care enough to ask, because there is another underlying variable."

"What's that?"

"There is a direct reflection on them (especially the family member) of how the individual is perceived. Think about this, in the world of financial services, how easy is it to lie, cheat, and steal. The product is an intangible from the start. Just words and numbers on paper. The broker that gets a tip on the inside. The sales manager of an insurance division. Here it is holiday time, and everyone is getting ready to meet friends and family for the annual Christmas party at Cousin Gary's house. Everyone's laughing, smiling, having a grand 'ol time. Conversations within conversations occur. *How's so and so, how's business, how's work?* All of that. A mother doesn't tell Niece Judy that their very successful business executive son who's in the other room wearing a $700 Brooks Brothers suit will lie through his teeth to close a deal. She only talks about his new zip code and the square footage of the new home her darling boy just bought."

"She (most likely) has no idea that her son is so unethical."

"Exactly. She is completely oblivious that her precious has an instinctual willingness to be so amoral. And I imagine (deep down) she doesn't even want to know, because if that information was valued it would reflect poorly on her."

"You make an interesting observation there. What is deemed valuable? What does it truly mean? Are the values of the mother and the business executive such that they both don't even care about the how? Because I'll tell you who does care, God. The executive that says; *look up here, not over there,* motioning with his arm and finger snap. They are the antithesis of an Andrew Myman."

"I've never heard the name. Who is he?"

"Unfortunately, it's a case of who was he. Andrew Myman was murdered when he was a young boy. Around twelve I believe. He was shot 5 times through the stomach by Muslims. He cried out, *I am so afraid, but I cannot deny Jesus Christ! Please don't kill me, but I will not deny him!* They left him on a sidewalk in a pool of his own blood."

"Greed has been around forever hasn't it. Before spices were traded as a currency. I was trying to think of when. When did it all get this way? So topsy turvy. But perhaps it has always been here in some way shape or form. Ever know a guy who always seems to *forget* his wallet when the bar tab comes or has *alligator arms* when the dinner check arrives? It's all calculated. Dare I say, diabolical. And chronological age can have nothing to do with ethical and spiritual maturity or accountability. Say, a couple is invited to attend a seminar regarding time-sharing. They fall for it hook line and sinker. End up buying three of them. Seventeen years later, when they are trying to get out of them and they can't, what do you hear; *It's the damn lawyers! They keep dragging their feet!* They're too proud, too ashamed, too immature to hold themselves accountable for the role they play in the scenario. It's the *presenter's fault* for being so suave in the first place and then it's the *lawyer's fault* for not being able to get them out of it. Just like in Genesis, after they took of the fruit and ate. Adam blamed Eve and Eve blamed the serpent."

"Are you saying we live in a fallen world?"

"Precisely."

"Do you know which regime these people that you speak of are so similar? It was not too long ago."

"Which?"

"The Third Reich. Tell me, how different is a vice president of that investment firm or insurance carrier from that of an SS officer to his immediate subordinates. How different was Uncle Adolf from a CEO today? It is my understanding that their fuhrer never had the guts to even go to Auschwitz or Dachau. To view the horrific results of his policy making. To view the reality of the perception he created. How many CEOs attend massive layoffs? They sit perched high in their office suites gazing out of their windows looking down at all us plebeians and serfs that they so easily label. As they have their conference calls to arbitrarily mandate which quotas will be set and for whom. My label for them is *RWT*."

"What's RWT?"

"Rich white trash. They are the biggest yellow bellies in the league."

"I hear ya, Eichman, Adolf, Mengele and even Eva Braun would sometimes be seen gathering atop some balcony overlooking Bavaria. Certainly, discussing next strategies and demands. All kissing their leader's butt just the way upper management does to those directly above them. It's amazing to even watch the body language. Never mind how they mimic each other in dress and verbiage. Look at the facial gestures and postures. A complete disregard for originality has run amuck."

"Like you said, they lie, cheat, and steal for it. Then in the same breath (and only in certain circles) at the right moment when it's convenient they'll say, *it's only money*. They're not even loyal to *their* master."

"I worked with this one guy (we had just got a new boss). The very next day after our new manager was implemented the first words out of his mouth were; *Aw Bill, he's my main man!* I overheard another manager address her client on the phone. Her voice went up at least two octaves; *Hi, this is Stacy Voss*. After she hung up, her voice immediately returned to her regular, deep, unexciting self. The level of pathetic is ... *pathetic*."

"They're incredibly cunning and intelligent. They'll intentionally ask you something about yourself such as, *What's your favorite music?* So that they can give the impression of having a connection or getting you to speak about what you enjoy. But it's not sincere. It's not real."

"Here's another angle on it, athletics. Somethin' tells me we've only tipped the iceberg. Remember when guys like Red Grange, Sammy Baugh, Dutch Clark, Ernie Nevers, George Trafton and Jim Thorpe played. Not only did they play both offense and defense. They had a full-time job in the off-season."

"Man, how much were the owners exploiting those guys. Like everything else, when it comes down to money (when the zeros add on) they compromise. Compromise their principals. Compromise what they were taught as children. And I'm not talking about missing the mark. We all sin. We all fall short. I'm talking about when did these men stop caring. So many people write it off as, 'Oh well, I already failed. I'm in. Might as well stay the course'. It's being a failure to be in consent with it. To get complacent about it. Succumbing to the low common denominator of societal popularity. I don't care how much fame, money and notoriety. It's not worth it. Think of the blatant hypocrisy of a sports team nowadays that wins so many multiple championships by cheating. All the while preaching hard work, preparation, and integrity in the locker room. The coach is in bed with the owner. The owner is in bed with the commissioner. The commissioner is in bed with the sponsors. The referees are sleeping with all of them. And we (as a society) end up forgetting. Or worse, adopt that mentality of, *if you ain't cheatin' you ain't tryin.* It wouldn't surprise me one bit if they are tellin' each other, *The public has a very short, short-term memory. All they care about is looking up and seeing those banners in the sky.* Do they really believe all the notoriety voids the unethicality?"

"It's only gotten worse hasn't it."

"In what way?"

"Back in the day it was known how corrupt the publican was. It was common knowledge. Their service and dedication to the Roman Republic excluded or flat out voided any meritorious behavior. Whether activities associated with insurance fraud in delivering goods during the Punic Wars or fraudulent practices in trying to get rid of unprofitable public contracts in the provinces. The masses were well versed in their unprincipled functioning and did their best to avoid doing business with them (when possible). Today it's not so obvious. Or perhaps we have allowed ourselves to become so disillusioned, desensitized, and conceding of the behavior. The principles that so many adopt. That it's easier to ask for forgiveness than to ask for permission. Or to blame the postal service for an unpunctual delivery when the individual knows the tardiness is due to their own accord. The actions are committed consciously and with a complete disregard for the truth. They think nothing of displaying irreverence toward the Lord with their *come to Jesus* meetings or even calling someone a god because they have been mentored and progressed up the corporate latter so swiftly. These tyrants are not only well disguised in our society. They are exalted. Put on a pedestal. And as you said, talked about at parties and barbecues as every mother's dream for a son. Here's a question for you, where does it all end?"

"Are you asking my personal opinion?"

"Yeah."

"When the four horsemen ride down."

"Do you have a time and date for this event?"

"So many have tried haven't they. Making their *predictions* and trying to stir up their own personal agendas with a precise hour of the rapture. They need to shut up. They are so foolish for stating their prognostication. They know (or at least they should know) that we are on the Lord's time. They have studied. They have read the text. They know it clearly states no one knows. Not even the angels in heaven know when the Son of Man will return. And yet they continue to try. In a way it reminds me of how so many New Testament theologians revert to the Old Testament in one specific area."

"Which area is that?"

"The tithe. I've heard them make statements that you are *robbing the Lord* if you do not offer the first 10% of your wages. Don't get me wrong, I absolutely believe we are to give to the church, and the more you get the more you owe, but that's a discordant way to put it in my opinion. To say that I am committing an infraction of one of the ten commandments (thou shalt not steal) if I don't give my first 10% to the church. Now here's where it gets even more interesting. These New Testament evangelists never mention 2 Corinthians 9 where the Lord said, "Give what your heart tells you to give." Why is it with money they always and automatically default to the Old Testament? Then the next lesson it's back to the New Testament. It was said that Jesus spoke more about hell than about heaven when he was here the first time. I heard a guy on the radio once say that Jesus spoke more about money than heaven or hell. I suppose we all know the *why* in the equation of the evangelists. The part that gets me is that these ordained preachers, ministers, priests, and reverends have made solemn vows to preach the Gospel. Possible, I say it's different than the individual who proclaims to have visited heaven or hell. Then writes a book about it and keeps all the proceeds."

"One of these days we're gonna see these guys in a commercial on that new-fangled electrical contraption saying; 'Come on down! to Happy Time Insurance Company! We got group life insurance, long term, short term disability coverage. You have a sub-chapter S or an S-corp? We're gonna price appropriately! Don't believe those other carriers. We've got actuaries working 'round the clock. Come on down to Happy Time! I'm Felix Jones! I'm *here,* to make life better ... for *you*!' "

"People never seem to recognize it in themselves, do they. Theologians condemn people for their lifestyle. Never realizing that when they habitually convey scripture inaccurately that *becomes* part of their lifestyle. Or Aunt Betty talking to Cousin Gwendolyn, 'Did you see how so and so, and look at so and so, well *we* never did that.' The hypocrisy never stops does it. All shapes and sizes. I once had to get up and walk out of a service because the Pastor told the flock to, *Just tell the dag gum truth.* Everyone was staring at me as I made my way toward the door. One guy stopped me. He asked, 'Are you alright'? I said no man, I'm not. I came here to hear the word and to praise his name. Not listen to a flirtation with blasphemy. He didn't even know what I was talking about."

"I'll give you an example from my own personal experience. My grandfather had just passed away. I was in the military at the time, and my first sergeant gave me the news. I was able to get immediate bereavement time approved to attend the wake and funeral. Family members came from out of state. I saw cousins who I hadn't seen in years. We all stayed at my grandmother's house the entire time. A day or two before the funeral I see my cousins going through all of our grandparent's dresser drawers. I say to them, 'What on earth are you doing'? 'She can't take it with her Leonard'! They yell back at me. That's how they justified stealing from their own family. And they actually believe they are different than any common thief. My question to them was, if you don't think what you're doing is wrong, why wouldn't you ask her if you can have it."

"That would be too honest wouldn't it."

"Too honest and too open for the opportunity of being told no. No, you can't have my jewelry. I worked hard for it and bought it. So fast forward a few years. My grandmother moves to Florida to be close to her daughters. She is getting up there in years and can't take care of the house anymore by herself. She has her estate set up where she leaves everything to her grandchildren. Me and my two cousins."

"The two that stole from her?"

"Oh yeah. She would never write them out. She said that since her daughters were already taken care of (they were both even on social security by now). Had husbands and homes bought and paid for, that they didn't need money. So, each of us were to get a third. That wasn't fitting for my aunt. Mind you, I found all of this out years later (after the fact). I was 3,000 miles away when it all happened. Anyway, my aunt coerced my grandmother (her mother) to get into the car. She drove her to the lawyer and influenced her to change her will and testament. I don't know how. I don't know what she said to her. All I know is the result. By this time in her life, gramma had full blown dementia."

"You know you probably could have contested the will and won. The second one."

"How so?"

"She was of sound mind and body when she drew up her first one right, to the three grand kids?"

"Yes."

"If there are medical reports stating signs of dementia or mental illness dated after that first will, it could be viable evidence to deem the second one voidable."

"Interesting. Yeah, as I say, all after the fact. So, my aunt forces her hand to sign a new will which leaves it all to her and her sister. Fast forward another few years when gramma passes away. We all went out to dinner the night before the funeral. Aunts, uncles, cousins again and extended family. The mood was light. She lived to be 97 years old so there wasn't too much sadness and grief. I'm sitting next to my cousin. His father is next to him, and my aunt is across from my uncle at the table. Remember, I had no idea what went down at this point. So, I'm talking to the wife of another cousin of mine and I use a phrase in jest. It was from an old favorite show of mine where this guy tries and tries to make it big and just keeps failing."

"What did you say?"

"I said, *You just gave me a million-dollar idea!* Man, all I was talking about was a goofy (nostalgic) way to bring in more patrons to a bar. I said, you set up a house acoustic guitar, amp and microphone. Anyone who wants to can go up and play a song. Maybe you get a free drink if you're good or have to buy a round if you get booed off stage. Ya know, whatever. My uncle immediately turns to my aunt (the one that's now controlling the estate) and says, *million-dollar idea, see Diane.* It confirmed he was feeding her ideas about me, and I just proved his point."

"And let me guess, he's never had the guts to discuss issues of the like to your face."

"Not a one. He assumes I'm frivolous and can't be trusted with money. The irony is that I drive a car that is over twenty years old. I hate to waste anything. I'm ultra conservative. My wife complains all the time how I don't like to spend money on myself."

"Sounds like your uncle flat out doesn't like you. What's that old saying, you wanna hurt someone you hit'em where it really hurts. In their wallet. You gave him an early birthday present."

"And I didn't even have to wrap it."

Ted's food came while he was still trying to read. He politely said thank you at its arrival and continued with his paper. Twenty-five minutes later. Without any indication, from the glare of the sunlight that ricocheted off the mirrors of the restaurant a deep hallowing voice echoed from the back of his left ear.

"Mr. Sullivan, would you have a moment to meet and talk with me and my comrade in the corner seating."

Ted swiveled slightly to his left to find a towering man standing behind him. He was wearing a plaid shirt with dark khaki pants and old worn work boots. He gave a gentle and kind smile to go along with his thick Russian accent as his hand was indicating the location of the booth area he was referring to. He then included, "When you are finished with your breakfast certainly."

Ted looked over and saw another man drinking coffee in a lone corner booth by a window. He appeared smaller in size, but he was sitting down. This man didn't look over. He continued to stare straight ahead or down at his cup. He knew they were both looking over at him, although he gave no concession of any kind.

Ted was completely stunned inside. He stopped chewing his food and didn't realize it. After a couple seconds longer the only words that came to him were,

"Do I know you?"

"No sir. We have never met before. I apologize if I startled you in any way. We would simply like the pleasure of your company for a few minutes."

The man turned to return to his seat then softly said,

"Oh, and my comrade has taken it upon himself to pay your tab with ... how you say, tip included."

There was a calming of Sullivan's nerves as the Russian walked back to where he was sitting. Ted folded his newspaper neatly back up the way he bought it. Taking his few last sips of his juice his hand was shaking bringing the glass to his mouth. His mind was racing. *What could they want with me?* He asked himself. He looked over and noticed the waitress just staring at him. Customers were trying to get her attention to place an order or get a refill. She had them filed elsewhere at the moment. This made him feel mysterious. He never saw anyone look at him that way. Was he even a little (possibly), dangerous in her eyes?

He continued to contemplate how to handle the situation. *What's my next move?* he thought to himself, *What could possibly happen? We're in a public restaurant in broad daylight with about 75 people all around us.* He felt safe enough and walked over to where the two men were sitting.

"Mr. Sullivan, once again a pleasure to make your acquaintance. Please have seat."

The man stood up the second Ted got close to them, and he extended a handshake upon his second introduction.

"My name is Nikolei Turgenev, and this is Vladimir Kuznetsov."

"Very good to meet you Mr. Sullivan." Vladimir said to him while staying sit and extending his handshake as well, but not having the kind facial gestures of Nikolei.

"We realize how peculiar this must be for you. Anything we can offer to put you at ease? Anything more from menu perhaps. Dessert?"

"No, I'm fine thank you," Ted replied. "If you could tell me what this is all about that would help put me at ease." Ted's knees were shaking under the table, but his voice didn't give anything away.

"It is our understanding that you are remarkably close to a certain design. We are simply asking if you would be willing to cooperate in attaining specific information regarding this design."

"Wait, what? What design? How do you guys even know me? How did you know I come to this diner? Is this real?"

Ted was completely baffled. He didn't know a thing about what they were talking about. He wasn't expecting anything, or he didn't know what to expect when he decided to sit down with them. For all intents and purposes, every bit of this was coming out of left field for him.

"I don't mean to brag Mr. Sullivan, but we are very good at what we do. We're very good at finding people. We're very good at finding out about people. I don't want to alarm you. And I don't want to frighten you in any way. We simply want to talk."

As big and robust as Nikolei was, he was the negotiator of the two. He had a way to put a mind at ease much better than Vladimir (and Vlady knew it). That's why Nikolei would always make the first introduction to a target. He would be the one to speak about the what and why of their agenda.

"Is this a shakedown? Is this a squeeze play? If it is, trust me fellas you've got the wrong guy. I'm a data processor that's moonlighting as a glorified data entry at the moment. I'm not in the Irish, Italian or Indian mafia (if there even is such a thing)."

Nikolei looked at Vladimir as if to say, *he doesn't understand.*

"Yes Mr. Sullivan, we know what you do. More importantly, we know where you were previously employed."

That's when it dawned on Ted that he should calm down and talk less (if he could).

"How do you know all of this about me?"

"Mr. Sullivan, it's not hard to trace school records and employment addresses, but that's not why we're here. We're here to simply ask you if you would be willing to provide us with certain information from time to time."

"You mentioned that before. Information. I have no information. Not of value. I have a Plymouth Reliant ... Valiant. What information?"

"Not you Mr. Sullivan. Your associate. A Miss Janine Jalinski is I believe her name."

Ted sat back in his seat. His knees stopped wobbling. He sat there and just looked at the two men sitting across from him as they stared back without a single expression on either. Vladimir felt the need to break the silence,

"She's a very talented young woman isn't she Mr. Sullivan. A very talented, very intelligent young woman."

"Yes, I suppose she is." Ted confirmed to him.

"We're merely asking if you would be able to provide portions of her work to us. In exchange you will be handsomely compensated."

Ted waited. Contemplated a few varying scenarios in his head then,

"How handsome?"

"The details will be worked out at another time. We just wanted to introduce ourselves to you. We can be reached at this number."

Vladimir handed Ted a business card that contained only a hand-written phone number on it. No name. No insignia. Just a white card. The two Bolsheviks stood up from their side of the booth to begin their exit. As Nikolei made his way, Ted was still looking down at the card.

"A pleasure to make your acquaintance Mr. Sullivan."

He smiled at Ted, shook his hand again and the two men proceeded to walk out of the diner.

Ted just sat there staring at the card. He glanced out of the window to view both Nikolei and Vladimir walking toward an old dark brown Chevelle. The only difference he noticed was with Nikolei. He wasn't wearing the same kind, gentle face that he displayed when they first met. He looked very stern and serious. The two men got into the car and drove off. Ted slid to the end of the booth and stood up. For a second, he felt dizzy. Like he lost his center of gravity. Then he was fine. Walking out towards the exit Florence was still at the welcome area.

"Everything alright Ted?" She asked him.

"You betcha Flo. Another day, another seventy-five cents."

On Monday Ted went to his (relatively) new job with a greater level of disdain for it. The monotony of the next eight hours was going to be mind-numbing. People he had only recently met were going to be walking by him and dropping papers into his inbox to be entered into the system. Some would say hi and smile to him. Some would drop off the work without a squint or a sound. Some would stop and chit chat.

"Hey good morning Ted."

"Good morning, Rick."

"Did you see Greyson last night?"

"Jerry Greyson? The vaudeville guy?"

"Yeah, he used to do vaudeville for years now he has his own variety show where he has different skits or situations. I don't know what they really call them. It's kinda like a show within a show."

"No, I've never seen it."

"He's got this one part to the show where he plays a bus driver in New York City and his character is a hot head. Always blowing his top, losing his temper, and getting himself into jams. There's an element to his character that comes up with these *get rich quick* schemes. He gets an idea, runs with it then falls flat on his face. The name of the show is called The Moonlighters and he plays a guy named Rupert Krendall. In the show there are four main players. His wife Agnes (who is a knockout by the way). She has to deal with his crazy hare-brained schemes along with his steaming temper, but she doesn't back down to him. She always stands toe to toe and gives it right back. His best friend lives upstairs with his wife. There's no kids between the two couples. I guess they figure nobody would want to see arguing in front of kids. His friend upstairs is named Elmer and he works in a sewer. Elmer's wife is Tracy and she's a housewife just like Agnes. Elmer is the complete opposite of Rupert. He's always in a good mood. Always laughing. Doesn't let stuff bother him. A happy go-lucky guy. So in last night's show Elmer invites himself to stay for supper (this already has Rupert a bit peeved but Agnes eases his mind and everything is okay ... for the time being). As the three of them are at the dinner table Rupert starts to open his mail. He gets a letter from the IRS. The Tax Department. He's excited and happy at first because he thinks it contains his refund check that he wants to use for a fishing vacation. He opens the envelope very calmly and says, 'There's a letter here, but no check'. Elmer comes in, 'Hey, what's the letter say Rupert'. 'Dear Mr. Krendall, could you kindly be at the office of Mr. Patter at bla bla bla address at this time and date'. Everything is ok, so far. No big deal yet. Elmer and Agnes are eating their food. Rupert hasn't touched a bite. Elmer says, 'Hey whatya' think it is Rupert'. Rupert ..., 'I don't know, I never got one of these before'. Agnes comes in with, 'Well, tomorrow's the 4th you'll find out then'. Rupert again very calmly, quietly raises his eyebrows, 'Can't be anything important'. Agnes ..., 'Oh no honey, I'm sure it isn't. c'mon eat your supper'. A couple more seconds of silence then ... *boom!* Rupert yells out, *'Why could they want me!'* And he slams his hand on the table all the silverware goes up in the air."

"Time out, Time out ... does this story even have a punch line to it?" Ted asked.

"Yeah, yeah, it's comin', it's comin', just givin' ya all the juicy intros. So, it's after dinner and the night goes on and Rupert is still ranting and raving. Agnes is worried he's gonna wake up the neighbors the way he is (so loud). She says to him, 'Rupert, just get a good night's sleep. Everything will work itself out tomorrow. C'mon just go to bed and get a good night's sleep'. Now it's back to being Rupert's turn again. He says, 'Agnes, will you stop telling me that! What do you think is gonna happen? You think I'm gonna walk into their office tomorrow, they shake my hand and say, 'Oh, Mr. Krendall so nice to meet you. Did you get a good night's sleep? Well let's call the whole thing off."

Ted sat there and watched Rick laughing hysterically. *Is this my life now?* He thought to himself. Rick quieted down some then asked him,

"Hey I'm goin' to the sandwich shop next door for lunch if you wanna come." Then walked off. Rick was one of those guys that knew he was a little different to be around but didn't care what people thought of him. Ted returned to his drudgery but had an appreciation for the way Rick was. And at least he made an effort to converse with him. It was more than what anyone else did.

That night Ted thought long and hard concerning his situation. His status in life. His place in society. Sitting at his kitchen table in the dark he saw one small cockroach make its way from the stained floor to in between the crack of the bottom cupboard and wall. Looking up at the clock, it was seven minutes after nine. He took out the business card he was given the morning at the diner from his wallet. Just stared at it. Thinking. Wondering. What if ...

A few minutes passed by in total silence. No next-door neighbor apartment doors slamming shut. No arguing from the couple adjacent to his unit that typically had marathon sessions of back and forth bickering from, 'Who ate the rest of the meat loaf' to 'Why don't you love me anymore' (and everything in between). Their sixteen-year-old son even took the brunt of it one day when he drank his father's beer. His dad was heard all the way down the hall, *Don't drink my beer! Drink the beer I bought you!*

Just then, in the deep still that he was in ... *Ring! Ring!* It surprised him more than any other phone call he had ever received. Made his heart skip two beats.

"Hello?"

"Hey man, watcha doin'?"

"Hey Vernon, just watchin' tv. What's up?"

"I think we need to get Ma some hearing aids. It's been getting worse and worse with her. I'm always repeating myself two or three times every time I go over there. Monica is always yelling when she talks to her. I think maybe it's time. Think it'd be a good thing. I spoke to her. She agreed and is willing to chip in. I looked into it and Medicare won't cover them. If we go in three ways, it will ease the burden. You able to do a third?"

"Yeah, I can help. How much are they?"

"They range from $500 to $5000. Don't know what kind she needs, and I guess we have to get them fitted to her ears. I'll have more details about it next week. I guess to be safe, plan on them being on the high end. So, $1,600 each should cover it."

"Does Monica have $1,600? I know she doesn't make too much as it is." Ted asked his brother.

"No, she doesn't. You and me will have to take care of most of it. Whatever we can get from her will be what it is."

"Yeah, okay."

Vernon expressed his concern,

"Hey, you alright? You don't sound the same.

Anythin' goin' on?"

"No, I'm fine. Just tired is all. Long day." Ted replied.

"Okay, I'll let ya' go. I'll give you a call next week with more details. Night."

"Night Vern."

Ted pressed down on the lever while still holding the receiver in his hand. Staring at the phone number on the business card he was given, he dialed the numbers and cleared his throat again.

"Hello."

"Uh, hello. I was given this number to call. To discuss. A couple of guys gave me this number last week. Not sure if..."

"Mr. Sullivan. Good evening."

A man with a good American accent (while still revealing his Soviet roots) answered the line.

"Yes, this is he." Ted confirmed.

"Thank you for returning our call Mr. Sullivan. Yes, I believe you met with my two associates a past week – end. Would you have time to meet with me in the evening of one night this week? Perhaps Thursday or Friday at 7:30pm.?" The voice requested.

"Yes, I can meet with you. Say Thursday 7:30pm at the diner?"

"If it's alright with you Mr. Sullivan I prefer a new location. Any other public dwelling of your choice."

Ted stood still at this point. He had been pacing back and forth as far as his telephone wire would allow him. He couldn't think of a place. He went blank. Couldn't remember the name of one single restaurant or bar even though he lived in the vicinity of dozens. The voice on the other end finally said,

"How about McGillis? I hear they are famous for their fish and chip."

"Yes. Yes, they are. Very good indeed. See you then."

"Good night Mr. Sullivan."

Mr. Sullivan didn't get much sleep that night. If he was Italian, the bags under his eyes would have been the size of a quarter the next day. He went to work so sluggish that he had his first cup of coffee since finals week his freshman year of college. Nobody at his job paid enough attention to him to notice if he was moving fast, slow, or indifferent. He finished the day without a sound. Nobody said goodbye to him, and he didn't extend the gesture to anyone as he was leaving. He was content with just getting out of there unnoticed.

The following evening, he arrived at McGillis' Irish Pub at 7:20pm. Walking through the double doors the band was setting up on the small home-made stage that was custom built to the area. The place was only at half capacity at this hour. Even though Ted didn't drink he knew Thursday nights were a big night for the younger crowd. They liked to get the weekends started early and Thursdays were it. He looked around. A young couple was shooting pool where the male half was lining up behind her to guide her stroke of the cue. On the other side, a couple of guys throwing darts whereby the sounds of a few expletives it was apparent they had some money riding on the game. A stumbling voice in close proximity proclaimed,

"How much ya chahge atcha bah!"

What looked to be a mechanic just off his shift, picked up the only pay phone in the establishment and answered as if he were an auctioneer,

"Reed Lavaca's Maint'nance. Reed Lavaca here, how's ya cah?"

A few of the waitresses had passed by in view. They tended to their tables and didn't stop to ask him if he wanted to sit anywhere. Ted met eyes with the bartender,

"What can I get you sir?"

"Coca-Cola please. No ice."

The bartender brought him his drink and he paid in cash. After taking a sip he looked around again. At the other end of the bar, in the rear of the establishment, sitting at a two-person table with his back against the wall, was a man wearing a grey tweed flat cap. He looked straight toward Ted and raised his glass to distinguish himself.

He walked over with less anxiety this time. For whatever reason, his nerves weren't at the peak they were on the phone. Arriving at the small table the man stood to greet him.

"Good evening Mr. Sullivan. My name is Ivan. Please have a seat."

The man extended his handshake with his right and motioned to the seat in front of him with his left. Ted sat down without making a sound yet.

"I would offer you this fine American vodka I'm drinking, but it is my understanding that you do not imbibe. Is this true sir?"

"Yes, that is correct. I must say, you guys really know how to do your homework."

"Thank you, Mr. Sullivan. If there is any type of food or drink that you would require during our stay together, please feel free to request it at any time."

"Thank you, Ivan."

"I guess we both know why we're here don't we."

"Yes sir, we do."

"And I imagine you have some questions. Am I right?"

"Yes sir, you are."

"Very good. So please, ask me anything."

"I suppose my first question is what exactly are you looking for? What is it that you would want? To which is it that you seek?"

Ivan sat there listening attentively to the way Ted was speaking. He knew he was nervous. Anxious, but he wanted to make every attempt to put his mind at ease. Establish a rapport with his prospect. Make him as comfortable as he possibly could, mentally and emotionally.

"For our first drop Mr. Sullivan, anything. Anything that you can get. Anything that you can attain in any amount and in any form."

"But what exactly would that be?" Ted asked.

"I'll leave that to you sir. You're certainly much closer to her and her work than I am."

Ted was realizing that it was the X's and O's that they were after. The details of Janine's work.

"And what is your offer Mr. Ivan?"

"For our first experience ... $10,000 American. For whatever you bring us."

Both men went completely silent. In the background was the sound of mic checks. Dishes being washed in the kitchen as the staff was going in and out of the doorway. Conversations and laughter of other patrons while silverware was being placed into the bins. Neither one of them made a crackle until,

"Can I get anyone anything?"

Their waitress who was at eye level to Ivan as they were sitting had just started her shift and was eager to make some tips that night.

"Another vodka for me please Miss. Mr. Sullivan, are you hungry? They have wonderful food here."

Ted was in a daze. Ten grand was almost two years' salary for him right now.

"Coke, please Miss."

And before the waitress could even write it down Ivan added,

"And please withhold the ice for my friend. He drinks it straight."

The young attendant retreated to leave the two alone again.

"May I presume by your silence that we are in agreement for this transaction Mr. Sullivan?"

There was a slight hesitation on Ted's part. He was almost ready to say $15,000, but then he stopped himself. He figured, *why look a gift horse, a bird in the hand*. All of that. Plus, it was more in one lump sum than he had ever received in his life.

"We are in agreement."

"Excellent. When you have what you have, please call this number."

Ivan gave him another plain white business card with a different phone number on it.

"Please don't feel rushed in attaining. Next week, the week after. The week after that. Whatever proves to be more convenient for you. Now that we have business out of the way. Tell me about yourself. What do you like to do for recreation?"

The two men sat together for another hour and a half getting to know each other. Ted talked about himself while trying to reveal as little as possible. Ivan reciprocated and spoke of his childhood in St. Petersburg Russia. Ted asked questions and Ivan obliged each of them. They were developing an affinity with one another. Each man listening attentively to the other and responding with mutual respect and courtesy. When it was apparent the overbearing noise from all the new patrons made it too difficult to have a conversation the two parted ways.

"I look forward to hearing from you Mr. Sullivan." Ivan said with a grin.

"Have a good evening, Ivan."

CH. 17

Janine's work was leading her to breakthroughs in computational analysis, but long hours at the office as well as at home were taking a toll on her social life and placing an added level of distance between her and her son. She had not seen Ted in a few weeks and for the first time ever she felt frustrated that her work had intervened so much in her personal life. Numerous attempts by Ted to plan an activity together had to be canceled. Janine routinely apologized to him and now she found herself missing him more and more. She replayed his quirky behavior in her mind. His bizarre ordering pattern at restaurants or observations in the car while driving were turning into hurt memories.

A new weekend was forthcoming, and Janine was meeting it with great anticipation. She was making progress every day in her statistical analysis. Her dissection of cross patterns opened new ideas and avenues to explore. Every hurdle that she encountered was surpassed with ease. This was the perfect time to make it up to her illustrious beau and plan a romantic afternoon and evening together. Perhaps start with a picnic in the park on Saturday afternoon. Watch the little ones on swing sets as they dine under an old oak (she thought). And then, in the evening an off-broadway show that would be in town. The possibilities were endless. Uninhibited delight was only a phone call away.

"Hello, my knight in shining processing! What say you to a weekend of frolicking and merry making that would leave every elf in the North Pole envious of us. I'm putting away the books and slide ruler this weekend to be completely devoted to you. I was thinking we could ..."

"Janine, I would love to" Ted interjected, "But I can't. My brother and sister-in-law asked me to help them install some paneling at their house. My brother gets lost on these projects so easily, so I kinda have to guide him. Otherwise, I would most definitely want to see you. I'm so sorry I ..."

"No, that's okay," she said. "I understand. I know I sprung this on you at the last minute."

"If it's any consolation, I would much rather be with you this weekend then be putting up some lame panels."

"It is. Thank you. Give my best to your family. Tell them I hope to see them again soon."

"I will, thank you. Everything alright, I hope?" Ted sensed a difference.

"Oh sure. I'll talk to you when you get back. Have fun. Drive safe."

"K. Bye."

"Bye for now." Then she hung up.

It was approximately 6:30pm this clear cool Friday evening when Janine found herself at her mother and father's house. She walked through the side entrance slow and solemnly. Diletta was washing the supper dishes when she walked into the kitchen.

"Hi, Ma."

"Oh, you scared me! Hi. What are you doing here? I thought you had a date with Ted tonight?"

"He had to cancel. His brother needed help removing some paneling at his house so we're gonna make it for tomorrow night. Where are the other two?"

"Around here somewheres. They were both starving so we ate a little earlier than usual. There's some leftovers if you're hungry."

"I'm fine for now. Here, let me do these for you. You go lie down."

"I need to take this girdle off. It's killing me."

"Go ahead. I'll wash the rest of these."

Diletta dried her hands and took her apron off to go to her bedroom. Janine found the yellow rubber gloves and put them on to finish up where she left off. Just then the boy walked into the kitchen with a couple of schoolbooks in his hand.

"Hi, Ma! I didn't know you were ... when'ja get here?"

"Hi honey. Just now. I had a change of plans so I thought I would stop by."

"You gonna stay over tonight?" He asked her.

"Yeah, I'll stay."

He sat at the kitchen table and opened one of his schoolbooks to start a little homework before The Dukes came on. She saw what he was working on and said,

"If you get stuck on any problems just let me know. I'll help you."

"Okay, I will."

A few minutes had passed as she was scrubbing the caked-on spaghetti sauce that coagulated at the corner of each plate.

"Honey can you do me a favor? Can you call Auntie for me while I'm thinking of it. I need to ask her if she is willing to pick up the set of glasses we were gonna get Grampa for his birthday."

"Sure Ma."

The kid went over to the phone and started dialing what he thought was her number. He got a busy signal and tried again. Same thing.

"It's not going through." He said.

"Do you have the right number?"

"I think so."

He dialed it again, busy signal. One more time. Same.

"It's not workin' right now Ma. Guess we'll have to try a little later."

"What number are you dialing?"

"508-555-1468."

"No son. Her number is 508-555-1486. *You can't even dial a f#!&ing phone number!"*

The boy dropped the phone because he never heard his mother use that word before or take that tone with him. Older kids in the neighborhood had used it. He overheard a couple adults say it as he passed by them on his bicycle. He knew it was the granddaddy of all curse words. And just as she said it Sven had come out from the den to get a cup of coffee. He roared immediately with such a loud thunderous declaration that vibrated the imitation chandelier above the table,

"Hey! Not that word! I don't ever want to hear that word in this house! Don't ever say that again!"

Just then gramma turned the corner into the room, "What's going on? What's the matter?"

"I said a bad word." Janine said soberly.

"What word?"

"The F-word."

"Is that all? Sven get with the times a little bit. It's not like it used to be."

"I don't like that word Diletta! It won't be used here."

Diletta looked over at Janine as if to say, *you know how old-fashioned your father is.* The kid picked up the receiver that was still lying on the floor and making a buzzing noise. He placed it on the hooks and went back to his homework. He wasn't able to concentrate. He just looked at the pages of his textbook and held his pencil in his hand. Janine looked down at the dishes and went back to washing. Grampa got his coffee and went back to the den to watch television. Five minutes before the show started the kid packed up his books and went in to watch with him.

Janine went outside and sat down on the cobblestone steps. Diletta noticed her out there and sat beside her. It was eating away at Janine, and she needed to get it off her chest.

"Ma, I don't know what it is, but my patience with him seems to get less and less."

"Yeah, I've noticed it. Your father mentioned it to me too. I haven't said anything about it, so I guess I will now. Why? What is it about him that bothers you so much?"

"I don't know how to describe it, but when I look at him, I see his father. I get so infuriated, I guess I take it out on him. I'm sure I've even blocked out a lot of the things I've said to him. Not even realizing it at the time or wanting to remember."

"We all know how you were treated by Fredo," Diletta replied. "It wasn't the way it's supposed to be. But now you've got to try and control your emotions with him. You can see the look on his face. He doesn't know what hit him. He's never brought it up to me. Never asked either of us about it. He's just been dealing with it on his own, his own way."

"Do you think I've started menopause?"

"Maybe, that would explain a lot. I remember how hormonal I was when I went through it. You've also had such bad allergies and been prone to infirmity. I don't know. Maybe it all has something to do with it. You and your sister are so different in so many ways. It pains me to no end sometimes with her. Your both my children and I love you both equally and unconditionally so if you repeat this, I'll deny it (Janine just grinned and looked down at the ground). My biggest grievance with Delores is that she doesn't even try. She has potential. She has ability. I don't know if she is so afraid of failure. I don't know if she is just so unmotivated. I don't know what it is. But she does not put forth a substantial effort. Remember when your father and I needed to be picked up at the airport from Irving Freedmore's funeral? I call her up and I says,

'Delores.'

'Hi, Ma. How are ya?'

'Your father and I have a funeral we have to go to out in California.'

'What happened? Who died?'

'One of your father's old war buddies. As the years go on, they just keep goin' one by one. Your sister is gonna drop us off at Logan, but she can't pick us up. She's got some meeting with her boss and shareholders and some other big shots that she can't get out of. Can you pick us up at the airport at 5 o'clock?'

'In the morning? Is that the only flight you could get?'

'Not 5am. 5pm. This Friday. I can give you a call before we take off to come back home to remind you.'

'No, that's alright you don't have to call. I'll remember. What's the flight number?'

'It's Delta flight 7046. Departs Oakland at 8:30am and arrives in Boston at 5pm because remember we got that time change.'

'Yeah, okay. I'll pick ya's up this Friday at 5. Night Ma.'

'Night.'

"So, we go to California for Irving's funeral. He was another good soul. Your father told me a bunch of stories of what they went through together. Poor Irving left behind a wife and three children. All grown up as well. His wife Ellen was well taken care of. Irving was very responsible and went to great lengths to provide for his family. He was a butcher by trade and always lived frugally with regards to himself. He put his three kids through college. Never denied Ellen a luxury item if she wanted it. Left her with his pension, social security, house all paid for and two life insurance policies. Ellen and her children were so grateful that we made the trip out there. They wouldn't hear of us staying in some distant motel. They insisted we stay at their house the entire time. When it came time to go, everyone was in good spirits. Ellen's son Luke was insistent on taking us to the airport so we wouldn't have to take a cab.

The flight back to Boston was smooth sailing the entire way. Even the flight crew kind of adopted us both as (their) parents. After departing the plane, we go to the baggage claim area for our flight. *This one and that one* I said to your father, and he grabs them both. We walked outside the terminal doors to the bustling of cab drivers and buses picking people up. *Do you see her?* I asked him. *No,* he says then looked down at his watch. It was 5:15pm. *She didn't get a new car, did she?* he says to me. Not that I know of. I tell him.

Another 15 minutes goes by and we're still waiting for Delores to pull up. I said, *where's the closest pay phone? I'll give her a call. Maybe she thought it's next Friday.* Daddy reached in his pocket and gives me a dime. *Maybe she's stuck in traffic,* he says.

I find the pay phone and call her. Came back five minutes later. No answer (I tell him). *I'll give it ten more minutes then I'm hailing a cab,* he says to me.

Ten minutes had come and gone. No Delores. Daddy flagged down a cab down and we're finally able to get home (at almost 8pm). *Long day, I'm tired,* he says to me. Took the luggage to our room and fell right to sleep. I took my shoes and stockings off 'cuz my feet were killin' me from all the standin' and walkin' around all day. Then I called your sister.

Hello, she says to me. Where the hell were ya? You were supposed to pick us up at 5 tonight. Did you think it was next Friday?

'Ma, I was there. Where were you? I got there at 5. I waited and waited. Didn't see you or daddy anywhere. People going in and out, out and in, left and right, right and left. You's two weren't nowhere to be found. I waited two hours and figured maybe yous just stayed longer.'

Delores, were you on the upper level of the airport or the lower level?

The upper level, she says.

That's the departures terminal! I tell her.

Yeah, I know. I departed my house to come pick you up. Where were ya's?

You pick people up at the arrivals terminal! You drop them off at the departure terminal.

Ma, I'm sorry. I seriously waited there for two hours looking for you. How'd you get home?

We took a cab. Good night Delores."

Janine spent that night at her parent's house and woke up early the next day to make her son breakfast. They ate together and got cleaned up afterward.

"I have to head back to the city a little early today. I have some important work I need to get done."

"Okay Ma, no problem."

An hour later she said goodbye to everyone and was on her way back to her apartment. Shortly after she got home her phone rang.

"Hello?"

"Hello Janine, how are you? I've missed you."

"I've missed you too. Did you get all the paneling taken care of at your brother's?"

"We did. It took forever 'cuz it was just the two of us."

"I thought you mentioned he has a son. Is he unable to help?"

"Yeah, Lance has some sort of slight disability, and his attention span isn't that long. He was diagnosed as a child. I can't remember the term they used. He said something yesterday that had us in stitches though."

"What was that?"

"It must have been around 5:30pm at the time. I had just arrived. My brother and his wife were sitting down with him (just the three of them). They were doing their best to describe death to him and specifically as it pertains to cuddles their cat. They said *son, cuddles has gone up to kitty heaven. She gets to play with other kitties forever up there and catch mice and birdies and everything is the best where she is now*. Lance sat there listening to everything they said ever so quietly with not a blip of emotion on his face. When the two were finished he looked them straight in the eye and said, *so what will we have now for dinner?* My sister-in-law and brother were beside themselves. I had all I could do to keep it together. I wanted to bust out laughing, but he was so serious."

"That is too much. So, what did they say?"

"They just looked at each other. I knew my brother was at a loss for words. His wife was, *uh, I believe chicken and mashed potatoes*. Lance stood up and walked straight to his room."

CH. 18

A few more weeks had passed. Work was consuming her again. She did not come to realize it until a Saturday afternoon phone call.

"Hi, remember me?"

"Hi, Ted. How are you? We haven't spoken in a while have we, I'm so sorry. I've been so immersed in my work that I lose track of things. Please forgive me."

"I was worried I said something wrong or did something wrong last time we were together. I hope that's not the case."

"No, absolutely not. I tend to focus on my agenda so much that ..."

"It's okay, it's okay. I'm just glad you're not breaking up with me. You're not breaking up with me, are you?"

"Heavens no." She affirmed him, (Ted gave a little smirk to himself on the other end of the phone) "Let me make it up to you Theodore, I'll take *you* out to dinner this time. Anywhere you want to go."

"Actually, I was thinking more along the lines of a quiet evening at home. Just the two of us. I could get takeout maybe or..."

"Lasagna! Let me make you my lasagna. It's my mother's recipe but I think I've almost perfected it. If you're here by 6:30pm we can sit down to eat by about 7:15."

"Sounds delicious. See you then, Bye."

"Bye."

She hung up the phone and immediately went to the fridge,

"Need ricotta, parsley, chicken broth, salad, okay, we can do this."

Janine flew down the street to the corner market to pick up the missing ingredients,

"Oh, he loves his dessert." She remembered and added a cherry pie to the list.

Arrived back home and started cooking immediately. She left in such a frantic whirlwind that all her work was still scattered throughout her apartment. Papers of equations were covering the coffee table. Diagrams of process models littering the floor and cushions of the sofa. Diverse scenarios of quantitative disciplines sowed the hallway walls.

6:30pm arrived as she was still preparing dinner ... Knock! Knock!

"Hello sweet princess, how are you? I brought a red and a white for you. Not exactly sure which one goes with lasagna and grape juice for me."

"Come in. Come in. I'm still getting it together. We probably won't eat until 7:30 or so."

She closed the door behind him. Gave him a kiss and when she opened her eyes,

"Crap! Look at this mess! I'm so embarrassed. I haven't even cleaned up this stuff."

"That's okay, I'll give you a hand."

Ted reached down and started to organize the multitude of documents which lay before him. Some of the words he knew the meaning of (just not in the context they were in). Others he had never seen nor heard of before and had no idea what they meant or why there were arrows leading to and from them on the page.

"So, how's work going?" He asked her. "By the looks of it ... actually, I couldn't even speculate. I have absolutely no idea what I'm even looking at."

"Really well in fact," she replied as she picked up everything in the hall. "A few roadblocks here and there, but that's to be expected."

Ted could tell by the sound of her voice the distance she was away from him. As he aligned all the papers on her coffee table, he folded three of them vertically and lickety-split, shoved them into the breast pocket of his jacket. Janine came out of the hallway and into the living room,

"Thank you. It looks so much better. Here, let me take these out of here so it's not so cluttered."

She took all the organized piles of paperwork and put them into one large assembly bringing them into her bedroom. Ted removed his jacket and carefully placed it over the arm rest of the sofa. Breast pocket down to ensure the most amount of material from the garment was over it.

"I haven't had homemade lasagna in years! This is the best news I've heard all week." He wasn't trying to over sell it. It's just the way he was.

"I'm so glad," she said with the same buoyancy coming back into the kitchen. "As I mentioned, it's not my recipe it's my mother's. She deserves all the credit."

"I can't wait to meet your mum and dad, if you want me to of course. It's completely up to you."

"Would you like to come to Sunday dinner tomorrow? You're welcome to come to church as well if you like. We usually eat around 1pm after getting home from 9 o'clock mass. It'll just be me and my mother going to the service. My father doesn't usually attend, and I think ... (she had to wait a minute). I think my son is with his dad this weekend. So, it would just be the four of us for dinner."

"I would really enjoy that. I didn't mean to put you on the spot with what I said. I apologize."

"No, not at all. I was going to ask you even before now. I just get so occupied with work."

Janine took the lasagna out of the oven to cool and prepared the salad while Ted took the initiative to set the table for two and pour each of their glasses. As her oven-mitted hands carefully placed the glass dish at the center of her table Ted said,

"I've been thinking so much about what we talked about last time and while I was driving around last week running errands, I came across this religious station on the radio. I must admit I don't usually keep the dial there, but this time I did. They were talking about something I've never heard before."

They both sat down across from each other face to face in a picturesque moment of elegance. The kitchen table may have been small and only three feet from the stove, but it was all very cozy. Modest, yet very peaceful and comfortable. She cut him a large portion of the casserole, delicately placed it on his dish then asked,

"What's that?"

He moved his chair to elaborate,

"This man, this theologian was discussing salvation. Specifically, salvation being lost. The way he put it he said your name can be *blotted* out of the Book of Life. He referenced a couple passages in Revelations. Revelations 2, 22 and 3. He also went to Matthew 24 and the Book of Jude, I think. I found it so interesting that all throughout this man's approach he was constantly saying the phrase, 'The Bible says' and two seconds later he would say, *I believe*. It was as if he didn't even realize he was contradicting himself. Over and over again it was, *I'm just telling you what the Bible says* and *Don't shoot the messenger*, then in the same breath he'd say, *What I believe Paul is saying here*. He was very demonstrative with his opinions and seemingly deceptive in integrating it with fact. Forgive me if I have gone astray."

Ted smiled and paused a second to take the first bite of his dinner,

"This is fantastic! I've literally never had lasagna this good. My extreme compliments to your Mum. What's her secret?"

"It goes back to the old country. I want to say my mother's, mother's, mother. But thank you."

"So, my first question may be somewhat trivial. This man mentioned the Book of Life as well as the Lamb's Book of Life. Is there a difference? And if so, what is it?"

Janine very properly dabbed the corners of her mouth with her napkin then replied,

"There are eight references in the New Testament to the Book of Life and two of them refer specifically to the Book of Life that belongs to the Lamb, Jesus Christ. Seven of the references appear in the Book of Revelation. Those whose names are written in the Book of Life are those who belong to God. Those who have attained eternal life. Paul refers to those who have labored alongside him as those whose names are in the Book of Life. From Phillipians 4:3. Again, identifying the Book of Life as a record of the names who have eternal salvation. In the same way Revelation 3:5 refers to the Book of Life in which the names of believers in The Lord are found. These are_those who overcome the trials and tribulations of earthly life, proving that their salvation is genuine. The Lord Jesus who is speaking to the churches in this part of Revelation, promises to acknowledge his own before Abba. Conversely, Revelation 20:15 reveals the fate of those whose names are not written in the Book of Life, eternity in the lake of fire. Revelation 17:8 states when the names of the redeemed are written in the Book of Life – 'The beast that thou sawest was, and is not; and shall ascend out of the bottomless pit, and go into perdition: and they that they that dwell on the earth shall wonder, whose names were not written in the Book of Life from the foundation of the world, when they behold the beast that was, and is not, and yet is'."

"That sounds like the King James lingo, right? I get easily lost with all the that's and thous and begats."

"You are correct sir! It most certainly was the King James. So now in Revelation 13:8 and 21:27 we find your reference to the *Lamb Book of Life*, in which as well are the names of all those who have been washed by the blood of the Lamb, Jesus Christ. The Lamb who has been *slain from the creation of the world* has a book in which are written all those who have been redeemed by *His* sacrifice. They are the ones who will enter the Holy City, the New Jerusalem and who will live forever in heaven with God. So, to answer your question, since the Book of Life is that which records all who have eternal life through the Lamb, the Book of Life and the Lamb's Book of Life are one in the same."

"It was amazing to me how specific this guy would get in one area and how blasé, vague and nonchalant (for lack of a better term) he would be in another area two seconds later. For example, he spoke of the precise non-capitalization (punctuation) in the Book of Job stating that, 'sons of God' is a very important lower-case s in sons. Not two minutes later a guy calls in with a question and his response to him is, 'Don't get hung up on this or that because you can make the Bible say whatever you want'. I couldn't get over how 180 degrees he could be from himself. And from what I understand, this man has been preaching for nearly forty years. What does that mean? But before I forget, you said a word in the context of which I've never heard before and don't know what it means."

"Which word is that?" she asked.

"Abba. What's Abba?"

"Abba is who. Not what."

He felt awkward when he was corrected by her although she said it so soft and gentle that he knew she wasn't being condescending.

She continued,

"In scripture there are many different names used to describe God. The word Abba is an Aramaic word that means 'father'. It was a common term that expressed affection, confidence, and trust. Abba signifies the close, intimate relationship of a father and his child, as well as the child like trust that a youngster puts in his daddy. Jesus addresses his father as *Abba, Father* in his prayer in Gethsemane. Abba Father is mentioned in relation to the

Holy Spirit's work of adoption that makes us God's children and heirs with Christ. It is a supreme term of endearment. A testification that we are God's children. Which leads me to address this man's testimony where he believes that salvation is something that can be lost, (or loosed) as the KJV has it written." She said it smiling and was waiting for him to get the little joke she made but there was complete silence. Her return to the topic was swift. "There are numerous references in the Bible that attest to the assurance of salvation. Which leads me to wonder what is this man's agenda on the radio? Sometimes it's striking to me how people attain their positions or even their titles. How many so called *experts* get it wrong."

"Ha!" Ted started laughing then interjected with, "And how much they are paid to get it wrong!"

"Yep, so true. More lasagna?"

"Yes please." (She loved the way he was devouring her food.)

"I guess my first reaction to this guy, this *theologian* (and I guess I use the term loosely with him) is that of frustration. I'm frustrated that he is allowed to spread such fallacious messages over the airways. If I ever met this man, I would look him straight in the eye and say what about Hebrews 13:5 – I will never leave thee, nor forsake thee. Deuteronomy 31:6 – Be strong and of a good courage, fear not, nor be afraid of them: for the Lord thy God, he it is that doth go with thee; he will not fail thee, nor forsake thee. Proverbs 10:30 – The righteous shall never be removed: but the wicked shall not inhabit the earth. Isaiah 55:12-13 – For ye shall go out with joy, and be led forth with peace: the mountains and the hills shall break forth before you into singing, and all the trees of the field shall clap their hands. Instead of the thorn shall come up the fir tree, and instead of the brier shall come up the myrtle tree: and it shall be the Lord for a name, for an everlasting sign that shall not be cut off. And while he's sitting there scratching his head I would go back to the Book of Hebrews and state 10:22 – Let us draw near with a true heart in full assurance of faith, then go to Ephesians 1:13 – Where in whom ye also trusted, after that ye heard the word of truth, the gospel of your salvation: in whom also after that ye believed, ye were sealed with that Holy Spirit of promise. I would most likely include some Romans 8:38 – For I am persuaded, that neither death, nor life, nor angels, nor principalities, nor powers, nor things present, nor things to come, nor height, nor depth, nor any other creature, shall be able to separate us from the love of God, which is in Christ Jesus our Lord. But to really bring it home for this guy, especially since he liked to reference Revelation and had the audacity to use the specific term of *blotting*. I would very calmly, very quietly, very properly refer him to Revelation 3:5 – He that over cometh, the same shall be clothed in white raiment; and I will not blot out his name out of the Book of Life, but will confess his name before my father, and before his angels."

Ted had stopped eating because he was in complete awe and fascination. He still had food in his mouth but was unable to swallow it. His mandible was dry and open.

"I've never heard anyone quote so much from the Bible in my entire life. I don't even know what to think right now."

"Are you familiar with a Hafiz or Hafiza being the female equivalent?" She asked innocently.

"Not even a little." He said with the same perplexed look.

"It's a term meaning *guardian* or *memorizer* depending on the context. It is a term used by Muslims for someone who has completely memorized the Quaran."

"How does someone even do that?" He asked. "No, how does someone even think that is possible at the beginning and then set out to accomplish it? My first reaction is that it isn't even possible."

"That's the difference isn't it."

"What is?"

"There are some people that ask themselves, 'What if. What if I tried, what if I did.' *If* can be a gateway to the miraculous. *If* provides hope. Hope is of the divine. Hope provides possibility. Hope is pure and positive. To the contrary, *can't* delivers a defeatist sentiment. *Can't* furnishes discouragement. I once heard this popular, very accomplished musician discuss his progression with his instrument. He's considered a virtuoso on the guitar. What's also so engaging is that the guitar is his third instrument. He informed the audience that piano was his first (it appears he was a classically trained pianist at an extremely young age). Then he desired to be a percussionist and by the age of 12 he had an insatiable desire to play guitar. He would skip school to play guitar. Friday nights his sibling would go out on a date only to come home late in the evening to find his brother in the same spot in his room learning pieces of music all by ear. It has been said that it takes 10,000 hours to master a practice such as this. If this is true, he surpassed 10,000 hours by age fifteen. He is highly redeemed for his unique playing style, complexity, and originality. The accolades he has received throughout his years active are rarely ever achieved in any field. What I found the most fascinating was his own description of how he developed his distinctive playing style. It appears that he and his brother would attend as many local concert venues as they could while they were growing up. One particular concert they attended showcased an already seasoned, highly skillful guitar player as its member. The way he described him on stage, he would use one hand to melodically play notes over and over at a specific location on the fretboard of the guitar and use the other hand to signal the audience a message of delight and excitement. The musician in the audience (as a younger child) said to himself, 'What if I move my hand up the fretboard, playing a similar style and add my other hand as well'. This was the beginning of his journey in creating a whole new sound. Other extremely accomplished guitarists have tried to mimic his style and methods. Often self-admittingly saying that they can sound similar to him, just not exactly like this man. I as a music lover see that as a good thing. I enjoy hearing a musicians' interpretation of another musician's work. It's not as much fun if we heard one piece of music played the same way over and over again. It would get stale."

Ted was feeling inferior at this point. An element of not trying had a certain level of humiliation that he was desperate to avoid but didn't know how. He quickly changed the subject,

"I hope this isn't too forward, but I was wondering if you would like to spend a weekend in Maine together? Perhaps leave early on a Friday and comeback Sunday. We could visit the Portland Museum of Art, walk along Cosco Bay and even visit the Acadia National Park if possible."

Janine was as giddy as she could be. "I would love that," she replied.

"Great," Ted said smiling. "I'll make all the arrangements."

The two spent the evening conversing and listening to each other with heightened attention. Every syllable he spoke to her was a treasure in her mind. And the cherry pie at the end was good for him too.

CH. 19

Ted arrived bright and early the following morning at 8am in his Sunday's best. Freshly starched white collar, neatly pressed slacks with even crease down the middle and finely polished Bostonians to accent his jacket. He walked toward the front of the door with unbridled bliss (and some flowers he picked up on the way from the grocery store).

Knock! Knock! (he didn't see the doorbell)

Diletta answered the door,

"Good morning, you must be Mr. Sullivan. I believe you will be joining us for service today, so nice to meet you. I've heard so much about you."

"Morning Mrs. Jalinski, pleasure to meet you as well. Here, these are for you."

"Thank you so much. Please come in."

Ted walked in to find the peaceful modest home he had expected. A rocking chair in the corner. A foot stool under the coffee table. One attention to detail that caught his eye, everything had a doily under it.

"Can I get you something to drink? A cup of coffee?"

"No, thank you I ..."

"No coffee, that's right. Janine told me. I'm sorry. I forgot. Juice or water perhaps?"

"Water is fine. Thank you."

"Please have a seat."

Diletta got him a glass and put the flowers in a vase to set them in the middle of the kitchen table.

"So, I understand you and Janine work together at Ratheon."

"We used to." He said, "I took a position with another company, so I'm no longer there."

"I see and read about that more and more these days. People get transferred so often now or one opportunity after another pops up. It must be exciting."

"Yes, it can be. Never a dull moment," Ted replied to her.

Just then Janine came down the stairs from her room and entered the kitchen.

"Well good morning Mr. Sullivan. Are these for me?"

"Well actually ..."

"No! They ain't for you. He gave them to me."

"Oh, I see." Janine said with a smile.

"Are you hungry at all Mr. Sullivan?" Diletta asked, "Would you like an English muffin perhaps before we leave?"

"Please call me Ted, I ..."

"Mr. Sullivan, I presume!"

Sven came up from downstairs to give his blustering greeting. Ted stood right up at attention.

"Good morning Mr. Jalinski. Pleasure to meet you sir."

Ted was as bright eyed, and bushy tailed as he could be. Nervous as anything on the inside, cool as a cucumber on the outside.

"Please sit down sit down. What can we get you Mr. Sullivan, cup of coffee? How do you take it?"

"Daddy I told you Ted doesn't drink coffee."

"Aw, crap. I forgot. Anything else then?"

"I'm fine sir. Thank you."

"I hear you're goin' to the house of The Lord with them today."

"Yes, sir I am."

"The Lord gave me a pass today."

Diletta had to jingle in,

"Don't you mean *every* Sunday!"

"Yes, I do believe The Lord has allowed me a sabbatical on more than one occasion." Sven looked at Ted in a jovial way, "I'll hold the fort down 'till you get back."

Diletta looked up at the clock,

"Speakin' of which, it's almost time to go. Let me get my purse and things."

"Okay Ma, we'll be outside. Bye daddy."

"Great to finally meet you Mr. Jalinski."

"Likewise. I hope you like corned beef and cabbage for dinner later. I've had a yearning for it like you wouldn't believe and I ain't even Irish."

"I love corned beef and cabbage sir. Looking forward to it."

Janine and Ted went outside and waited by the car. "I'll drive us," he said. "You just have to tell me where to go."

"It's St. Mary's," she replied in a silly goose manner. "Did a fine Irish-Catholic boy forget his way?" Janine was on her tippy-toes leaning into him as she spoke with prodigious innocence.

"We went to St. Barnaby's," Ted replied with a slight hesitation. "The other fine, catholic, establishment, similar to ... where we're going."

"Ah, I see Mr. Sullivan."

Janine spoke as giddy as she had ever been, trying to do her best Irish accent. It wasn't really there but Ted wasn't about to tell her. It was still early in the a.m. and he had just made a good impression with everyone. *Everyone except her son,* he thought to himself.

"Okay, Let's go!" Diletta came out with her floral sun hat on and rosary beads dangling from her purse. It was almost as if she was going straight to the Kentucky Derby right after church.

"Ted said he'll drive Ma."

The three attended the service as a quasi-family. Diletta knew she would be fielding questions either after the mass or later in the week at the Mug n' Muffin regarding the fresh-faced male escort her and her daughter had with them.

When they arrived back home, Sven was mending the birdhouse he had mounted to the big oak tree in the yard.

"Try not to fall off the ladder again!" Diletta yelled out to him as she slammed the car door shut.

"When did daddy fall off the ladder?"

"He didn't. He knows I'm messin' with him."

They went into the house and Diletta began the preparations for Sunday dinner. Janine couldn't wait to give Ted a guided tour of the over-size Cape. She grabbed him by the hand, "C'mon, I'll show you around."

She took him to every room of the house as a tour guide would present their guests through Buckingham Palace. It was,

"Now over here we have the living room which has a sofa and chairs where we entertain guests rather sparingly. Much of the assembly is done in the den, kitchen or breezeway area. Here we have my parent's bedroom. They haven't slept in the same bed for years. I guess when you get old it's more comfortable to have your own bed."

Ted noticed a third little bed in the corner of the room that had a Bruins hockey puck pillow on it. He held it in for so long now he just had to ask,

"Is this where your son sleeps?"

"Yes, that's his bed. And over here we have the upstairs bathroom which is adjacent to mine and my sister's old room."

Again, it was a case where he wasn't going to inquire at the risk of changing the mood.

"Everything is so poised and proper." He said, "I wish my place was as neatly kept."

"That's right!" It just struck her. "I've never been to your place have I."

"There's not much to it, and the tour will take all of one minute, but you're welcome any time."

The two smooched for a couple minutes in her old room then went back downstairs to the kitchen.

"Do you wanna watch tv while I give my mother a hand?"

"Sure."

She led him to the den (the only room in the house that had a television set). "I'll check on you in a little while."

He sat down in grampa's chair after turning on the Nascar race (bypassing all the ball games and candlestick bowling that were on) to watch his famed driver in Rolondo Polotzo. The faint sounds of oven doors opening, and closing were muddled in the background compared to the vrooming engines as they turned each corner. Janine came bouncing back in on cloud nine almost as if she was fourteen,

"Hey, do you want a ..., race car driving? I had no idea you were into race car driving."

"Yeah, I've always had a passion for it. I used to go up to Bristol, New Hampshire all the time. Had season tickets there for a while. See that car there. Number 43. That's the king. He's the best there is."

"Why didn't you ever tell me you were so much into this?"

"I don't know. I guess it never came up."

"That's two surprises today. I've never seen your place and race cars. Would you like a ginger ale? We're out of cola."

"Sure."

When the four of them sat down to eat, Janine noticed a slight difference in the décor of the room. There was something missing or out of place. It took her a couple seconds but then,

"Hey daddy, where's your fishing trophy from The Lobolos? It was always on the mantle over there."

"Your mother made me take it down. She said it stuck out like a sore thumb."

"And it did!" Diletta exclaimed. "Nothin' from that silly lodge belongs in the living room."

"There's nothin' silly about The Lobolos." Sven said to her. "It's an indispensable organization. A highly valuable asset to the community. And stick this in your pipe and smoke it, Mrs. Weisenheimer. There's a luxury that benefits the both of us due to my association with this vital organization."

"Oh yeah, what's that?" She said *smart-alecky*.

Sven cleared his throat,

"We have a lifetime free membership to fish at Ned's Landing with unlimited usage."

Diletta just looked at him with a *big deal* expression.

After dinner Ted offered to assist cleaning up, but Janine wanted to display her domestic side.

"You go watch tv or something," she said. "My mother and I will get these."

"Where'd your dad go?" He asked.

"He's either outside or downstairs in the basement with his hearing aids turned off. He does that so he doesn't have to hear my mother."

A little while later Ted made his way down the steps of the fabled staircase. He turned the corner and noticed Sven at his desk going over some numbers. Most likely from his checking account.

"Mr. Jalinski pardon my intrusion. Do you have a few minutes?"

Sven saw that Ted was walking toward him and moving his mouth,

"One second son. Let me turn these up so I can hear you."

"Pardon my intrusion sir. I was hoping you might have a few ..."

Then Ted noticed an 8x10 frame with bizarre writing. He had no idea what is said or what it meant, and its uniqueness stopped him dead in his tracks.

"Um, may I ask. What does that ... What is ...?"

Ted pointed to the odd fixture that was neatly hanging above the desk. It read:

¿ A Lesson in Latin ?

Ci Billi Ci Ergo. Forti Buses Enero. No Billi Demistrux. Ci Watzinm. Cowzndux.

"Oh that, that's my only lesson in Latin. Can you read it?"

"No sir, I can't."

"It says, See Billy See Her Go. Forty Buses in a row. No Billy. Them is trucks, See what's in 'em. Cows n' Ducks."

"Never in a million years would I have gotten that sir."

"Ha! Yeah, I use to give them out to customers at the grocery store I managed. That's the only one I have left. Janine told me there's some machine that makes copies now, Borox ... Forox ... Clorox ... something like that. I never got around to it."

"May I sit down with you sir?" Ted asked him.

"By all means."

Sven got him a chair. As he was waiting to sit down Ted was contemplating what to say. He wasn't nervous. Just a little off as he had never done this before and wasn't sure how it was supposed to go. He waited a second then looked Sven straight in the eye.

"Sir. I love your daughter with all my heart. I want to have a life with her. With your permission I would like to ask her to marry me."

"Son, I admire your traditional values. It's my understanding this doesn't happen very often anymore. It certainly didn't with her first husband. I remember asking Diletta's father for her hand. I was nervous that day. I think I asked to mend a fence or milk a few cows on their farm just to get a little workout before I did it. I appreciate you taking the time here. You certainly have my blessing to ask her."

"Thank you very much Mr. Jalinski."

"I guess you can call me dad soon enough if you prefer." Sven said smiling.

The two shook hands and Ted put his chair back. As he made his way up the steps and back to the kitchen he thought to himself, *everything is as planned.*

CH. 20

Janine and Ted were married in the summer of that year. Her son was placed as ring bearer and looked around every ten seconds for where to stand and what to do. Her parents were pleased that she was so happy. When the newlyweds returned from their honeymoon in Europe, they bought a raised ranch out in Norwood on a cul-de-sac. The kid was never asked to come live with them. He stayed with his grandparents.

CH. 21

The years continued to pass by. The research and development of project Avianet was going as anticipated. A minor break through, then a major set-back. The team would collaborate at various intervals and then separate to research independently. It was during these moments of separation that the *boy's club* developed. Ed had been working on a method of grouping data. Larry was experimenting with various transmission mediums and Michael would review communication channels. They would each converse individually and then get together collectively to bounce ideas off each another.

The Wednesday of that week Michael and Larry paid a visit into Ed's office. A little discouraged by now because they were stuck in their tracks. They both just sat down before giving a greeting.

"And good morning to you too." Ed said sarcastically to each of them.

Michael couldn't help himself,

"I'm still, man ... I'm stagnant. I can't see where to go from here. Everything I try is a dead end. I've explored linear sequentials, malvol deductions and stored simple links. Nothing. Nothing at all."

"I know what you mean." Larry was in the same boat. "I've tried secured targon equations and monopole secretions. Same results."

"Let me show you both where I was headed down this rabbit hole." Michael opened up his briefcase and put a stack of papers on the table. Ed put down his coffee cup and happened to glance over at what Michael was putting down.

"Where'd you get that?" Ed asked him.

"That?" And he pointed. "You don't want to know."

It was a publication of the Vell Labs Technical Journal. An in-house scientific journal for employees (specifically research and development technicians) of Ella Vell Laboratory, Inc. It was published annually by Ella's own team of scientists, journalists, editors, and writers as a resource for its exclusive team members to use as a tool for expansion. The theory being any groundbreaking discoveries would pose as an inspiration to other team members. Each discovery or pattern meticulously detailed in its explanation. This publication was a highly coveted instrument within the disciplines of electrical engineering, computer science and telecommunications. Very few indexes were printed and each one had to be accounted for at all times throughout the year. No one was ever allowed to make copies as no one was allowed to take one home.

Ed turned to Larry,

"Did you know he had this?"

"I had no idea. I'm as surprised as you are."

"There's something I'm missing here." Ed's astonishment continued, "What do they produce, two of them every year?"

"Yeah, something like that."

"And they're under lock and key all the time. Guarded like Fort Knox. Someone or Someones are going to be highly accountable when they realize one is missing. How did you do it?"

"You really want to know."

Both Larry and Ed just looked at each other and nodded. Michael continued,

"I couldn't get someone to get me a copy after they were already created. That would pose too many problems. There is too much margin for error. With the security guards and system, the ultimate recognition that one has been lost or stolen could possibly jeopardize any future publications. No, the best way to achieve this is to make as if it never existed."

"And how do you do that?" Larry interjected. "Since obviously we know it exists. My first instinct is that they know it's alive since they produce it from start to finish. I mean look at it. Their custom binding on the front and back cover."

Michael just shook his head,

"Well, it isn't *they,* over there that know about it. It's *he*. And *he* has sworn me to secrecy not to divulge his name so please don't even ask."

"Okay, we won't, so how much did you pay him?" Ed's gut was there all along.

"$15,000."

"Fifteen grand? Man, that's a nice house." Larry confirmed.

"So back to the *make as if it never existed* part. How is this accomplished?"

"I actually don't know the details of that. When we were negotiating the terms, I had to stop him from telling me everything. I said wait, (believe it or not) in this deal there are some things that I don't even *want* to know. From where he was in the explanation, two copies became three and two are put here while one is put there. This guy wanted to give me the keys to the kingdom."

"Literally!" Ed proclaimed with conviction.

"Yep, and viola. Here she be."

Larry still had some questions on how it all went down,

"So how did you meet this guy and initiate something like this to him?"

"That was more or less a coincidence. It was a Saturday night, and I was downtown at The Sill. I think I was with Evelyn or Dotty that night (I'm not sure. Can't remember. The one I first met in Austin, Texas one year. She said she is half Czechoslovakian and half Mexican, she's Czech-Mex.), when I recognized this guy from somewhere, but I couldn't place where. He was sitting all alone having a drink. We walked over and I said, 'Hey, aren't you'? He said yes and the three of us chatted it up for a while. I put the request to Evelyn (or Dot) to call one of her girlfriends and come join us. She did. They did. We did. And the rest is history."

"It's amazing," Larry exclaimed.

"What's that?" Michael asked.

"How all the stars align for you. Reminds me of a guy I worked with right out of college. He was Irish, but the luck of the Irish only scratched the surface with this guy. We were working together at a plastics distributor. We'd get the raw materials, resin as well as adhesives (sealants) and be able to cut the tubing or sheets to a customer's requested specs. We were both inside sales reps at the time. One day, out the clear blue sky, *bam!* This guy up and quits. No two-week notice, nothing. I see him at the grocery store a couple weeks later. We started talking and catching up on things. He tells me, *Awe man, I've had to move back home with my parents. Can't afford the rent anymore, a car payment, food etc ...* I'm trying to empathize with him. I tell him if I can help in any way just ask. You need a couple bucks here ya go (I think I gave him $10 bucks that day), and then we went our separate ways. A week and a half later I see in our directory this guy is an outside rep for our Braintree office. I called him up, 'Hey Phil how ya doin'? What the heck is goin' on around here? He says, *Hey Larry how are ya? You won't believe it, I'm sitting at home watching some lame ass soap opera because that's all that's on at 11am on a Tuesday thinking to myself, what did I do? I got up off my parent's couch and started to walk to the phone to call*

Dave our old manager. I say to him, 'You mean my current manager'. He goes on, *Yeah, I guess. I was gonna beg and plead him to take me back when all of a sudden, my mother yells down to me from upstairs. She needed me to run some errand for her (for the life of me now, I can't even remember what she wanted me to pick up). I go to the store for her, come back and there is a note by the phone telling me that Dave called, and he wants me to call him back. I call him up and the first thing he says to me is, 'Phil, what's it gonna take to get you back here'? I said (with a smile to myself). Oh, I don't know Dave things are lookin' good right now. What's your offer? He gave it to me. I took it and here we are'*. I said to him, that is absolutely incredible. You got a raise and a promotion from a job you quit abruptly and just wanted back. All he said was, *Yep."*

Michael turned to both Ed and Larry,

"A man after my own heart."

"I bet you didn't even get the $10 bucks back," Ed added.

"Nope, he took a job with a competitor for more money shortly after. Our old boss was so pissed. I didn't have the heart to tell him the story right then and there. I waited a couple weeks to let him catch his breath. When I finally mentioned it to him, we were eating lunch in the break room. He didn't even finish his ham on rye. Just left it on the table and walked back to his office. I gave him my two-week notice a month later (as if it mattered)."

"You're a more considerate man than I," Michael said. "I would have quit on him the day I found out he gave him the promo."

"Yeah, I didn't want to leave him high and dry. Besides, things have a way of working out for the best."

CH. 22

Sven and Diletta passed away due to natural causes. Sven first then Diletta a few years later. The kid was never picked up by any college to play hockey. He tried to make it as a walk-on at Northeastern University, but they told him his services would not be required. There was a tryout for a new league forming in Florida the year after. He packed up everything he had and drove his Buick station wagon (with the wood grain) all the way down to the sunshine state. The league never came to be as the investors were embezzling money from various sources. He turned around and came back to Boston. Finally hung up the blades and enrolled in community college. Got a job in a restaurant as a dishwasher to pay for rent and tuition. He told me of the day they got a new hire in the kitchen that was brought on to scrub pots and pans as well. He was an older gentleman. The man was soft spoken as he didn't speak very good English, but he was extremely kind and had a gentle spirit.

The two had just started their shift together. Other staff were bringing them their dirty plates, silverware, and sauté pans to be cleaned. Standing side by side the two introduced themselves with a welcoming grin. As the kid was looking down at his sink filled with the small stock pot, mixing bowls, baking sheets, and scrubbing with an industrial strength steel wool pad, the gentleman rolled up his sleeves to begin. The kid happened to glance over and noticed a set of numbers tattooed on the inside of his left forearm.

CH. 23

Janine's work was unparalleled in its innovation. Ted had witnessed the most vital element to the entire project that *was* Avianet. It was simply a matter of attaining it, assessing its value, and proceeding with the exchange. His confidence was at a pinnacle. There was no reason to believe anything other than the usual protocols over the past few years would occur. He would call the new number given to him at the previous exchange. The location would undoubtedly be fresh as no two drops were ever at the same place. There was the possibility that a new operative would be introduced as it had a couple of times previously, but that placed no concern. Ted decided to proactively place the call to attain the details regarding the logistics of the next encounter.

"Hello."

"Good evening Nikolei."

By now they knew each other's voice and accent very distinctly.

"Good evening Mr. Sullivan. How are you tonight?"

"Just fine thank you."

"May I presume you are inquiring regarding the details for next?"

"Yes sir, I am."

"I as well are anticipating they will be given to me by my superiors as I am currently without,"

Just then Ted heard a clicking in the line. He didn't say anything about it as Nikolei was still talking, but then the Russian made an interjection on himself.

"Mr. Sullivan, could you please hold for one minute. I believe I have a call on the other lines."

"Sure, thing Nikolei."

Nikolei then pushed the blinking white button that was flashing vigorously at the bottom of his phone. He answered in Russian as the voice on the other end responded in their native tongue. What they were completely unaware of was that somehow, someway the lines got crossed and Ted could hear everything they were saying to each other. He had no idea what they were saying, and it was difficult for him to confirm who the third party was. Nikolei sounded different to him as he was talking faster than when he spoke in English. *Was it Ivan?* He thought. Certainly possible, but still no level of concern need be raised. None the less, Ted placed his hand slowly over the bottom of the receiver to ensure even his breathing would be undetected.

There was an English word he caught. *Doogans.* This must be the location for the next encounter. It was more out of the city than usual, but that placed no concern. As he continued to listen attentively it was apparent their conversation was coming to a close. The last instructions Nikolei was given were, *Tushit Sullivan.*

Ted didn't know what he just heard. He only knew his name was said. He started to pace back and forth. While still keeping his hand on the phone he heard another slight click then,

"Mr. Sullivan. Are you still there?"

"Yes Nikolei. Still here."

"I apologize for the interruption, but at least I now have the itinerary. Are you familiar with Doogan's Grill? I believe it is north with a patio area outside. We could meet on the east side parking lot. Will that be adequate for you Mr. Sullivan?

Doing his best to stay tranquil and not arouse any suspicions he agreed calm and quietly,

"Yes, that will be fine."

"Is next Wednesday good for you Mr. Sullivan? Seven o'clock in the evening perhaps."

"I will see you next Wednesday at seven."

"If I am unavailable to be there Mr. Sullivan one of my associates will, to assist you."

"Thank you Nikolei. Good night sir."

"Good night."

Ted's hand was shaking strenuously as he placed the receiver back down. He was unable to sleep more than five minutes at a time that night. The next morning, he arrived at his work an hour earlier than usual. Only a few fresh faces were around at this hour. The security guard, a maintenance crew member, the janitor. The dilemma at present was a means to decipher what he heard the night before. He had no friend or relative that spoke Russian. No one at his office ever even hinted that they could be bilingual. Let alone be fluent in an eastern bloc native tongue. The one-time old joke he heard kept replaying in his mind, *what do you call someone that can speak three languages ... trilingual. What do you call someone that can speak two languages ... bilingual. What do you call someone that can speak one language ... an American.*

The only thought was to go to the library at noon. He had an hour for lunch but was going to need more time since the closest public library was in Roxbury. He ducked out fifteen minutes early unnoticed. If traffic wasn't bad, he could get there a little after twelve.

After pulling into the almost empty parking lot, he entered the facility with direct intent. The information desk was governed by an elderly woman who may have moved slow physically but was sharp as a tack mentally and knew every detail of her surroundings.

"Excuse me ma'am," he asked her. "Could you point me to the section that would have a Russian/English translation dictionary?"

"Yes sir. That would be in education. Follow that hallway to the end. Turn right and it will be in the fourth section on your left." She stood and pointed to assist him as the most detailed guide could without holding his hand.

"Thank you, ma'am." He returned.

Ted walked down the corridor in complete silence. The aroma of must from all the books that surrounded him permeated his nostrils. The faint creaking of the floorboards spoke with every step. He arrived at the proper section just as the sun was breaking through the side windows over the individual desks that neatly aligned the far wall. The glare hit the thin plastic shield that covered each volume of hard copy and bookends that faced him. In alphabetical order it went Aramaic to English, Armenian to English, Croatian to English, Greek to English, Polish to English, Romanian to English, Russian to English translation. He slid the one he needed out from the shelf as the bordering book leaned slightly to the right after its retrieval.

Ted chose a solitary desk that appeared unused for some time. He didn't bother to take off his coat. Upon opening the reference manual, he tried to say the word to himself over and over ... *tint*? ... *tushtt?* The spelling of the word was unsure and proving intricate.

Going through the T's as close as he could and relying on syllable pronunciation next to each word, he came to *tywnt* pronounced *tushit*. He recognized this from the third voice on the phone. The English translation ... *extinguish.*

Ted ever so slowly closed the manual and sat there. Staring at it. Ultimately contemplating the fate that awaited. When he finally returned, he arose and placed the book back to its location. Slowly making his way to the exit the kind &

helpful woman was still seated at her station as he walked past her.

"Were you able to find what you were looking for sir?" she asked him while standing up and raising her eyebrows above her bifocals.

He was incapable of speech. He nodded ever so slightly looking straight ahead as he walked out.

Sullivan lay in stir that night thinking; how did he get himself into this. And more importantly, how to get himself out of it. He had a short window from now until the next interaction. He needed more time.

Three days had passed he had eaten two bologna sandwiches, one order of small fries and 14 colas the entire time. Work was just a function of necessity. He was thinking of calling in sick for a few days, but then where would he go? What would he do?

It was 6:30pm that evening. He placed a call.

"Hello."

"Hello, Nikolei."

"Hello Mr. Sullivan. No, this is Vladimir. How may I help you?"

"Hello Vladimir. I need some more time before the next contact. Our schedules have been so conflicting and hectic lately. She's been working late and odd hours. I need more time to get this crucial piece."

"How much more time will you require?"

"Another week or two, maybe three at the most. I don't ever want to raise any suspicions when I attain."

"I understand Mr. Sullivan. I don't see that to being a problem. We shall re-convene with a new date, no?"

"That will be fine Vladimir. Good night sir."

-Click- he hung up.

CH. 24

Nikolei and Vladimir's residence was an old, abandoned mill. They were always ordered to remain as inconspicuous as possible. The dark, damp, and musty walls that lead underneath never bothered either of them. They were trained to ignore things like the weather. And they excelled at it.

Vladimir opened the door to the poorly lit room to find Nikolei boiling water on his hot tray for tea.

"Is this our new comrade?" Nikolei said to Vladimir in Russian.

"Da." He replied.

Next to Vladimir stood a blond hair blue eyed young man not a day over eighteen. He was thin and muscular. Not a wrinkle or blemish on his skin to be found.

"What's your name comrade?" Nikolei asked him in their native.

"Viktor." He replied without any hesitation.

"Very good. That's a strong masculine name. Do you speak English Viktor?" Nikolei stated in Russian.

"Yes, sir I do," Victor replied in perfect English without the slightest hint of a foreign accent.

"Perfect," Vladimir added. "This will be helpful. Please have a seat."

Victor was given a chair behind an old wooden desk that was placed toward the back of the room. He sat down and watched the two men make themselves comfortable.

"Do you have the target Viktor?" Nikolei asked him.

"Yes, sir I do." Victor assured him.

"Good." Nikolei replied as he reached into the lowest drawer of his desk. Pulling out a .45 caliber pistol wrapped in a torn sackcloth and sliding it across the desk. In his reassurance Nikolei stated to Viktor,

"Do well, and it will lead to greater opportunity."

CH. 25

Ted came home that evening with a heightened sense of insecurity regarding his course of action but disguised it with gentleness in mannerism.

"Would it be alright if we stayed in tonight?" He asked his wife. "Don't feel the need to cook. We can order out and I'll go pick it up."

"Yes, sure." Janine said with no disappointment. "Everything alright or do you just prefer a quiet Saturday night."

"Yeah, with all the running around I've been doing lately a relaxing evening with dinner and the late show sound pretty good."

He ordered her favorites from the Hong Kong Gardens restaurant. That night as they were watching television Janine rested her feet on his lap as they took in an old Charlie Chan movie. She felt he was much more reserved and silent this evening than most but accepted his prior explanations as sufficient.

At the end of the movie and only five or six one syllable words exchanged throughout the entire intermission, Janine felt it impossible not to inquire.

"I don't mean to pry honey. We've been married for many years now. I hope you know you can tell me anything. Your concerns are my concerns. Your problems are my problems. I hope you know that."

"I do Janine. I've never been so close to someone in all my life as I am with you. You're absolutely everything to me. I can't get to sleep sometimes at night until you come to bed. I love you with all that I am."

"So, talk to me. Tell me what you are thinking about." She implored.

Ted hesitated for about twenty seconds. Stood up and turned the television off. The shadow from the evening lamp left the side of his face completely dark. His outline on the wall was extended and two sizes larger than his actual. He looked her straight in the eye and without the slightest facial expression said,

"Let's get out of here."

"What? It's late. Everything is closed at this hour."

"I don't mean now and just for tonight. I mean forever. I have a lot of money set aside that will take care of us for the rest of our lives."

Janine sat up straight. Hands folded on her lap. Knees clenched tightly together, and the heels of her feet were three inches in the air.

"What are you talking about? Where is this coming from?"

She was scared, curious, disoriented and bewildered all at the same time.

"There are things about me that I have never told you," Ted said to her with a *matter-of-fact* element to it. "I'm sorry I've kept things from you Janine, I truly am, but it doesn't change how I feel about you. It doesn't change how much I love you and want to spend the rest of my life with you. I know how this must sound to you right now. And I know that it's coming at you from out of nowhere."

Both her heart and mind were racing. She didn't know what to think, or more importantly what to say right now. The only thing she could think of was how she felt at this precise instant.

"What is happening right now? *How* is this happening right now? What do you mean you have a lot of money? What about your family? What about my family? What about your job? What about my job? What makes you think we can just pick up and move never to be seen from again?"

"Because we can," he said with his hands in his pockets still standing. "We can go anywhere in the world we choose. There's just one caveat, when we go, we have to stay gone. We can't come back ... ever."

"Ted, you're scaring me. You've never talked like this. You've never been like this. This is irrational. What exactly have you kept from me?" She waited with a lack of discernment that he was all too familiar with.

"I don't believe what you believe," he said. "Theologically, I know I've led you to think that I do and for that I apologize as well."

"What does that even mean? Theologically?" (He knew she wasn't asking the definition of the word)

"I'm agnostic. Up until now I've been going through the motions because I know how important it is to you. I was afraid to tell you because I thought you might leave me."

Janine didn't know how to process everything she was hearing. Her emotions hadn't hit a vortex like this since her first marriage. She wanted everything back to normal again. Back to the way it was twenty minutes ago.

"I think it's something we can work through," she said with her accustomed optimism. "I'm sure we're not the first to go through something like this. With counseling and time, this is something we can overcome."

Ted listened attentively and awaited the right moment of silence to reply,

"I've also had some business associates the past few years. They've proven to be very lucrative."

"What type of business associates? You're a data processor."

"This has been more or less a side business. A little unconventional. None the less, highly profitable."

"What sort of business?" She asked slowly.

"Information," he replied while looking at the ground this time. "There is a tremendous value in information, and we can benefit from it for the rest of our lives. I know what I'm about to say will sound terribly radical, but please keep an open mind."

She closed her eyes to prepare herself for another level.

"We need your son to drop off the software that contains the algorithms to Avianet."

She opened her eyes ... "My son? What does *he* have to do with any of this?"

"Nothing," Ted assured her. "That's why we need him. All he will be doing is dropping off a package. That's it."

Then it came to her. Janine asked,

"What's Avianet have to do with any of this?"

"Russian operatives have paid very handsomely for the work you've produced. With this one final drop we can take off. Anywhere, unsuspecting, free and clear."

"So, you've been selling my work to the Soviet Union right under my nose?"

"Yes, but this is where I'm coming clean to you. No more half-truths. No more withholding anything from you. I'm terrified of what you might think."

"I honestly don't know what to think right now."

"I know how so much has changed for you simply in the past hour. Just know nothing about the way I feel toward you has ever changed. I want to spend the rest of our lives together."

"So why do you need my son to make this final, what is it ... *drop*?"

"It will give us time. Extra time we can use to blend in wherever we go. Time to learn customs and courtesies that will be beneficial. We will need to disappear and amalgamate ourselves as local natives in our destination."

"You're saying I'll never see him again? My only son. You're telling me that's it."

"I know it will be hard. Especially at first, but you can do this. You have the strength."

"How are you able to be so cavalier about all of this? How long have you been contemplating all of it?"

"I had to discipline myself. You've showed me that I can be stronger and more focused than I ever thought I could be. And believe me, I never would have asked you while your parents were alive. Saying goodbye to my brother and my sister won't be easy. I've entertained the thought of not saying anything, for *their* sake. Sort of it's better and safer if they don't know anything. I recommend that with your boy. Just give him the details of the where and when of what we need done. Just asking him a favor and not raising any suspicions. In time the wounds will heal."

Janine stood up from the couch and proceeded to walk to their bedroom. Her hands were shaking. Her mouth was dry. She tried to take a deep breath but wasn't able to inhale as much as she needed. Ted stood there and watched his wife as she slowly made her way out of the living room. He sat back down on the couch in complete silence. With his right leg crossed over his left knee he pursed his lips and calmly brought his finger to rest under his nose. A million questions started running through his mind, *What could she be thinking? How will she react to this?* He even pondered the most extreme and crucial, *Will she leave me?*

Janine reached her bed and laid down staring straight up at the ceiling. She could feel her heartbeat in her ears. Her pulse was more distinctive to her than it had ever been. She blinked once every thirty-five seconds. She never counted that before.

An hour passed by that felt like a minute. Neither of them had moved a muscle. Another twenty minutes had gone by where all that was heard was the settling of the house and an appliance in circulation. Janine walked back to the living room to find Ted sitting there. Their eyes locked without saying a word. She picked up the phone to dial. Each number felt like in eternity.

"Hello?"

"Hi honey it's me. I'm sorry to call you so late. Are you still up?"

"Ma, are you alright? Yeah, I'm still up. What's wrong?"

"Nothing honey, nothing is wrong. I just need you to do me a favor. Can you drop off a package for me tomorrow? Ted and I have a function to go to and won't be able to. It's all work related so it's extremely important."

"Yeah, sure I can, are you sure everything is okay?"

"I'm sure honey. I'll leave it in our mailbox with the instructions of where and who to deliver it, okay?"

"Okay."

"I love you Lum Lum. I love you now and forever."

"Love you too Ma."

-click-

ACKNOWLEDGEMENTS

This book is a result of a culmination and an accumulation from a lifetime of events and experiences. I wouldn't be where I am today without the Lord above and the care of my grandparents. They kept a roof over my head, food on the table and the heat on my entire life and never asked for a dime in return. How does one even put into words the level of thanks and gratitude they deserve?

I am also extremely grateful to my mother. We may have had a tumultuous past Ma, but I love you very much and I know you love me too.

Pamey, what can I say! Your assistance, knowledge, and patience with me is so incredibly appreciated. I am forever thankful to you. I love you so much.

To the reader I extend my most sincere thank you for taking the time involve yourself with this piece of literature. I am also in tremendous appreciation for each and every trial and tribulation (we all eventually face). I sincerely hope that this book will assist others in seeing that we can use all the negativity in our lives and re-channel it into something positive. God Bless You.

ABOUT THE AUTHOR

Matt grew up in the metro-west area of Boston, Massachusetts. His dreams and aspirations of becoming a Division 1 ice hockey player were cut short at an early age. He entered the U.S. military and served his country honorably for 4 years. Upon discharge he completed his bachelor's degree in marketing as well as subsequent masters level courses. After spending 14 years as a corporate professional his creative desires to write became apparent in both song and literary work. His original music is diverse in both melody and lyric while his literary creations encompass a vast array of themes and subject matter. Sight See Unseen is his debut novel.

www.ingramcontent.com/pod-product-compliance
Lightning Source LLC
LaVergne TN
LVHW091042080826
845145LV00002B/586

* 9 7 8 1 7 3 5 9 9 4 4 3 7 *